Diana, A Spencer Forever

Praise for *Diana, A Spencer Forever*

"*A well written series about Diana. The first two were fantastic, and this one does not disappoint! Fans of the Royals will love this series. Enjoy!*"

"*The last book in Deb Stratas' Spencer trilogy is wonderful! The last two years of Diana's life were chaotic, as she tried to carve a role for herself and find love. Ms. Stratas does an excellent job of portraying the princess' life during this time. Again, royalty fans rejoice!! Highly recommended!!*"

"*Best Diana trilogy ever! So well written. I couldn't put them down, yet I wanted them to last forever. Awesome author. Love her.*"

"*Glad to see this third book in the series. I wasn't disappointed. When's the next one? Great research and true-to-life stories. So sad when she died. It brought back such sad memories.*"

"*I have to say this was my favourite out of the series. Of course, we know the tragic ending, but to go through the final years of Diana's life where she worked tirelessly for causes close to her heart and finally finding love again – we see her really happy. We are reminded of the good works she did, and those causes her sons carry on to this day.*"
Royal Central

Also by Deb Stratas

Diana, A Spencer in Love

Diana, A Spencer in Turmoil

At Home with Diana

The Royal Key

Diana, A Spencer
Forever
A Novel

Deb Stratas

DEB STRATAS

Diana, A Spencer Forever

Author: Deb Stratas
Website: debstratas.com
Editor: Robin Djokoto, Susan Sparling
Cover Art: Katrina Robert

First Printing: November 2018
Second Printing: January 2020

ISBN: 9781660722433

Acknowledgments

Diana, A Spencer Forever is dedicated to everyone who loved or still loves the late Diana, Princess of Wales. For all of you dedicated Princess Diana fans, this one is for you!

I'm also dedicating this book to my Mom, who is long gone, but never forgotten. Thank you for instilling in me the never-ending love of reading and writing.

I'd like to thank Kwesi Pencil for the incredible piece of art - not a photograph, but a one-of-a-kind *pencil art* drawing. Kwesi is a Ghanaian artist who strives to break the boundaries of Pencil arts and portraiture.

Table of Contents

Preface

Welcome to *Diana, A Spencer Forever* – the third and final novel in my Diana Spencer trilogy. I hope you've already read and enjoyed *Diana, A Spencer in Love;* which tells the 1980-81 story of Lady Diana Spencer and her marriage to Charles, the Prince of Wales. And, the second book in the series, *Diana, A Spencer in Turmoil,* which follows the Princess in her life with Charles, as she bears two princes, and struggles in a difficult marriage in 1991-92.

I knew I had to tell Diana's story in three parts – her first extraordinary year of royal life, the tumultuous times culminating in her separation from the Prince of Wales, and the final tragic year of her young life. To do her story justice, looking back at her experiences, challenges, relationships, and accomplishments could not be told in just one volume. The core of her Spencer strength is a theme throughout all three novels, and vital to show who she was, and who she became.

As with the first two novels, I thought it was important to complete the trilogy with *Diana, A Spencer Forever* from her point-of-view, not as a dispassionate onlooker. What was she thinking and feeling as she left the royal family for good? Why was she compelled to participate in the *Panorama* interview that came to define her? What about the new loves in her life? Was she really moving in a new and healthy direction? *Diana, A Spencer Forever* explores her thoughts and feelings, along with an updated version of her daily, incredible life – a glimpse into the self-assured woman, mother, friend, icon, and humanitarian that captivated the world – then, and even now.

Writing *Diana, A Spencer Forever* was a bittersweet odyssey for me. Of course, I wanted to finish Diana's story. I needed to paint a true picture of the emerging world figure who was confident, and poised to make a real difference in issues like abolishing personal landmines. I also wanted to explore, and ultimately dispel myths about her love life – especially in that last summer when the world's eyes saw her in love with Dodi Fayed. And naturally, writing about her tragic death and the aftermath was painful and challenging.

After three years of writing about her, and three decades of following and reading about Diana, her story will be finished. This was sad for me, and at times, hard to let her go. As a writer, your life becomes entangled with your lead character, and it was like saying goodbye to her for the second time.

As with the first two installments in the series, I've based many of the settings on real events and people. I've tried to maintain historical accuracy as much as possible, while imagining what a thirty-five-year-old Diana was thinking and feeling, as life tossed her around once more. There are differing viewpoints as to how she really felt that summer of 1997 – was she in love with Dodi? Was she just trying to make a handsome doctor jealous? Was she simply enjoying herself on a beautiful yacht in the south of France? Based on my research, I'm presenting the version that I think speaks best to her character, personality, and way of thinking. No one will ever know for sure, but I've truly tried to bring the Princess' voice to life. And as usual, I've invented a few escapades that may or may not have actually happened.

I've continued to use a British voice, language, and expressions throughout the story. Please refer to the glossary at the end of the book for the definitions of any unfamiliar English words or phrases.

So, it's time to sit back and return to the late 1990's. Take this last journey with our beloved Princess in *Diana, A Spencer Forever.* I really hope you treasure the final months, days, and moments of the one and only Diana.

CHAPTER ONE

Without a Net

Shots rained down on the tinted windows of the green Audi. One of the car's passengers shrieked, whilst the other simply sighed.

"Diana, are those gunshots? What should we do?" Nora clutched the arm of her friend, as the rat-a-tat sound crashed around them.

Her Royal Highness, the Princess of Wales snorted. "There's nothing to bloody do, Nor. It's the wretched photographers. They bang their cameras on the glass – it sounds like gunshots, and is meant to make us open the windows, so they can snap my picture. It's a pathetic trick. Pay no attention."

Nora gasped, and impulsively hugged her dear friend. "Diana, what you have to cope with is unbearable. How can you endure the paparazzi stalking you like this? How did they even find out we were going to the opera tonight? There must be at least twenty photographers out there." Nora shook her brown curls angrily.

"They always know where I am, and where I'm going to be," the Princess replied wearily, her normally brilliant blue eyes troubled. "Whenever I think it can't get worse, matters turn even more horribly wrong. When I gave up my protection officers after the separation, I thought I'd finally gain my longed-for freedom. Hah! Now it's open season – the media are relentless." Diana opened her grey silk clutch bag, and applied an unnecessary coat of coral lipstick.

Diana and Nora had been close chums for well over a decade. They had been through so much together – good and ghastly – and nothing could come between them.

"Do you ever regret relinquishing your royal protection?" asked Nora timidly. This was a sore subject with the Princess.

"Never," responded Diana vehemently. "Charles – and his mother – pleaded with me to keep my PPOs at their expense. But after the separation was official, they had no say. Besides, those bodyguards were always there spying on me, and reporting back all my movements and conversations to the palace. Finally, I can breathe again without someone overlooking me twenty-four hours a day. It's the freedom I always longed for." Diana tossed her blond head in defiance.

Nora thought that this kind of freedom – with the unchecked press banging cameras on the windows of the limousine – was not a trade for the better. Surely Diana had been safer with the experienced and expertly-trained palace security machine? But Nora wisely kept her counsel. Diana would never admit she'd made a mistake in dismissing her security detail in its entirety. Best to leave it. She turned back to her friend with a reassuring smile, determined to make a proper night of it.

Tonight, the Princess of Wales was dressed in a Catherine Walker grey silk satin frock with simulated pearl embroidery, and matching pumps. Her short blond hair and makeup were freshly done, and she looked fabulous with diamond drop earrings and a matching bracelet.

Nora was as dark as Diana was fair. She was tiny at just 5'2", so her friend towered over her – especially in heels. Nora had shoulder-length curly auburn hair, sparkling green eyes, and was cheerful and bouncy.

Tonight, she had dressed in a short red skirt and gauzy white chiffon blouse.

It was October 1995, and unseasonably warm for London – a lovely autumn evening. Diana had been looking forward to an outing at Covent Garden to see *La Bohème* with Nora, and resented the intrusion of the press – bitterly. It had been almost three years since her formal separation from Prince Charles, and the public interest in her was as intense as before – perhaps even more invasive. She was as used to it as anyone could possibly get, and it still wore her down desperately at times. Why couldn't they just leave her private life alone? she asked herself for what seemed like the thousandth time.

Nora could see her friend was starting to get vexed. As the car pulled away, and the din of photographers receded, she was determined to get their evening back on track. Too many had been ruined in the past.

"Tell me, darling. Did Harry like my birthday gift? I'm very sorry that Clemmy and I couldn't make it to his party. She's still not entirely over the chicken pox yet." Prince Harry had turned eleven years old on September 15th, and unfortunately, Nora's daughter Clementine had been too ill to attend the celebration.

"Yes, he adores the mini-table tennis set. He and William have been playing it non-stop. William usually wins, but Harry is gaining strength all the time. How's my sweet Clemmy doing? Itching like crazy?" Diana had easily done a turn, and was centred on her friend and nine-year old god-daughter.

"Thank goodness, the worst seems to be over. Now she's just rather cranky to be stuck in the nursery whilst her friends are out playing. No scars, thankfully." Nora smiled to see her friend in better form.

"Well please give my little love a big hug and kiss from Auntie Diana. and tell her I'll bring her around some jelly babies very soon." As the car slowed, Diana sat up, straightened her long legs and prepared to exit the vehicle, clutching her bag to her upper chest to forestall photographers zooming in on her cleavage. Predictably, a crowd had been forming around the theatre in anticipation of a glimpse of the lovely Princess.

"You know Nora, I read that Marilyn Monroe was able to turn on and off her glamorous persona whenever she liked. She would walk down the street in a kerchief and sunglasses, unnoticed. Then she would say to her companion 'do you want to see her?' and would rip off her disguise and, in instant, become the dazzling movie star."

Nora knew that Diana had long harboured a fascination for the famous starlet who had died so tragically at the young age of thirty-six. She felt an affinity for the tortured star, who had suffered a troubled childhood, difficult marriages, personal problems with anxiety and depression; and who had been exploited by Hollywood and the press.

Nora laughed. "Well, you could certainly give her a run for her money. I never saw you shrink from your duties or obligations, and you've always shown a smiling and gracious face – even in the pouring rain at the dullest engagements. And I know how rotten it's been for you at times, darling. Putting a brave face on things when you were terribly sad or let down."

Diana gave her friend a small smile in gratitude. The car pulled up to the theatre entrance, and the crowds were shouting "Diana, Diana!" The Princess grinned and said, "do you want to see her then?" Nora nodded in encouragement.

The door opened, and the flashbulbs started to pop - blinding the two friends. Diana stepped out with an athletic bounce and a dazzling smile on her face, as she greeted the evening's hosts with her usual charm and grace. She stooped to receive a bouquet of flowers from a small girl, and gave her an encouraging hug. They exchanged a quiet word before Diana waved to the crowd, and disappeared into the theatre.

Nora scrambled to keep up with her friend, plastering a smile on her face as she fought a wave of nerves. You show 'em girl, she thought to herself with more than a little sense of pride and admiration. The Princess of Wales had arrived.

A few hours later, after an agreeable night at the opera and late supper with Nora, Diana returned alone to Kensington Palace. Her car passed through the security checkpoint without incident, and Diana alighted outside the doors to Apartments eight and nine – home. Waiting for her with his usual ready smile was her KP butler, Paul Burrell.

"Good evening, Ma'am," Paul greeted her with his habitual head bow, as he opened the heavy black double doors. "I trust you had a pleasant evening with your friend?"

"Hello, Paul," Diana smiled. "Yes, it was lovely, thank you. Any messages?" She swept into the foyer. A whisper of her signature Hermes 24 Faubourg perfume trailed behind her. She bounced up the staircase into her sitting room, as Paul strove to keep pace with her.

"Ms. Simmons said she tried your mobile but the line was engaged, and she wanted to ensure you knew she called. Also, Mr. Jephson rang to say he'll be a trifle late for your daily meeting in the morning. He has an unavoidable appointment, and he's very sorry for any inconvenience." Paul reeled off the messages as his boss entered the sitting room, kicked off her shoes, and flopped onto the sofa.

"Fine, fine," she replied. "I think we have a light day tomorrow, in the event." She paused. "Paul, the opera was brilliant. Never quite as good as a ballet performance, but very stirring. And Nora really needed a night out after being cooped up in the sickroom with Clemmy for the last week." Diana proceeded to fill in her butler on the myriad details of her evening. Living alone, with her boys at boarding school, she relied heavily on this senior staff member to be confidante, as well as head of household.

"Tea, Ma'am?" he offered, while remaining standing. No matter how long the Princess would take to regale him of the day's events, Paul never forgot his place as an employee. Diana had begged him time and again to take a seat during their long chats, and he always refused. She never offered anymore.

"Chamomile please, Paul, if it's not too much trouble?" The Princess smiled.

"The kettle is boiled and waiting, Ma'am. I'll be back in a tick with your tea." He bowed his head, and quickly left the room. Diana seized the opportunity to slip upstairs to her bedroom to change out of her evening frock into a long dressing gown, remove her makeup and jewelry; and return to the sitting room. Paul was waiting for her with the tea tray.

"And the photographers, Ma'am? Not too troublesome I hope?" Paul asked with real concern.

Diana gratefully took the proffered teacup, and gave Paul a wry glance. "Horrid as usual. Nora was quite stunned by the camera clacking ploy. Until you get used to it, it's quite realistic – and frightening -- as gunshots popping. But rather commonplace for me." She shrugged and paused. "Any new jokes for me, Paul?"

Diana had a racy sense of humour, and was forever on the lookout for new and spicy jokes to add to her repertoire.

"No, I'm afraid not, Ma'am," he replied with chagrin. He did not share his mistress' love of the dirty joke.

Paul Burrell had been with the Princess since 1987 – first as the Highgrove butler when he served both the Prince and Princess of Wales – then as the Kensington Palace butler since the separation in 1992. He had started his royal career in service as a footman to the Queen, and had thought long and hard about taking on the post of Highgrove butler. Leaving the Queen's service had been a tough decision, but the lure of the countryside, along with having his wife Maria as a housekeeper, and his two sons nearby had been too irresistible. He had become close to the Princess during that time, as had Maria. The young princes played with their sons Alex and Nick; and country life had been idyllic. From time-to-time, he had filled in as the KP butler, but never envisioned the move to London. After the separation, the households had been divided. Because of the Burrell family's closeness to the Princess of Wales, they were firmly seen to be in her camp; and a job and life change to Kensington Palace was inevitable. That was in 1993, and although the transition had been trying – especially on Maria - they were now settled back in the heart of London. Paul was loyal, steadfast, and completely devoted to the Princess. He routinely worked fourteen to sixteen hours a day, and it was not uncommon for Diana to call him back from his cottage on the KP property late at night, for another chat over a personal crisis, or urgent errand.

"Well, you're in luck then, Paul, because I heard one from the driver tonight. What three words will ruin a man's ego?" She giggled and waited expectantly.

Paul sighed. He had played this game before – many times. "I don't know, Ma'am. What three words will ruin a man's ego?"

"IS IT IN?" Diana cackled, while her butler winced. "Get it, Paul? It's so small that the woman doesn't even know if it's in!" As usual, the Princess was her own biggest fan when it came to off-colour humour. She dissolved into peals of laughter.

"Very amusing, Ma'am. Thank you for sharing."

"Don't be a poor sport, Paul. Men are so sensitive about that area of the body. It's just a joke." Diana was still smiling, as she blew on her tea to cool it, then took a sip.

"Just so, Ma'am. Will there be anything else tonight?" Paul was eager to get home to his little family, and it seemed the Princess was winding down.

She waved him away. "No Paul, thank you kindly. Give my best to Maria, and see you in the morning."

After Paul left, Diana carried her teacup to the desk and sat down. The lamp was already lit so she pulled out her personalised KP Princess of Wales stationery, and quickly penned a thank-you note to the hostess of the luncheon she'd attended that day for *Barnardo's* Children's Charity. She signed with her distinctive *With Love from Diana*, and left it propped against the lamp for Paul to post in the morning. She toyed with the idea of ringing back her friend Simone Simmons, but decided it was too late, and she'd just turn in.

As she fell asleep alone in her beautiful palace, Diana thought back to the comments she'd made about Marilyn Monroe to her friend Nora. She herself had put on a public face for so long, that it came automatically – too much so. She needed to get involved with a cause that was more important, bigger than herself. She resolved to speak to Patrick about it in the morning.

Several days later, Diana was alone again at KP, but this time it was by choice. She had given all the staff the day off for Guy Fawkes Day, and had even convinced

Paul she didn't require his services that Sunday. This was going to be a very special day.

For a long time, Diana had been considering giving a live television interview to a sympathetic reporter. As she had felt when collaborating with Andrew Morton on *Diana, Her True Story,* the urge to convey her own side of the story – the truth – was almost overpowering. Although she regretted some of the things that had been written about her in the book, it *was* all true. She needed the world to know that Charles had cheated on her with Camilla Parker Bowles, and had been in love with *that woman* for the entire duration of her un-fairy tale marriage.

Albeit public sympathies had been overwhelmingly with the Princess, the cost to Diana on the personal front had been enormous. The book had been the catalyst to the formal separation, which had been part of her aim. The fallout, however, to Princes William and Harry had been far greater than she'd ever imagined. William especially, had been very hurt and embarrassed about what was written about his parents. And she had been frozen out by the royal family – they were barely civil to her at the few engagements she'd been invited to attend since then. Prince Philip had snubbed her openly at Royal Ascot.

In an effort for Charles to get his side heard, his friends and aides encouraged a biography by Jonathon Dimbleby called *The Prince of Wales,* which had been published in 1994. Although it only lightly touched on the royal marriage, it was intended as a public relation undertaking to portray Charles in a more sympathetic light. After all, he was the heir to the British throne, and needed a boost to his image. It had been followed up by an ill-advised television interview with the Prince by the book's author. The biography and film were commissioned to mark the twenty-fifth anniversary of Charles' investiture as Prince of Wales. Mr. Dimbleby was given unparalleled access to the future sovereign, and followed him around for a year and a half.

The interview had been a disaster, with the Prince admitting to adultery on camera.

"Did you try to be faithful and honorable when you married Lady Diana Spencer in July 1981?" asked Dimbleby.

"Yes, absolutely," replied Charles with a steady eye.

"And you were?" pressed the questioner, and well-known British journalist.

"Yes," Prince Charles answered. Then after a slight pause, he added, "Until it became irretrievably broken down, us both having tried."

The last had dealt a massive blow to the Prince, who was doing his utmost to be honourable and honest. It backfired, the public was aghast at his admission, and support had poured in for the Princess.

Since that broadcast, Diana had been considering her own television interview to set the record straight once and for all. And there was a secondary motivation – her increasing anxiety about her apartment being bugged, and information leaking constantly to the palace. She was convinced that even the country's national security service, the MI5 were watching her. She'd confided in her closest friends that she was truly concerned for her life – that someone or some people were out to destroy her reputation, and maybe even arrange for her death. She'd had her KP apartment swept for bugs on a regular basis, and had become extremely careful about where she held private conversations.

For weeks she had been in contact with Martin Bashir, a television presenter and reporter for BBC's Panorama programme. Her brother Earl Spencer had met Martin, and the two had discussed Diana's security concerns. Charles had then put him in touch with his sister. Diana had spoken to Martin a number of times at her friends' safe houses, and felt he was the right person to tell her story. She believed he would treat her with respect and dignity. He had provided her with the questions in advance, and she had rehearsed the answers on her own, until she felt confident and assured.

Today, Martin and his camera crew were to be smuggled into the palace to record the interview in deep secrecy. Diana had not asked Buckingham Palace for permission, nor had she told Charles of the impending taping. And surprising for Diana herself, she had not confided in any of her friends, save one. She had asked many of them separately for advice about consenting to a television interview, and they had all given her the same counsel – a solid and alarmist *no*. Even some of her favourite press associates like Richard Kay and Richard Attenborough had advised strongly against it. She had not told her private secretary Patrick Jephson, nor her press secretary Geoff Crawford that she had decided to do the interview. She wanted nothing to stop her from this enterprise, nor anyone to try and talk her out of it. Despite all the negative advice, she trusted her instinct that this was not only the right move for her, she *had* to do it. Today was the day.

As she began to dress for the event, her mobile rang. It was Nora.

"Hello, Diana. It's just me. How are you feeling today?" She attempted a breezy tone.

"I'm ace, Nor. You didn't need to ring me. I'm not going to change my mind." Nora was the one person that Diana had chosen to confide in. Not her butler, nor either of her two sisters, her mother, or her best friend Carolyn. Just Nora.

"It's never too late to call it off, Duch," replied Nora, with an edge to her voice. "You're the bloody Princess of Wales. You can halt the whole thing in an instant, you know."

Diana laughed shortly. "Nice try, Nora, but it won't do. I'm determined to see this thing through. The financial settlement is moving at a snail's pace, and I want custody settled, and my residence to be firmly resolved. This limbo is killing me. If everyone – and I don't just mean the public, but the palace too – can see my side, it can only help expedite matters." She lowered her voice. "And you know I need to go on the record as a credible and sane Princess to stay safe. I know all the questions, and my answers are prepared. Please just stand with me on this." Diana's tone began to take on a touch of impatience.

"Alright, darling. I'm sorry. Of course, you know what's best. Just be careful. Your public adores you, but think of the children. They're older now and will remember everything." Unseen by Diana, Nora was pacing her own sitting room.

"I always think of the boys," Diana retorted crossly. "Everything I do is for them." She paused. "I must go, Nora. I need to get dressed. They'll be here soon."

"Don't be annoyed with me, darling. You know I must always at least try to paint an objective viewpoint. That's one of the reasons you keep me around, remember?" Nora attempted to soften the Princess.

"Alright Nor, but please just leave it. Trust me. Everything will be fine. I'll speak to you later. Bye." Diana put down the phone in a hurry. Nora rang off more thoughtfully.

Diana resumed her careful toilette. Her hairdresser had come as usual that morning, so her hair was professionally styled. She did her own makeup, and penciled in dark eyeliner under her eyes. She was going for a subdued look.

She wore a black skirt and jacket, with matching tights. A white blouse softened the look. Gold earrings completed the ensemble. Diana gazed into her reflection in her dressing room, considered it suitable, and went downstairs to meet the journalist and camera crew.

They had decided to film in the boys' sitting room, which had been Prince Charles' study before the separation. As the lighting equipment was being set up, Diana chatted with Martin, whilst reviewing her notes.

"No need to be nervous, Ma'am. It will be just as we agreed. You have the list of questions. I'll ask them in order slowly. You don't need to gaze into the camera – just look at me. Any time you want to take a break, just stop. You can take all the time you need, and then we'll resume. The rest we can do in editing later. Do you have any questions?"

Diana shook her head no. She felt calm and prepared. This was her chance! "I'm ready whenever you are, Martin," she replied with a small smile.

Martin had been rather surprised at her demeanor and appearance. He was used to seeing the Princess in bright colours, with a ready joke on her lips. He took note that she wanted to make a certain type of impression on camera – to be taken seriously. He would do his best to treat her respectfully.

Outwardly Martin was the epitome of serene composure. Inside he was trembling with excitement. His weeks and weeks of laying careful groundwork were finally coming to fruition. He was about to conduct an exclusive interview with the Princess of Wales. Barbara Walters had tried and failed. Piers Morgan and countless other famous journalists had attempted to gain an interview with the powerful Princess. But only he had succeeded. Over the weeks they had been meeting, Martin had slowly been gaining Diana's trust. She was eager to tell her story, but after years of being hounded and abused by the media and photographers, she didn't want to be pressured and pushed. Martin's polite and serene style really appealed to her. There was something about this soft-spoken thirty-two-year-old British-Pakistani journalist that touched a nerve with her. As always, she trusted her instincts.

Very few topics had been determined to be off-limits. Diana would be willing to speak about her romance with Captain James Hewitt, but not any other men with whom she'd been linked in the press. She was prepared to talk about the royal family, and even Camilla Parker Bowles – the Prince's long-term love. Martin knew that if the Princess were forthright about what had really transpired in the royal marriage – this could be the most explosive interview ever broadcast. He smiled at Diana.

"Right-o then, Ma'am. You can sit here in front of the fireplace, and let's get started, shall we?"

Diana sat poised and ready for the first question.

"Your Royal Highness, how prepared were you for the pressures that came with marrying into the Royal Family?"

For the next three hours – including many breaks – Diana answered question after question. "Were you overwhelmed by the pressure from the people initially? How did you handle the transition from being Lady Diana Spencer to the most photographed, the most talked-about, woman in the world? What was the family's reaction to your post-natal depression? According to press reports, it was suggested that it was around this time things became so difficult that you actually tried to injure yourself...? The depression was resolved, as you say, but it was subsequently reported that you suffered bulimia? Is that true? When you say you were never given any credit, what do you mean? Around 1986, again according to the biography written by Jonathon Dimbleby about your husband, he says that your husband renewed his relationship with Mrs. Camilla Parker Bowles. Were you aware of that? Do you think Mrs. Parker Bowles was a factor in the breakdown of your marriage? What effect do you think the book (*Diana, Her True Story*) had on your husband and the Royal Family? By the December of that year, as you say, you'd agreed to a legal separation. What were your feelings at that time? There were also a series of telephone calls which allegedly were made by you to a Mr. Oliver Hoare. Did you make what were described as nuisance phone calls? Do you really believe that a campaign was being waged against you? What was your reaction to your husband's disclosure to Jonathan Dimbleby that he had in fact committed adultery? Were you unfaithful? What role do you see for yourself in the future? Do you think you will ever be Queen? Do you think the Prince of Wales will ever be King?"

At times, Martin was frustrated at the vagueness of her responses: "I received a great deal of treatment, but I knew in myself what I needed was space and time to adapt to all the different roles that had come my way. I was crying out for help but giving the wrong signals." "We struggled a bit with it, it was very difficult." "Oh, a woman's instinct is a very good one." "It was already difficult, but it became increasingly difficult." "Well, my husband's side were very busy stopping me. But I am a free spirit - unfortunately for some."

He pushed with follow-up questions as much as he dared, and received bits of clarification. He was still left unsatisfied, but overall, the interview had been a huge success. Diana had admitted to bulimia, injuring herself, having an affair with James Hewitt, and most tellingly – that she didn't think Prince Charles was fit to be King. Martin knew he had a box of unexploded dynamite in his care.

After a grueling afternoon, the lights were turned off, and everyone breathed a sigh of relief that it was all over.

"You were brilliant, Ma'am. Simply brilliant. You couldn't have done any better." Martin beamed.

"Do you really think so, Martin?" Now that the cameras were switched off, Diana reverted to her usual ebullient self. She giggled. "I was a bit uneasy at times – especially about the questions about when I was unwell. For the most part, I feel I did a bit of all right, though. Thank you for staying with the questions we agreed to. Albeit some of the follow-up probing was unexpected." Diana shot Martin a black look. "I'm counting on you to stick to our agreement. I don't expect to see any surprises come out of the editing, Martin." She turned icy blue eyes on him, as her displeasure was crystal clear.

Martin bowed his head. "Of course, Ma'am. Sorry if I pushed a little hard." He held up his hands, and smiled his boyish grin. "Once a journalist, always a journalist, Ma'am. But don't be concerned," he rushed to add. "You'll be delighted with the finished product, I promise. Your image will shine even brighter."

Diana felt slightly mollified. "I'm relying on it, Martin. And on you," she replied meaningfully." The reporter and camera crew finished packing up, and left KP as surreptitiously as they'd arrived.

That evening, an impromptu party broke out at Kensington Palace. Diana had called Nora full of the news of the filming, and her friend had insisted on hearing it first-hand. When she'd arrived, she'd been surprised to see the Duchess of York, Sarah Ferguson, already sipping white wine in the Princess' sitting room. Paul Burrell had been called when the former sisters-in-law had been searching for the corkscrew, and insisted on coming back to look after them. The mood was light and celebratory.

"Nora, darling. Come through. Paul, please pour my friend a glass of wine. We're about to make a toast." Diana had changed into black leggings and a long, pale blue jumper. Her piercing blue eyes sparkled, and she was slightly flushed from the wine. She rarely drank, and it tended to make her either giggly or more tearful – depending on her mood. Tonight, she was joyful.

"Hullo Nora. Lovely to see you. Surviving the chicken pox, I hear. I trust Clemmy is on the mend?" Red-haired and exuberant Sarah gave Nora a double kiss, as she made a place for her on the pale green sofa. The two knew each other quite well through Diana and various children's parties, but were more acquaintances than friends.

"Fergie. Bril to see you, too. How are the adorable Princesses? Clemmy was heartbroken not to have seen them at Harry's birthday party. And yes, she's turned the corner, and is now just crabby, not sick." Nora was surprised to see Diana's former sister-in-law here on this Sunday night. Diana tended to keep her friends in different compartments – fun friends, charity contacts, travel companions, other moms, special confidantes, family, etc. Rarely did she put them together in groups. She talked to each of them individually – some about her innermost thoughts and feelings; and others about shopping and the latest Hollywood films. Nora knew that this was quite deliberate on the part of the Princess. She tested her friends' loyalty often, and didn't want them sharing information and speaking to each other about her. She must be feeling quite jubilant tonight to include both her and Sarah in the Bashir interview debrief.

Sarah was also in top form. "Bea and Eugenie are just ducky, Nora. Thanks for asking. Already thinking about Father Christmas coming in a few weeks. Making their lists and all that. But enough of the children – Diana, give over. Tell us what happened this afternoon!"

"I think I really succeeded in my aim to portray myself as strong, in control, and most of all – perfectly sane. I stayed calm. I didn't cry, Sarah! And I got across all my major points. I think people will be talking about this interview for a long time to come." Diana sipped her wine, and smiled at her two dear friends.

"Like what, Duch? What did he ask? "prodded Sarah.

"He asked if I thought Mrs. Parker Bowles was a factor in the breakdown of the marriage, and I answered: 'Well there were three of us in the marriage, so it was a bit crowded.' How's that, Charles?" Diana broke into her infamous giggles.

"Bravo for you, Duch. That was one we had talked about. Charles will simply die when he sees it." Sarah joined in a hearty laugh. "Did he ask you about James?" It was clear the cheerful Sarah had been in on some of the pre-interview planning.

"Yes, and I think I handled that well, too. He asked if I'd been unfaithful. And I said 'Yes, I adored him. Yes, I was in love with him. But I was very let down.' It felt good to say it out loud. I've been waiting a long time to strike back from the humiliation Charles subjected me to when he admitted to adultery on that Dimbleby programme. Not to mention the biography that went along with it. And I want James to know too how much he hurt me for writing that horrid book about our romance. What a cad. No wonder the press is calling him the 'Love Rat.'" Diana had nothing but contempt now for her former lover for collaborating on a tell-all book called *Princess in Love* about the couple's affair.

Nora couldn't help herself. She gasped. "Diana, you're not serious. You didn't say that on national television?" Nora looked at her friend in horror.

"I bloody well did, and I would do it again," Diana replied with a familiar obstinate tone. "I needed to do this on *my* terms. And I know my public will always bolster me. Especially when they hear how the royal family has treated me, and the surveillance and bugging that's been going on. Don't lecture me, Nora." The two friends faced each other.

During this exchange, Paul had been refilling glasses, serving crisps and fruit; and standing by in case he was needed. However, he was severely dismayed. What was his Princess thinking, giving this interview and sharing the dirty linen of the royal marriage to the whole world?

"Paul, did you know of this interview? Could you not talk your boss out of this absurd idea?" Nora turned to the butler for support.

"Her Royal Highness did confide in me her desire to raise her voice in a television interview, yes. But I wasn't aware of today's taping." He paused and turned to Diana. "Ma'am, did you get the Queen's permission? Is His Royal Highness, the Prince of Wales aware of this scheme?" Paul posed these last questions carefully.

"No, of course the Queen and Charles don't know anything about this, Paul. Do you think they would have let me participate in this interview the way I wanted to, if I'd tried to get advance permission?" The Princess snapped at her butler. He turned white, knowing of the disastrous effect this would have on the palace and royal family.

"Diana, darling, you're playing with fire," offered Nora simply. "You must advise them before the interview is broadcast." She rose to take Diana's hands in her own. "Surely you see that?"

Diana dropped her friend's hands. "Of course, I know that. I'll let them know before the show airs. But why are we concentrating on that? This is supposed to be a celebration of my success. I thought you were my friends?" Diana's eyes began to fill with tears.

"Well, I for one, think you are very brave, Duch. Were you able to talk about all the other topics we discussed? Your statement about becoming the Queen of People's Hearts was masterful!" Fergie took another sip of wine, and tried to boost the spirits of her sister-in-law.

"Ta, Sarah," murmured a mollified Princess. "I hope

that no matter what happens between Charles and me, that I can always play that role – it's vital I help people as the Princess of Wales." She paused. "And, yes, we touched on almost everything – the press, my past and future roles, my sickness, the children, and so on. I *was* feeling good about the whole thing until these two nervous nellies started raining on our party." Diana pouted as she looked in the direction of her closest staff member and best friend.

"Ma'am, I'm very sorry. You know I'm always here to help you and smooth any rough waters. Please tell me how I can assist." Paul apologised profusely and sincerely. He truly only wanted the best for the beleaguered Princess.

"I'm sorry too, Diana, but as your friend, I have to caution you when I think you're going a tad too far. Why don't you tell us everything, so we can all be on the same page and support you with one voice?" Nora was now down to the business end of damage control. Like Paul, she would do anything to help her friend – even when Diana was her own worst enemy with the media.

"I think another round of wine is in order," Fergie jumped in. "And it's jolly good that the last sweep didn't find any bugs in here, Duch. We surely wouldn't want anyone to listen in on this conversation."

The little group was more subdued now, thinking of the inevitable fallout that would be produced from Diana's interview on the BBC Panorama programme. They spent the next hour reviewing Diana's notes, and hearing from her as best as she could recollect, exactly the questions Martin had posed, and her own responses. They parted with hugs and kisses just after midnight. Diana shooed Paul back home to his family, and returned alone to her sitting room.

Sitting by herself with a small pool of light from a lamp keeping darkness at bay, Diana felt satisfied with her performance today. She was tired but exhilarated. Only one small point niggled at her brain. She hadn't told any of her little gang of supporters about the final questions in the interview. Something had held her back – perhaps a small fear that she may have overstepped the mark? She shook her head no. It was nothing. She'd not implicated Charles in any way, or cast him in a poor light – at least no poorer than the one he'd focused on himself with his adultery.

She cast her mind back to the questions and answers.

BASHIR: "Do you think the Prince of Wales will ever be King?"

DIANA: "I don't think any of us know the answer to that. And obviously, it's a question that's in everybody's head. But who knows, who knows what fate will produce, who knows what circumstances will provoke?"

BASHIR: "But you would know him better than most people. Do you think he would wish to be King?"

DIANA: "There was always conflict on that subject with him when we discussed it, and I understood that conflict, because it's a very demanding role, being Prince of Wales, but it's an equally more demanding role being King. And being Prince of Wales produces more freedom now, and being King would be a little bit more suffocating. And because I know the character, I would think that the top job, as I call it, would bring enormous limitations to him, and I don't know whether he could adapt to that."

BASHIR: "Do you think it would make more sense in the light of the marital difficulties that you and the Prince of Wales have had, if the position of monarch passed directly to your son Prince William?"

DIANA: "Well then, you have to see that William's very young at the moment, so do you want a burden like that to be put on his shoulders at such an age? So, I can't answer that question."

BASHIR: "Would it be your wish that when Prince William comes of age, that he were to succeed the Queen rather than the current Prince of Wales?"
DIANA: "My wish is that my husband finds peace of mind, and from that follows other things, yes."

Diana chewed her fingernail. Surely that was woolly enough to not be incriminating, whilst also casting doubt on the Prince's abilities? Surely, she hadn't gone too far? Surely? Diana sat by herself for a long time, hoping she'd not just made the biggest mistake of her life.

CHAPTER TWO

New Life at Kensington Palace

The next morning, Diana's private secretary Patrick Jephson, arrived for the morning meeting and briefing. As usual, he was accompanied by Diana's long-time lady-in-waiting Anne Beckwith-Smith, and press secretary Geoffrey Crawford. Besides reviewing the week's schedule with particular emphasis on today's diary, Patrick shared with her the news of the day, as well as vast amounts of royal correspondence. This could be any number of invitations, memos from the palace, briefs about upcoming overseas trips, school flyers, and masses of personal post – letters and cards from people Diana had connected to over the years, personal friends, and so on. Now that she was no longer on the royal roster for official duties, she didn't receive an official *bag* of mail to be dealt with daily, but the post was always a daunting task; and one that both the Princess and Patrick worked hard at to maintain control.

Diana had pared down her staff significantly since the separation. Besides this trio that supported her in official capacities, she had a daily hairstylist, a dresser, chauffeurs, bodyguards, and of course, the ever-present Paul, on whom she relied heavily. This was in addition to the KP staff of chefs, maids, and cleaners. But she felt she needed to keep her inner circle small and intimate – it was a thorny prospect knowing who to trust.

Anne had been with her since her marriage to Prince Charles fourteen years ago. She was trustworthy, reliable, efficient at her duties, and had become as close a friend to the Princess as a staff member possibly could. Diana liked to call her media-proof, since she had never once spoken to the press, nor succumbed to offers of vast sums of money to share details of the Princess' life. Anne was wholly dedicated to Diana, having never married. She was ten years older, did not compete in the looks department, and had a no-nonsense air of going about her duties. In short, she was irreplaceable, and Diana was quite fond of her.

Patrick Jephson had been with the Princess of Wales since 1988, first as an equerry, and most recently as her first very own private secretary. He was of Irish descent, and had served in the British Navy before assuming royal roles. He was devoted to serving the Princess, and was efficient in his own quiet way. He had a wry sense of humour, and was sometimes able to make controversial suggestions to the Princess using his unique brand of diplomacy and humour. He had been working tirelessly since the separation to help carve out a role for the Princess that would leverage her incredible strengths and widespread popularity. This was an uphill battle with all the media skirmishes being waged on both sides of the War of the Wales. Patrick was committed, however, to furthering the causes of his boss with the Queen, and palace machine. Besides handling correspondence and the diary, Patrick was also responsible for organising and managing Diana's overseas trips, and he performed during these demanding tours with tact and efficiency. He had masterfully overseen jaunts to Nepal, Zimbabwe, Japan, and Russia so far. Argentina was up next.

Geoffrey Crawford was the newest member of the little team. He had been with the Princess since 1993, and was the liaison between Diana and the media. He was her official spokesperson – albeit she, like the other members of the royal family, rarely issued press releases. They all believed that no comment was the safest response to almost any news item concerning the Windsors. It was also Geoffrey's responsibility to keep the Princess apprised of what the press was saying and printing about her, although Diana kept up with this incredibly well on her own. She had all the major British papers delivered to her daily, and poured over them looking for pieces about her and her appearances. In the past, she had also scoured the news for any items about her husband and *that woman*. She had finally given that up, but she still obsessively read every piece printed about her. Even though everyone in her circle had advised her against this daily ritual, Diana had simply not been able to give it up. She needed to see and read what the newspapers were printing about her. And she also craved the positive feedback about her charity work, mothering accomplishments, and fashion triumphs. All her staff knew, however, when something negative had been circulated about her. She would be moody and glum all day when given a bad review, or had spotted an unbecoming photograph.

Geoffrey rounded out the threesome supporting the Princess of Wales. Today, on this Monday morning, there had been favourable press and photos of Diana at the opera, so she was in a fine mood.

She had bounced into the drawing room, freshly showered and made up after a morning run through the Kensington Palace gardens. She tended to do this early in the day or late at night when no one would have suspected the tall blonde with the sweatshirt, leggings, sweatband, and earphones clamped to her head was the Princess of Wales. She also belonged to the Chelsea Harbour Club, and frequented it almost daily. Her workouts included strength training, and sometimes a round or two of competitive tennis with friends. And she still adored a punishing ballet workout when she could fit it into her diary.

"Good morning, one and all. Not a bad day for November," she chirped to no one in particular. Diana looked smashing in a forest green pantsuit with a delicate white blouse, and gold earrings and necklace. Although she had always looked terrific, her work on her muscle strength and endurance in the last couple of years had given her a toned and lean look that made her even more beautiful. She had all but conquered her on-again off-again battle with bulimia. Her skin was clear, her eyes bright, and she had a ready smile.

"Good morning, Your Royal Highness" replied Anne, Patrick and Geoffrey in unison. Paul offered tea and coffee to the small team, and they settled in for the daily briefing.

Patrick took the lead. "Ma'am, this week isn't too hectic, if I may say. Shall we go through the diary?" He was prepared with his notes and omnipresent leather valise. The royal diary was set six months in advance, albeit there were more holes now in the schedule since the official separation. Diana also liked to be spontaneous, and to feel she had some flexibility in her schedule, so these meetings were crucial to keep everything in balance. If the Princess felt too hemmed in with unwanted engagements, she tended to be cross and more difficult to sort out, and surprise everyone by adding in unexpected plans that needed to be accommodated in a rush. He hoped this week had a good blend of business and personal commitments to keep her engaged and fulfilled. He looked up at the Princess expectantly.

"Yes, yes," she waved her hand. "Let's get on with it."

"Very good, Ma'am. Right, so today you're having lunch here with Ms. Simmons at one p.m. Then you're to visit your acupuncturist, Ms. Oonagh Shanley-Toffolo at her clinic at four o'clock. This evening, you are scheduled to attend the British Red Cross dinner to raise funds for the troops fighting in Bosnia. There's just a meet and greet, then the dinner, Ma'am. You're not expected to speak or present whatsoever." He paused here for a reaction. Getting none, he plunged on.

"Tomorrow, you have your standing weekly colonic irrigation appointment at eleven a.m. Then you're free until three o'clock, when you're due to meet the journalist Mr. Kay for tea here at the palace. You asked for the evening to be kept open, but your friend Ms. Monckton inquired if you could meet her for dinner?" Patrick paused again.

"Rosa? Yes, goodie, that will be splendid. Can you make a reservation at San Lorenzo for nine p.m. please, Patrick? And then, what about Wednesday?" Diana was eager to get through this rather tedious routine.

"You requested the morning free for personal errands last week, Ma'am. I believe you wanted to finish your Christmas shopping?" Diana nodded. "Very good, then you have no luncheon plans, but your afternoon is reserved for some dress fittings and a facial, I believe?" At this last, he looked over at the lady-in-waiting for confirmation. She nodded. "And then you have a private dinner scheduled here for Wednesday evening, Ma'am."

Diana smiled. "Yes, that's excellent, Patrick. And what about Thursday, then? Not too early a start, I hope?" Diana's clear blue eyes pierced those of her private secretary. "Not at all, Ma'am," Patrick replied formally. "We have time on the diary to discuss your upcoming Argentina trip, and you kindly asked me to stay for luncheon after our eleven a.m. meeting? Is that still satisfactory?" At her nod, he continued. At half-past three, you have a massage here, and then Mrs. and Miss Truscott are coming for dinner and a video night."

"Nora and Clemmy? How lovely. Anne, we'll have to sort through the boys' videos to find something a little girl would like. Or perhaps you'll need to go and rent something new at the video store?"

"Very good, Ma'am," acknowledged Anne, as she made a note.

Patrick carried on. "Friday is an awayday for you, Ma'am. You're scheduled to attend the tenth anniversary celebration of St. Luke's Hospice in Sheffield. They're opening a new cancer ward, and you'll be saying a few words. I have the short speech ready for you to review. And Geoff has also looked it over."

The Princess nodded. "Yes, that is an important engagement. People dying with dignity is of the utmost importance. Anne, we need to consider my wardrobe for that visit." Diana could always be counted on to support any causes or functions for those in the greatest need. "What time will we return, Patrick? I need to be here when William arrives from Eton." With this, she broke into a huge grin.

Life had been lonely for the Princess at the palace since her youngest, Harry, had followed in his brother's footsteps in attending Ludgrove Boarding School. William had just started at the prestigious Eton College this fall, and Diana had been longing to see him. This weekend was only his second exeat this term. Unfortunately, young Harry's exeat was not in sync with William's, so she wouldn't be seeing him this weekend. He had already been home three times. Now having been at Ludgrove since 1992, the settling in period was well over and Harry was thriving.

"Remember when our days centred around the school runs for the boys, Anne?" asked Diana wistfully, as she rose from the sofa to look out the window. "Now this house seems so empty and quiet without them."

"Yes Ma'am, but it's only a few days until Prince William is home, and then you'll have a proper weekend all to yourselves to see how he's getting on at Eton. And he is close by. Doesn't he walk to Windsor Castle every Sunday to have tea with Her Majesty?" Anne wanted to jolly along her mistress, so they could complete the task at hand.

"You're right, Anne – best to look forwards, not backwards. And yes, William has started having tea with the Queen every Sunday afternoon. It's her beginning the training he needs to someday take on the future role of King. So far, he seems to quite enjoy it. He loves history, thank goodness. I expect I'll hear all about it on Friday."

Diana turned to face the little group. "Well, that's the diary sorted then, isn't it? I want the whole weekend kept free for William – until he goes for tea and back to school on Sunday. I'll have to start planning ahead for all his favourite foods and treats. Anne, let's think of some fun things for us to do. And banana flan for William's welcome home pudding!" The Princess clapped her hands in excitement. Nothing made her happier than spending time with her boys. Absolutely nothing.

Patrick and Geoffrey exchanged a knowing look. "We're not quite concluded yet, Ma'am. Geoffrey would like to go over the latest news items from Buckingham Palace, and the protocol for the St. Luke's hospice visit."

Diana sighed. "Must we, Geoffrey? Is there anything in that pile of crown-covered paper that matters to me at all?" Diana waved towards the stack of important-looking documents that her press secretary was shuffling.

"Nothing urgent, Ma'am. Some notices about the schedule for the boys for the upcoming holidays, a status report on Her Royal Highness, Queen Elizabeth the Queen Mother's hip replacement surgery, and a few other affairs. Nothing you can't review at your leisure. About the hospice visit though…" Geoffrey attempted to summarise the day's correspondence to suit the Princess' mood.

"Geoffrey, haven't we done enough of these visits to execute them in our sleep? Must we pour over every moment in excruciating detail?" Diana was eager now to call her time her own. She still had a mountain of personal correspondence to sort, and she needed to start her daily round of telephone calls.

"Ma'am, you said yourself this is an important engagement. It will just take a few minutes to review the names and titles of your hosts, history of the hospice, sequence of events, room layout, your short speech, the photographs we've approved for the press, and so on. The usual. It won't take but a few minutes."

"Can we please do it tomorrow, Geoff? Or better yet, type up a brief, and I'll read it over a supper tray one night this week? You're my A-Team – surely you can find a more efficient way to sort these engagements?" Diana's tone was weary, not from fatigue, but from the boredom of repetition.

Patrick and Geoffrey exchanged another glance. They knew they'd been defeated. "Of course, Ma'am, as you wish. The brief will be on your desk before lunch, and I'll ensure we include time on the diary this week for a short review. Will that suit you?"

"Perfectly, Geoff and thank you." She smiled to indicate the meeting was over. "So, if there's nothing else?" she asked hopefully.

Patrick cleared his throat. "Just one more item, Ma'am. Is there anything you'd like to share with us? Any news or upcoming events that we should be apprised of?" There had been some easiness and tension amongst the palace grapevine, and he wanted to be sure he was kept in the know about anything affecting the Princess of Wales.

Diana raised one eyebrow. "Not a thing, Patrick. My weekend was boring as hell."

"Very good, Ma'am." Patrick and Geoffrey rose to leave, as they gave head bows to the Princess of Wales.

"Oh, there is one more thing," said Diana as the two men waited. "Please send a bouquet of flowers with my best wishes for a speedy recovery to the Queen Mother. I understand she's doing remarkably well for a ninety-five-year-old woman who's undergone this type of surgery. She's a tough one, I'll give her that." Although Diana and Prince Charles' beloved grandmother were not close, Diana held a grudging respect for the mother of the current Queen.

The two men nodded again, and retreated. Anne stayed to help with the Princess' letter-writing, and to settle the week's menus.

A short while later, Simone Simmons arrived at Kensington Palace. She'd been a frequent visitor there since 1993, and was easily waved through security, and greeted warmly by Paul.

"Hullo, Paul. Did you have a good weekend? How is the family?" Simone was short with dark wavy brown hair and a beautiful smile. She had originally been engaged by the Princess to cleanse Kensington Palace of negative energies, and been a firm confidante since that time. Simone was an energy healer who worked out of her London flat, and had spent many hours listening to and supporting Diana since they had first met. Single and the proud owner of three cats, Simone could dedicate loads of her time to the Princess – be it over the phone in long, rambling conversations, or visits such as this – either to KP or Simone's small flat. Diana seemed to like Simone's positive yet sometimes provocative points-of-view about her life and events.

"Good afternoon, Ms. Simmons. Maria and the boys are well – we had a lovely weekend, thank you for asking." He took Simone's jacket, and nodded up the staircase. "She's in the sitting room. I'll bring along some beverages. Luncheon will be served in about thirty minutes." Paul was his reliable, efficient self.

Simone thanked him, and bounded up the formal staircase. As always, she paused to look at the portrait on the landing. It was one of Diana's favourites – the Princess standing looking off into the distance with a serious, faraway gaze. She wore a frilly white blouse and long, turquoise satin skirt, and Queen Mary's emeralds as a choker. Nelson Shanks had painted her in 1994, and over the fifty sittings it had taken to complete the piece, Nelson and his wife Leona had become dear friends of the Princess. She was well used to the mind-numbing business of portrait-sitting, so tried to keep the threesome giggling and laughing throughout the project.

It was a large, magnificent portrait that showed an independent Princess, perhaps a little despondent for the past, but firmly eying the future. No guest failed to gasp or comment on its stunning almost full-length impact.

Kensington Palace had been Diana's home for thirteen years. They'd moved in here just before William was born in June 1982, and not a moment too soon. Diana had been longing for a home of her own, and had been eager to move out of Prince Charles' Buckingham Palace apartments and the haunting memories of his bachelor days.

She and Charles had also shared Highgrove House, a country retreat in Gloucestershire – mainly at weekends – for most of the marriage. After the separation, it had permanently become Charles' haven and sometimes headquarters for the business of being the Prince of Wales. He loved the estate, especially the gardens over which he'd lovingly laboured since the estate's purchase in 1980. The boys adored the outdoors life there. Diana had enjoyed it at times, but at heart she was a city girl, and was content to leave Highgrove behind after the separation in 1992.

Built in 1689, the red-bricked Kensington Palace was in central London in the fashionable Knightsbridge district, and close to shopping at Kensington High Street. William the III had been its first royal inhabitant. Queen Victoria had been born at KP, and had been awoken there in 1837 to be told that her uncle, King William IV had died, and that she was now Queen. She then promptly moved to Buckingham Palace. During World War II, Kensington Palace was severely damaged during The Blitz of 1940. It had been hit by an incendiary bomb that exploded in the north side of Clock Court, damaging many of the surrounding buildings, including the State Apartments. KP had been rebuilt, and ongoing renovations and refurbishments were a matter of course.

Kensington Palace was a series of apartments, housing senior royals who were mainly close relatives of the Queen. These were known as grace-and-favour apartments – homes granted for life for nominal rents in exchange for service or familial proximity to the crown. The Queen's sister Her Royal Highness Princess Margaret lived at number ten, next door to Diana at Apartments Eight and Nine. Although they had been on friendly terms since Diana had burst on the royal scene, relations had been frosty since the Morton book had come out. Princess Margaret had felt it a betrayal to her sister.

Two of Queen Elizabeth's II's first cousins (through their grandfather King George V and Queen Mary), lived at KP. The Duke and Duchess of Gloucester lived in the twenty-one rooms of Apartment One, with the duke's aged mother Princess Alice, Duchess of Gloucester. Prince and Princess Michael of Kent had an apartment next to Diana and had lived at KP since 1978.

Diana's older sister Jane was married to the Queen's private secretary Sir Robert Fellowes, and also had a home on the grounds of KP. They inhabited a cottage with their three children in a small complex known as The Barracks. Paul Burrell and his family lived in the same block.

In total, KP housed four royal households, and well over a hundred people – besides the State apartments and public spaces. Each of the individual dwellers lived independently with their own households of chefs, security detail, private secretaries, equerries, ladies-in-waiting, nannies, butlers, housekeepers, maids, footmen, valets, dressers, chauffeurs, and cleaners. The inhabitants rarely saw each other, or kept abreast of each other's movements. Although, Diana had regularly seen HRH Princess Margaret discreetly lift the curtains in one of her upstairs windows to see guests enter or leave Diana's home. Diana sometimes waved back in defiance.

Charles and Diana had combined Apartments Eight and Nine into one larger L-shaped space, with three stories and twenty-five principal rooms. It was located on the palace's north side. Staff, kitchens, and security rooms were located on the lower ground floor, with reception rooms found at street level. Bedrooms, family space, and guest rooms occupied the second floor. The nursery was housed in the attic space on the third floor.

For the public area, a large reception room could comfortably seat seventy-five guests. The drawing room could easily accommodate more intimate gatherings of fifteen or so visitors. A focal point to this room was the large Flemish tapestry depicting villagers in a country scene, which took up most of the wall opposite the sofas. It had been the backdrop for many photos and interviews during the time of the royal marriage. The formal dining space could easily seat sixteen around a unique round mahogany table. It was used to entertain visiting dignitaries, royal family members, charity executives, pop stars, and other important company. Even Oprah Winfrey had enjoyed lunch with the Princess at this table.

A sweeping white Georgian staircase led to the family space upstairs. A large master bedroom with a custom-made four-poster bed that had been built for King Edward VII occupied a prime spot. Diana had completely overtaken this and the dressing rooms after Charles had vacated KP in early 1993. The bed was entirely covered with Diana's cuddly toys; and pictures of Diana's family – especially the boys – and many knickknacks, dotted the walls and tables.

Diana's private sitting room was her oasis of dusty pinks and light blues. The sofas were covered with light floral chintz and pale green. The Princess was often found sitting at her lady's desk between two windows, penning thank you notes to friends and party hosts on her personalised cream-coloured KP stationery with her embossed name. Her fountain pen and ever-ready bottle of Quink were well-used and stood at the ready. Her old wooden school trunk from boarding school days sat on the window sill. It still bore the carved name D. Spencer. A rosary that Mother Teresa had given the Princess was lovingly draped over a religious figurine on her desk. Circular tables dotted the room, and were covered with fine blue silk tablecloths, and many framed photographs of William and Harry. Other pictures of beloved family members like her father the Earl, and photos taken with celebrities like Elton John and Liza Minnelli cluttered the tables and walls. Cabinets and bureau tops were crammed with her beloved Herend glass animal collection, stuffed animals, children's drawings, and other prized possessions like embroidered cushions with sayings like *You have to kiss a lot of frogs before you find a Prince.* Diana kept the room filled with her favourite lilies and warm candles. It was a cozy and girlish chamber. Diana spent much of her time alone there.

The young princes were also comfortable in the sitting room, lounging on an overstuffed leather hippo cushion in front of the fireplace, as they watched television or did homework.

Charles' former sitting room had been taken over by the princes as a playroom/study/games room. The nursery upstairs remained virtually unchanged since the boys had first occupied the bedrooms, staff quarters, kitchen, and playroom on the third floor. Only the toys had gotten more sophisticated over the years. William and Harry loved video games, and sported an impressive collection.

Since the separation, Charles had taken a few pieces of art, sculpture, paintings, and personal effects, but had left KP much as it had been during the marriage. Diana had done the same at Highgrove – each of them wanting the boys to feel at home in their separate residences. Diana had made the place a little more feminine with lighter colours and less heavy furniture. She had always considered it both a gilded cage and a safe haven. As she did still.

Simone knew her way to the Princess' sitting room and was not surprised to see her friend listening to the stereo. Diana often took refuge in music - mainly classical – and especially appreciated Russian composers like Boris Tchaikovsky. She even played his music to soothe her jangled nerves on the Steinway piano in the drawing room, or at the family seat in Althorp.

"Darling, how are you?" Diana jumped up as soon as she saw Simone. "You look smashing as always." Diana was quick with a compliment, and hugged her friend with affection.

"It's you who is looking so well. What has brought that sparkle to your eyes today, Diana?" Simone was chuffed to see her friend in good spirits.

Diana ran her fingers through her fully coiffed blonde-highlighted hair, and smiled an impish grin. "I'll tell you, but only after we've settled for lunch. I think Paul said it was fish and salad again. I hope that's alright?" The Princess ate lightly most of the time, and often lunched on salads accompanied by chicken or fish. Rarely did she eat dessert, although it was always on offer.

"Of course, Diana. The meals here are always exquisite. Much better than the takeaways at my flat." Simone grimaced.

"Just so," giggled Diana. "Do sit. Luncheon is almost ready. I must tell you – I had a dream about Camilla last night. You must help me interpret it." Diana had long ago given up the name-calling of Charles' mistress. After the separation, a lot of her anger and frustration had dissipated, and she understood that Charles was directly to blame for his infidelity – not Camilla. Diana no longer called her *The Rottweiler* or *that woman.*

Simone sunk into her favourite seat in the room – the oversized stuffed hippo, and leaned forward. "Do tell, Diana," she encouraged.

"Well, we were at Highgrove. I was rushing to leave with the boys – somehow, I felt a sense of urgency, as if I needed to escape before someone was coming. And – like I often dream – the boys were much younger – perhaps five and three." She paused. "I wish you could have seen William and Harry then, Simone. They were so adorable in their short trousers and matching shirts." She smiled at the memory, and took up her recollection. "I was bustling them into the car with the nanny, when suddenly Camilla drove up – by herself – and got out of the car. She was dressed in dowdy country clothes, but she wasn't afraid or nervous or anything. She approached me straightaway, and said, 'This is my house now, Diana. But no need to hurry on my account. Perhaps you'd like to stay on for tea?' And she held out her hand for me to shake it. I was so shocked I didn't know what to say, so I shook her hand back, mumbled an excuse, and dove into the back seat of the car next to the boys. The funny thing was – when I woke up – I wasn't angry or sad. It was almost a relief, really to speak to her face-to-face. For how many years did we go to unnatural lengths to avoid each other?" Diana paused again, and shook her head ruefully. "So, what do you reckon, then?" She looked cool and composed.

"Firstly, I reckon that you are pretty pleased yourself at your own reaction. That in itself shows tremendous growth, Diana. Can you even imagine a few years ago having any kind of positive feelings about Charles' girlfriend?" Simone was herself delighted. "And it almost seems as if your unconscious mind is accepting Camilla's place in Charles' life – despite some lingering anxiety about it, as represented by your haste to leave. And the fact that you have reconciled that Highgrove is now Camilla's home, and not yours, also tells me that you're letting go of a lot of that negative energy – which is very healthy. All in all, I'd say a terrific dream for you, Diana." Simone finished with a smile.

Diana beamed. "Yes, I rather thought so too, but I'm so relieved to have you confirm it. For so many years, I was haunted by her, had to know what she was doing, was she with Charles? And becoming exhausted by it. It's such a relief to let that go. I can't see us ever being friends," she giggled. "But I certainly don't feel any hatred towards her anymore. I wasn't even distressed when she and Andrew divorced earlier this year. A lot of that spiritual work is thanks to you, Simone. Talking though all this bitterness and resentment has lightened me up in a way I can't truly explain." She gave her friend another quick hug. "Remember I told you about my Myers-Briggs interpretation several years ago? Ambrose said I was an Extrovert – and that I love to work things out by talking out loud. How true that is!"

About five years earlier, Diana's dear friend Nora had arranged for a personal interpretation for the Princess. Diana had learned all about personality type, and how people's inborn preferences can actually predict how they behave. She had found it fascinating, and read voraciously about MBTI since then. As an Extrovert, Sensing, Feeling Perceiving type, she loved to *typewatch*, and adjust her style to get better communications results from others with different preferences. It also helped her to understand her own actions and reactions to others.

Just then, Paul entered, waited silently to be noticed, and announced lunch. The two friends chattered easily as they strolled into the dining room.

"Alright, Diana, enough of this small talk," Simone said a short while later, as they enjoyed coffee after their light lunch. "What do you have to tell me? I always know when something is bubbling under that serene composure of yours."

Diana laughed. "You know me too well, darling." She leaned forward in a conspiratorial manner. "I've done it, Simone. I've given Martin Bashir the television interview." She sat back with a tiny smirk, and waited for the reaction.

"Diana, you haven't!" shrieked her friend in dismay. "I thought we had agreed – you had agreed – that was a very unwise move. We discussed this so many times, Diana. Whatever changed your mind?" Simone had that awful feeling in the pit of her stomach when you realise something really dreadful has happened.

The Princess frowned. She had hoped for more praise and support. "I talked to loads of people about it, Simone. In the end, I decided to trust my instinct. It's never steered me wrong, and I just *knew* I had to get my side out." Simone had heard this before. She chose not to point out to the Princess that her instinct had failed her on more than one occasion – the Morton book being the most catastrophic, certain choices in men another. She selected her words carefully.

"Darling, what did you say? What types of questions did he ask?" Simone was watching her friend intently.

"I had the questions in advance, so there were no surprises. Everything I expected, really – how did I adjust to my royal role when I was so young? What did I think of the unrelenting press interest in me? What about my eating disorder and harming myself? My thoughts about Charles and Camilla. And so on," she waved an elegant arm absentmindedly.

"Hmm," replied Simone. "And you admitted to the bulimia, and trying to hurt yourself?" This was a bombshell in the making.

"Yes, I did. I wanted to make sure everyone knew *why* I did those things. Because of the adultery, the royal family disregarding me, no help whatsoever over the years, never once saying *well done* or *good job*." Diana warmed to an oft-repeated theme.

"Anything else?" Simone asked ominously.

"Well, I did admit to my affair with Jamie Hewitt," the Princess fidgeted nervously with her napkin. "I just *had to* Simone, after Charles humiliated me by acknowledging his own affair. Don't you see that?" Diana's cornflower blue eyes locked with Simone's green ones, pleading for understanding.

Simone avoided the question. "When will the interview be aired?" she asked in a deceptively casual voice.

"I think November 20th," Diana replied softly. "I need to let both Charles and his mother know, I suppose. But everything I said was the truth, Simone, I swear it!" Diana's eyes started to fill with tears. She knew her friend disapproved of this rogue action.

One version of the truth thought Simone to herself. "There, pet. Don't cry. I'm sure you were diplomatic and careful in your responses, right? I just worry that with editing, lighting, and even promotion of the programme – *your* truth may be twisted to hurt you."

"I really don't think so, Simone. That Martin Bashir was so very soft-spoken and lovely. He didn't put any pressure on me. I didn't even cry once – you'll be so proud of me when you see it. I really wanted to come across as mature, in control, and most of all – sane. And I'm sure I did just that. It will be a triumph. Just wait and see. Trust me."

Simone patted her hand. "I'm sure it will, darling. I can't wait to see it. But do please go ahead and advise the palace and Charles. You can't let this be a surprise to them." Simone smoothed things over, but inwardly she was appalled at her dear friend's poor judgment. Nothing good could come of this, she thought to herself darkly. She gave Diana a reassuring smile.

Diana nodded, and the two took their coffees back to the sitting room.

November 14, 1995. His Royal Highness, Prince Charles' forty-seventh birthday. Diana had decided that it would be the most appropriate day to let the palace and her hubby know about the upcoming Panorama interview. Happy Birthday to you, Charles. Diana smiled to herself as she rose.

As usual, she'd gone to the Chelsea Harbour Club for a strenuous workout. She drove herself, and the usual paparazzi were waiting impatiently to take her photo. In an oversized sweatshirt, spandex shorts, baseball cap pulled low over her face, and white trainers, she hardly saw what the fuss was about; but she'd given up long ago trying to understand what the press found so fascinating about her. She parked, got out of the car without showing her face, and proceeded to walk backwards until she'd safely entered the private gym without a good shot being taken of her. A small victory for the day! Her personal trainer put her through a grueling ninety-minute workout, including cardio and weights. It always felt good to push herself, and she adored the adrenalin high she got from exercise. After showering and dressing, she sipped some carrot juice whilst speaking to a few acquaintances in the gym's café. She left the club with the same backwards gait, got in her car, and sped back to KP.

Showered and changed into slim jeans and a navy jumper, Diana picked up the phone in her sitting room to ring her brother-in-law, Sir. Robert Fellowes. He picked up promptly.

"Hello Robert, Diana here. How are you doing?" Her tone was breezy and light.

"Very well, Diana. I trust you and the boys are in good form? I heard from Jane that you enjoyed your recent weekend visit with William. He's growing so very tall now." Robert and Diana had a strained relationship at the best of times. As the Queen's private secretary, Robert was a senior royal staff member, close to the monarch. He had served in various capacities since 1977, been promoted along the way, and was a seasoned courtier. His natural style was reserved, reticent, and traditional. Although he had known Diana since he had married her sister Jane in 1978, he had never understood his sister-in-law's unpredictable and emotional ways. He had been embarrassed by her on more than one occasion, and in fact, had offered his resignation to the Queen amidst the uproar over the Morton book. Under careful and repeated questioning, Diana had vehemently denied any knowledge of the author and the book. This had been relayed to the Queen; and the palace had therefore supported the Princess during the ensuing public frenzy.

To this day, she stood her ground, albeit had become obvious to anyone close to Diana that she had played an integral role in the book's content. The Queen had graciously refused Robert's resignation, but he still considered this a black mark on his record. He always tread cautiously where the Princess of Wales was concerned.

"Yes, he is, rather. I think he gets his height from us Spencers," replied Diana with a slight tease in her voice.

"How may I help you today, Diana?" asked Robert in his most officious tone.

"I'm ringing to advise you about an upcoming television programme that I've taped, Robert. It will be broadcast on BBC on November 20th, so I'm notifying you in advance. As you know, the press has an unholy interest in whatever I seem to do, so I thought it prudent that I apprise you now." Diana's voice even sounded slightly smug as if she were doing the Queen a favour.

"A television programme? What television programme?" asked Robert in a panic. He struggled to maintain a calm demeanor. What the bloody hell had his sister-in-law gotten herself into this time?

"It's called *Panorama*. The presenter is Martin Bashir. I taped it a week or so ago."

"Does Her Majesty know of this?" he asked in a state of shock.

"No," replied the Princess brusquely.

"Has the Prince of Wales been informed?" he persisted.

"No, you're the first person I'm telling, Robert. You know the best way to proceed in these affairs," she replied primly.

"I must inform Her Majesty immediately. Diana, I can't believe you did this without royal sanction. I'll ring you back directly."

"Goodbye Robert," Diana said sweetly, and rang off.

Robert telephoned the Queen straightaway, and asked for an immediate audience. She met him in her private sitting room, where she was attending to her constant pile of correspondence. The Duke of Edinburgh was in Canterbury at an official engagement.

A footman admitted him, and Robert gave his customary head bow to the Queen of England. "Your Majesty, I'm sorry to disturb you, but I have a matter of some urgency to relay to you."

The Queen nodded. "Please sit down, Robert. Would you care for tea?" At age sixty-nine, the reigning monarch of the British empire was a vibrant and intelligent woman. She had served as Queen for forty-three years, and was adored and respected world-wide. Now graying gracefully with a step not quite as youthful as it once had been, nonetheless she was in the prime of her reign, and took on board any new developments – good or bad – with her stoic and enduring regal presence.

Robert refused tea, and made straight for the point. "I'm afraid Ma'am, that the Princess of Wales has agreed to, nay, already filmed a television programme to be broadcast next week. Are you familiar with the *Panorama* television show, Ma'am? It's a current events series."

The Queen didn't blink an eye. "Diana has taped an interview for the BBC? Whatever for?"

"I'm not quite sure why, Ma'am. She just called and informed me a few moments ago, so I wanted to advise you straightaway. I suspect it may be in answer to His Royal Highness, the Prince of Wales recent television interview with Jonathon Dimbleby."

The Queen shook her head. "I told him it was foolish to go on television. Once something is said, it can never be unsaid. And look at the damage it's done. But he insisted. And now Diana is inserting herself into the public eye again with her own version, I'm quite sure."

"Yes, Ma'am. I fear it could be quite damaging." This last was rather an understatement, but was typical for an exchange between the monarch and her private secretary. No need to raise voices. Let's just resolve this matter and carry on.

"Does Charles know about this?" The Queen asked Robert.

"Not according to the Princess. Unfortunately, he is on an official overseas tour of Germany as you know, Ma'am. I'll get in touch with him directly, once you've given me orders."

"Rather convenient, the timing, isn't it, Robert?" The Queen commented drily. "And on his birthday, too. Please ring his press secretary to advise him. No comments to any of the media until we see how we can halt this interview from being aired. Please call Marmaduke and put a stop to it, Robert." Sir Robert Marmaduke was the Chairman of the BBC, and the husband of one of the Queen's Women of the Bedchamber, Lady Susan Hussey. Robert nodded.

At the same moment, Diana was relaying the news to her own secretary, Patrick. He too, went white with shock.

"Ma'am, I don't understand. Can you please explain the purpose of this interview?" He attempted to be polite, but was filled with horror.

"The purpose, Patrick, is to explain how things really are in the royal family. To describe the utter hell I've been through, and to set the stage for my new role as an ambassador-of-sorts for Britain." Diana laid out her arguments.

"And you're saying that you did this without the knowledge or permission of the Queen, palace or the Prince of Wales?" he asked incredulously.

"That's exactly what I'm saying, Patrick." She gave

him a steely look. "We both know if I'd asked permission, I would only have been refused. I had to do it in secret."

"But you've advised Sir Fellowes?" he confirmed.

"Yes, and so by now the Queen and Charles know. It won't do any good though, the broadcast is set for next week – the twentieth – it's too late to stop it."

"I see, Ma'am," replied Patrick, although he had never felt so snubbed and disparaged in all his years of royal service. The Princess did not care that she'd made herself, the Queen, the Prince of Wales, and her staff look foolish and uninformed. On a whim (or so it seemed), she'd done exactly what she wanted – again. He nodded, excused himself, and literally ran out of the room to begin making a series of phone calls.

When her brother-in-law called her later to further discuss the issue, Diana was visiting Broadmoor - a high security prison for the criminally insane - and conveniently couldn't be reached. She avoided Robert's calls for the remainder of the week.

And the Princess proved to be right. The BBC would not bend under the pressure of Buckingham Palace, so it was a matter of waiting to see what the volatile Princess would say to the world on November twentieth.

The largest viewing audience ever for the *Panorama* programme tuned in that night. Over twenty-three million viewers watched the somber Princess reveal an even darker side of her royal marriage than she'd exposed in the Morton book.

Reaction was swift and divided. In general, the public applauded Diana's performance, and her bravery in speaking up about sensitive and profound issues. Within days, thousands of letters started pouring into KP supporting her. Women especially, shared their own stories of self-mutilation, unhappy marriages, and eating disorders. Diana felt triumphant and vindicated.

The response from the palace and the press was somewhat different. The Queen, Prince Philip, Prince Charles, and the rest of the royal family were almost apoplectic that Diana would go on record saying the heir to the throne was not fit to be King! The Queen Mother and her other daughter Princess Margaret were appalled at the lack of grace and deference that Diana had shown to the family who had supported her for well over ten years. Princess Margaret wrote Diana a scathing rebuke; a letter that truly wounded the Princess of Wales with its acrimonious condemnation. Charles also called Diana, and delivered a scalding reprimand, but it fell on deaf ears. Diana was basking in the glow of public support.

The press had a field day with the interview. Never before had such a senior member of the royal family aired dirty linen in such a public way. Many thought Diana's performance was staged, scripted, and rehearsed. Some believed she came across as vengeful and mean-spirited. Courtiers in Charles' camp were outraged on his behalf, and struggled to find ways to support him. One of Charles' closest intimates Sir Nicholas Soames went on a public television programme accusing the Princess of being in the advanced stages of paranoia.

Within days of the interview, a planned appearance by the Princess of Wales at a large Red Cross event was cancelled by the Palace.

CHAPTER THREE

New Loves

Diana sat back in her first-class seat, clapped on her headphones, and slowly let out a breath, as the air hostess began reciting the standard safety instructions before the plane took off. It had been four days since the Panorama interview had aired in England, and it had been a stroke of brilliance that the Princess had planned ahead for this working trip to Argentina. She desperately needed to get away from the pandemonium that had taken hold of London.

The Princess gazed out the window, her troubled blue eyes seeing nothing, as she pondered the events of the last several weeks. She hadn't banked on the negative reception to the news of the impending broadcast by those closest to her. Patrick had been withdrawn and remote since she had confessed to her complicity in the Panorama interview a few days before the air date. After peppering her with questions and rushing to report to the palace, he had served her with dutiful respect and nothing more. She'd told him everything would be alright, and he'd find the programme moving and powerful. He deflected. He'd carefully briefed her on the upcoming Argentina trip, but remained distant and coldly polite when she'd tried to joke him out of his black temper. She realised she'd crossed a line with him, and didn't know how to bridge the chasm between them. She chewed her nails.

Her long-serving lady-in-waiting, Anne Beckwith Smith, had not shown her dismay at the news of the looming programme, but Diana knew she disapproved. Anne had been strangely quiet the morning after Panorama had been broadcast. She had been flattering with praise when pressed, but her words seemed hollow. Diana lowered the airplane window shade as night engulfed the aircraft.

Her press secretary Geoff Crawford has unexpectedly resigned over the affair. He'd been quite civil and absolutely final.

"Ma'am, it's apparent that you don't trust me. You've taken this course of action with regards to the Panorama interview, without even consulting your press secretary. As such, it's impossible for me to carry out my duties as you engaged me to do. I wish you every success in the future." He had handed Diana his letter of resignation, bowed and made to the leave the Princess' sitting room.

"Wait," cried Diana. She opened a desk drawer, and removed a signed and framed photograph of herself. "Geoff, you've handed out many of these in your job. Please take one for yourself. Thank you for your helpful service. I'm sorry to see you go." The Princess was compassionate but dry-eyed. She *was* sorry to see Geoff go, but if he wasn't loyal to her, she had no choice but to accept his resignation. He bowed again, thanked her, and left. She hadn't seen that coming, and it really unnerved her. Since, she had resolved to put the matter completely behind her.

She had taken a particularly acrimonious call from Prince Charles, which had left her shaken. What had been the absolute worst reaction she had received, without question, had been William's response. Diana had driven to Eton the day before the telecast aired to talk to him about the interview in person.

"Darling, how wonderful to see you!" she had called to him as he met her in the private Visitor's Lounge. He looked so handsome in his school uniform, and was getting so tall!

"Mummy," he smiled to greet her with a hug.

"Darling, I've pulled you out of class to speak with you about something serious." The two sat down with Diana still holding onto her son's hands.

"What is it, Mummy?" a worried William queried. At thirteen, he was a serious and studious young man. "Is Papa alright?"

Diana patted her son's hand. "Yes, Papa is fine, busy with engagements, as usual. No, this is about me. There's going to be a television programme tomorrow night. I've been interviewed by *Panorama*. You know the media – they like to ask hard questions. I wanted to prepare you for some of the things you might be hearing." William nodded.

Diana hesitated. "William, you know I have struggled for some years now in the royal family. So, I spoke about some of those troubles and my reactions to them. Being ill at times, and some of the bad moments when Papa and I would row all the time. You remember that, don't you?" William nodded again, but still said nothing.

"I think what may surprise you is that after Papa and I knew that we couldn't stay married to each other, I had a relationship with James – a special friendship."

"You mean Uncle Jamie?" asked William, his blue eyes starting to darken. "He taught you how to ride, and then gave Harry and me our own army fatigues and toy guns. Is that the special friendship?"

"No-o-o, not exactly, William. We loved each other and cared for one another very much."

William jumped up. Diana had never seen him look so angry.

"You mean he was your boyfriend, don't you, Mummy? All those times he came to Highgrove, he was really coming to see you, not us! How could you do this to Papa? I hate you!" William turned from his mother, rapidly wiped his tears, and strode from the room in fury.

"William, wait," cried Diana, as she raced after him. But he was too fast. He had run down the hall, and disappeared behind the Students Only door. Diana sat back down and began to sob. Oh, what had she done?

William refused to take her calls for almost two weeks. Diana had sent him copious letters begging for his forgiveness, trying to explain the situation to a hurt and embarrassed thirteen-year-old.

The headlines on November 21st had been outrageous: "Princess Diana Tried to Take Her Own Life," screamed *The Daily Mail* in a front-page cover story. "Diana Admits Adultery in TV Interview" shouted the *BBC*. "Diana Admits 'I Loved Hewitt,'" reported *The Daily Express*. And on it went, endlessly. The reaction had been far more volatile than she had dreamed.

"Diana, whatever made you think this was a good idea?" her mother had pressed her on the telephone. Diana and her mother had an uneasy relationship at the best of times. The Princess yearned for a warm and loving connection with Frances Shand-Kydd, but the two were very different; Diana open and giving, whilst Frances was closed and private. Although the relationship was cordial, it had never been the all-consuming mother—daughter relationship that Diana craved. She wasn't surprised that her mother had not been supportive of her – again.

"Mother, as usual the press has got it all wrong. You

know they only pick out the juicy bits, and plaster them all over the newspapers. Did you watch the entire programme? Didn't you see how composed and in control I was?" Diana tried to keep the little-girl pleading tone out of her voice, but with only limited success.

"Diana, it was ruinous. Why ever did you feel compelled to disclose such personal information to the world? Did you know that the interview drew the largest viewing audience in *Panorama's* forty-some-odd-year history – something over twenty-one million viewers?" Frances was aghast.

Yes, Mother, I'm well aware," replied her daughter, gritting her teeth. Inwardly, Diana had been pleased that her interview had drawn more attention than Charles' had; only fourteen million people had watched his programme the year before. But she dared not gloat to her outraged mother. "That's precisely why I did it. To get out the truth – the real truth – so no one can dispute it, or paper over it with Buckingham Palace rubbish. I thought I did rather a good job of it," she finished lamely.

"But to imply that Charles is not fit to be King, Diana. How could you have dared?" Frances almost whispered. Such things should never be spoken aloud.

Diana attempted to breeze this away. "I only meant that Charles is conflicted about a lot of things, and worries over them. I never said he shouldn't be King," she defended herself.

"Don't be foolish, Diana. You knew exactly what you were saying, and how the Queen and the establishment would interpret your remarks. I'm ashamed of you, I really am." Frances was never one to mince words. She herself had been the victim of terrible media attention after she had left her husband and four children, and had never fully recovered. Her husband, Viscount Althorp at the time, had agreed to a trial separation, and then later refused to let her take the younger children to her

London apartment, as planned, after a family Christmas in Norfolk. In a harsh and hostile custody battle, the courts had given primary care of the children to Johnnie Althorp, thanks in part to testimony by Frances' own mother – Lady Ruth Fermoy. This had caused an unspeakable rift between that mother-daughter relationship that had never been repaired. Although she had remained in her children's lives, Frances had never really healed from this heartbreaking event. In fact, she had inherited some of the icy steel of her mother Ruth (close friend and Woman of the Bedchamber to Queen Elizabeth, the Queen Mother) which she was demonstrating now.

"Well, in that case, I don't need to keep listening to you then, do I Mother? The papers can do the job well and proper. I don't need a ticking off from you. I'm ringing off now. I must prepare for my trip to Argentina. The show must carry on, you know." Diana was hurt, but retreated to a place of safe distance. Goodbye."

"Goodbye, Diana. And please stop talking to the newspapers and for heaven's sake, don't give any more interviews!" But all Frances heard was a dial tone. Her daughter had rung off.

As the plane sped through the air to Buenos Aires, Diana shook her head to dismiss the lingering conversation with her mother. She could hear Simone's voice in her head, telling her not to waste negative energy on something she couldn't change. She shifted her mind to her loyal butler, Paul. *He* had been sympathetic and reassuring after having watched *Panorama* with his wife Maria.

"You were splendid, Ma'am," he said approvingly. "Very stately and assured. And just look at this post pouring in." He motioned to the large batch of cards and envelopes addressed to the Princess of Wales. Diana had been delighted that public opinion had been with her yet again. As with the Morton book, despite family and royal disdain, the millions of people who adored her, had stood by her. Women who had struggled with eating disorders, self-mutilation, suicidal thoughts, and bad marriages had written to the Princess pouring out their own hearts, and words of support. Diana had really been overwhelmed with the thousands of letters and cards. They had soothed the pain from the negative responses raining down all around her.

She was brought back to the present with a small throat-clearing by Anne. "Best to try to get some sleep, Ma'am. It's a very long journey to Buenos Aires, and you have an itinerary that's crammed to bursting over the next three days. The Princess smiled and nodded, as she turned to look out the window again.

As promised, the next few days in Argentina were chock-full of engagements. It was lovely to be out of damp and cold London in November. It was sunny and warm in Buenos Aires, and Diana was thankful for the light, pastel shift dresses, and short-sleeved suits that Anne and her dresser had packed for her.

Although she encountered a few protestors, for the most part the Argentinian people had welcomed her with open arms. She was moved by the visit to an infant paralysis centre, and also visited a rehabilitation home for the disabled. She put her heart and soul into these engagements – touching and speaking to as many patients as possible - especially the children. It also soothed her own battered spirit to reach out and give back to these brave young people.

Many photos were taken of her during the short trip. She had lunch with President Carlos Menem and his daughter, Zulemita; and had taken a side trip to

Patagonia for whale-watching. Patrick and Anne had ensured the hectic schedule had been executed with precision, and as planned. All too soon, it was time to travel back to London to face the storm once more.

"Rosa, it's marvelous to see you!" Diana was back in her KP sitting room when Paul showed in her dear friend. The two embraced, and Diana looked Rosa directly in the eyes. "Did you stop in at the grave on your way up?" she asked softly.

Rosa nodded, and the Princess could see she had been crying. "Yes, of course, Diana. Thanks to you and the key you gave us, I come often. It's such a comfort to know little Natalia is buried right here in the walled garden of Kensington Palace. Dom and I can never thank you enough." Diana gave her friend an impulsive hug, with an accompanying smile of reassurance.

The previous spring, Rosa had suffered a tragic stillbirth. She and her husband Dominic had been inconsolable. In an impetuous, compassionate gesture, Diana had offered for the stillborn baby to be buried in consecrated grounds on the KP property. The Lawsons had gratefully accepted. Under a veil of secrecy, Paul and the previous butler Harold Brown had dug the grave, and with the help of a young Catholic priest, had put the small baby to rest in the walled garden. Diana had given Rosa a key, and insisted she visit anytime. It had cemented forever an already close friendship. Not even Charles knew of the arrangement.

"I'm so pleased," replied Diana quietly. "I often go there myself for peace and solitude. I love the stillness there." The two embraced again. Diana changed the subject to lighten the atmosphere. "Rosa, you are looking smashing for a new Mum. How is my dearest Domenica

– lucky number seventeen of my godchildren?"

Earlier that year, Rosa and her husband had welcomed another baby girl, a little sister for Savannah, now seven. Domenica had been born with Down's Syndrome, and Diana had fallen madly in love with the sweet and sunny-natured baby. The Princess had been a tireless comfort to Rosa through the birth and adjustment to having a child with special needs. None of them could imagine life without this very exceptional child. Diana had been honoured to become Domenica's godmother.

"She is a pet, she watches the world with such bright eyes, and beams such a beautiful smile,". gushed Rosa with all the pride of a new mama. "We're just starting her on some pablum and soft fruit – what a mess she makes of things."

Rosa was a dark-haired and dark-eyed London businesswoman, who managed a branch of Tiffany's, the luxury jewelry shop. Diana had met her through a mutual friend, Lucia Flecha de Lima, the socialite wife of the then- Brazilian ambassador in London. Rosa and Diana had become fast friends, and spent countless hours together.

Rosa had descended from a family with a history of proximity to the British royal family. Her grandfather Walter Monckton had drafted the abdication speech of King Edward VIII in 1936, and was the only Crown official to witness his ensuing marriage to the American divorcee Wallis Simpson. Her mother Marianna was a member of the Maltese nobility, and had been close to Queen Elizabeth II in the early years of her marriage to Prince Philip. Rosa was likewise loyal and steadfast to the Princess. They had holidayed together, and often frequented Diana's much-loved London restaurants for girls' luncheons.

"Sounds lovely. I so would have loved a little girl. You're very lucky, Rosa," Diana offered wistfully. She was dressed for a day at home in an oversize Tommy Hilfiger sweatshirt and leggings. As ever, she looked fresh and lovely.

"Well, it's not too late, you know, Diana," teased Rosa with a smile. "Perhaps with a certain Pakistani doctor?" she added playfully.

Diana blushed, and seemed rather flustered. "Really, Rosa. Sod off. I've only been seeing DDG for a short while. But he *would* make beautiful babies; a little girl would be divine." She sighed.

DDG was Diana's nickname Drop Dead Gorgeous for a Pakistani doctor. She had met Dr. Hasnat Khan whilst visiting the husband of a friend. The two had felt an immediate connection based upon their shared compassion for the sick and suffering, and had been dating ever since. It was early days yet, but Diana felt the promise of a great love.

"Well judging from that glow, I'd say the romance is thriving, darling," Diana threw a cushion at her friend. "Alright, alright. I'll leave off it for now." Rosa decided to change the subject. The two were sitting companionably in their typical positions – Diana on one sofa with her bare feet curled up under her, and Rosa sitting in an opposite chair. It was late in the day, and Paul was preparing an afternoon tea for the chums.

"Diana, after your bad luck with men, you truly deserve someone that loves and spoils you. Heaven knows you've had a few duds in your time. Take James Hewitt, for example. Who would ever have thought such a dashing military man would become such a cad?" Albeit Rosa and Diana had only been chummy for about two years, Rosa was well acquainted with the story of Captain James and the Princess. Who couldn't know when James had co-written a tawdry tell-all book that spilled all the secrets of their love affair? He'd been vilified by the press and public alike, and given him the nickname The Love Rat.

Diana snorted. "That *was* a blow. I didn't think he had it in him. But then again, he didn't actually write it. He probably just sat there with a pint in his hand, dictating his warped recollection of things. I really couldn't believe he'd betray me like that, though. He was so sweet and attentive to me – in the beginning. Just the salve I needed from the wounds in my marriage. And I miss his mum, Shirley. I visited her often in Devon with James." Diana looked rather melancholy.

"You really did love him, didn't you, darling?" asked her friend gently.

"I truly did, Rosa," replied Diana fervently. "He was everything that Charles was not – emotionally available, interested in me and what I was doing, sympathetic and supportive to my difficult role, all of it. He taught me how to ride. He was smashing with the boys – they adored him, too. They called him Uncle Jamie." She gave a small smile. "And he was fireworks in the bedroom. We couldn't get enough of each other. Again, not like Charles. He was never very interested in that department." It was obvious that Diana still felt the prince's rejection keenly.

"You two saw each other for quite a long time, didn't you? Did you ever really consider leaving Charles and the royal family for James?" Rosa was curious. She knew how deep Diana's romantic streak went. She also understood just how strongly her practical side ruled her.

"Yes and no, really," responded Diana slowly. "Yes, of course I had the dream of having someone strong who loved me to look after me. And we were very compatible. I'm not sure of his personality style, but he liked to live in the moment, like me. But no, I just couldn't see myself as an army barracks wife, moving from camp to camp, cooking supper on a tiny hob in a cramped kitchen somewhere. With William's role as it is – well, there are just certain things I can't do. The Queen and the men in grey would have had convulsions if I'd bolted for a commoner. But that's done and dusted, now. James is firmly in my past." She looked resolute, her stunning blue eyes clear and calm.

Just then, Paul discreetly knocked and brought in the tea trolley. The chef had created a tempting array of light sandwiches, tea cakes and sweets, the essential scones with clotted cream and jam; and of course, a variety of teas from which to choose.

"Ladies, may I tempt you with a light repast?" Paul was standing by, ready to pour.

"We'll help ourselves, Paul, ta very much," Diana smiled in his direction. "We're in the middle of discussing my gloomy love life at the moment." She giggled.

"Very good Ma'am." Paul put down the teapot, bowed and left.

"So, let's put a big cross next to James' name, then," joked Rosa. "What about James Colthurst? Did you have romantic feelings for him?"

Diana laughed. "Not at all. I think he may have been a little in love with me, but we were always just friends. He was an enormous help to me as the liaison for the Morton book, and I'll always be ever so grateful to him for that, but it was nothing more." The Princess nibbled on a dainty smoked salmon sandwich and picked up a grape.

"I think every man that meets you falls a little in love with you, Diana. You have a way of making everyone feel special. Not to mention you are drop dead gorgeous yourself."

"Please Rosa, you are too much. Help yourself to more sandwiches and cakes." Diana was pleased nonetheless, with the compliment. No matter how many she received, it never seemed to be enough to fill that gaping hole of insecurity inside her.

Rosa obliged, and tucked into a plate of sandwiches, a raspberry tart, and a slice of Battenberg cake. "Bollocks, Diana. You light up every room you enter. Now what about Mr. Hoare? That seemed like rather a disastrous affair?" Although Diana and Rosa had discussed the men in the Princess' life before, she wasn't always as forthcoming as today. Rosa chose to delve a little deeper while the door was temporarily – and temptingly - open.

Diana rose to pour them both some tea. "I quite fancied him, too. He was just my type – tall, dark, handsome, and well-to-do. Unfortunately, he was also married." Diana grimaced. "I don't think my man-picker is functioning in top form. That whole rubbish affair makes me feel a proper fool, if I'm honest, Rosa. Believing he was going to leave his wife for me, that they were more like room-mates than a married couple, the marriage was over, and so on. Utter rot. Why are women so stupid to believe that from a man?" Diana *did* feel a fool for believing Oliver's love words and promises. Yet another romantic letdown.

"I don't know the man, darling but I can only assume he got in over his head. He was dazzled by the beautiful princess, whilst still firmly attached to his wife and family. You are an outrageous flirt, you know?" Rosa reached for another pastry from the tea trolley.

Diana batted her eyelashes coquettishly, and fluffed her hair. "I can't help it if my charms and graces slay men," she giggled. "Oliver was very passionate, you know. There's something about middle-eastern men that really appeals to me. That dark swarthiness combined with a gentle spirit, I don't know," she finished. "We met at the Chelsea Harbour Inn. He looked proper fine in his workout shorts. And remember, *he* approached me. Men are so intimidated by me; they rarely make advances in my direction. It's surprisingly difficult to date as the

Princess of Wales, you know." Diana sipped her tea thoughtfully, as she voiced this gross understatement.

"Diana, I've always wanted to know – *did* you make those nuisance calls to Oliver when the relationship broke down?" This was a touchy subject with the Princess.

Diana focused her blue eyes steadily upon her friend's. "Absolutely not, Rosa. How could you even ask? With my hectic schedule and all the places I'm meant to be, how could I possibly have time to make that massive number of calls? And you know it was proven to be some local schoolboy, in the event."

Rosa remained unconvinced, but tactfully kept her silence. It had been well documented across all the papers that the Princess of Wales had made over 300 nuisance calls to Oliver's mobile and home phones. She would call and then hang up, presumably trying to get Oliver's attention. Diana had staunchly refuted these accusations, but Rosa knew that Diana had been driven to this kind of behaviour in the past. It was rumoured she'd done the same type of call and hang up routine with Camilla Parker Bowles at times over the years. Since Oliver had been the one to break off the affair when he had found the Princess' needs for his time to be too demanding, it was likely the stories about the nuisance calls were true. Rosa felt deeply for her friend. All Diana had ever wanted was a man to love her completely, and with the same all-consuming passion that she gave in a relationship. But this seemed to remain eternally elusive.

"And what of the rugged rugby player Will Carling? Any truth to that bit? He seems a trifle short for you," offered Rosa.

"Another innocent friendship overblown by the media, Rosa. I simply engaged Will to help me with my strength training at the gym. I wanted to contour my shoulders and arms in a more structured way. He helped. We had coffee a few times. That's all." She dismissed this one out of hand. "And yes, he was a bit shorter than me. Sorry, but I need to look *up* to the main man in my life." She giggled again, and held up her hand in a stop sign motion. "And don't even start with me about James Gilbey. Did I flirt with him? Yes? Did we have an affair? Absolutely not. At the time, I was devoted to my other James."

"Sure, whatever you say – Squidgy!" retorted Rosa laughingly. She referred to the incriminating tape that had been released just before the Prince and Princess had separated. The recording was a private conversation between Diana and James Gilbey (of the Gilbey gin family) that hinted at an intimate relationship at worst, a close friendship at best. Rumours swirled whether it was an amateur ham operator who had happened upon the *Squidgygate* conversation, recorded in 1989; or a more dire conspiracy attempt amongst palace courtiers out to threaten the Princess. The furor had died down, but it had been one of the catalysts to the December 1992 separation. Diana and James still maintained an ongoing friendship. He was a laugh, and fun to be around.

"Any more lovers in your closet, Diana? Besides the dishy doctor?" The two friends were now getting rather giddy and playful.

"I've had a few – nothing serious – but none that I care to discuss," Diana replied with a prim smile. "I had high hopes of a future in America at one time, but that has come to naught." She paused. "Time will tell about Hasnat. I'm really enjoying his company at the moment. We'll just have to wait and see where it leads – if anywhere," she finished enigmatically.

She glanced at her watch, and leapt to her feet. "Now that I've given you tea and spilled all my secrets, that's enough for one afternoon. I must get changed, and dash to my acupuncture appointment, darling."

The two women grinned at each other. They truly

loved the easy camaraderie between them. They parted cheerfully with promises to meet up soon.

The next few days were spent in busyness preparing for another overseas trip – this time to the United States. Diana had squealed with delight when Patrick had told her that she had been chosen to receive the Humanitarian of the Year honors from the United Cerebral Palsy of New York Foundation.

"Oh Patrick, I've never received an award like this – any award for that matter!" She couldn't help herself. She jumped up, and impulsively thrown her arms around Patrick's neck. Her private secretary reacted stiffly, awkwardly patting her back. "Well, except for the Pet Care Award I got at Riddlesworth Hall," she giggled, and stepped back. "Don't look so wretched, Patrick. A hug won't kill you." The Princess twirled around in an elegant ballet move in her sitting room.

"Of course, Ma'am," Patrick responded crisply. "It is a great honour. There's a dinner in New York City, and you'll be expected to say a few words. I'll draft a speech for your review." Patrick was still deeply wounded to have been kept in the cold about the *Panorama* interview, but he knew his duty – extremely well.

"Lovely, Patrick. That would be brilliant. I must think what to wear."

That had been a few weeks ago, and Diana was eagerly anticipating the American junket. She adored everything about the United States, and always received a very warm welcome from the people. Not the least of her keenness was her need to get away from the swirling negative mood in London – even a short escape was welcome.

She took the Concorde to Manhattan, and received a

tremendous American reception. There were record crowds wherever she went, and a constant throng outside The Carlyle Hotel where she always stayed. Her suite was sumptuous, and had a spectacular view overlooking Central Park.

"William, I definitely want to bring you with me the next time I come to America. You'll love the hustle and bustle of the city, and the people are so warm. I can see horse-drawn carriages from my hotel room." Diana gazed out of her window, as she spoke to her eldest son. They had forged an uneasy truce since the argument after the *Panorama* broadcast. Diana had written William numerous letters begging for his forgiveness, and the two had managed to get back to a place of uneasy peace. Neither one liked conflict, nor to be at odds with each other, but William still harboured resentment towards how his mother had handled the situation, not to mention the humiliation at the hands of bullying school friends. Nonetheless, he loved her dearly, and was willing to move on.

"Mummy, you must finish all your Christmas shopping whilst you're there. You should be able to find all the new video games on my list at the big toy stores." William and Harry still loved to spend countless hours playing competitive videogames together.

Diana smiled, knowing she had completed all her holiday shopping back in October – including everything reasonable on William and Harry's lists. "I don't think I'll have much time for the shops, darling. It's just a swift trip, you know." Diana's voice held a teasing note.

"Mummy, can you please bring me back the latest Nike trainers? I promise I won't even wear them till after Christmas," pleaded the young prince.

"Of course, darling. But only if you keep focused on your studies. It's not time for the holiday break just yet." A serious note crept into the Princess' voice. William would one day be King of England and the Commonwealth. He needed to work hard at his lessons so he would succeed at the best schools in Britain. Diana and her husband were in accord on this topic, if not much else.

"Thank you, Mummy," replied William cheerfully. "I must ring off now. My time is up, and the next boy is waiting to use the telephone."

"Goodbye, darling and see you in a few days. I love you, William."

"I love you too, Mummy. I'll watch you on telly for your speech. What do the Americans say? Break a leg!"

The next night was the United Cerebral Palsy of New York Foundation's gala. As dozens of cameras snapped relentlessly, jaws dropped when the Princess stepped out of the car. She was dazzling in a slinky long, black Jacques Azagury black cross-back dress, with an embroidered sequin bodice. It showed off her daring décolletage and athletic figure perfectly. Set off with sparkling diamond pearl-drop earrings and coordinating sapphire and diamond cuffs, Diana looked and felt spectacular. Still wearing her engagement and wedding rings, she embodied the Royal Princess in every way.

Sitting next to the former U.S. Secretary of State Henry Kissinger at dinner, she turned on the charm to high-powered celebrities like General Colin Powell and Barbara Walters. She and Kissinger talked easily about the Princess' quest for a future meaningful role for herself, and he advised her to pursue humanitarian causes for which she had great and long-standing passion. The two struck up an unlikely friendship that was to last beyond the gala dinner. He introduced the Princess, and presented the Humanitarian of the Year

Award to her.

As she began her speech, a heckler shouted out "Where are your children?" Diana looked up, did not skip a beat, and briskly responded "at school." She then finished her speech: "Today is the day of compassion. Let's not wait to be prompted. Let us go out tonight, tomorrow and the days that follow, and let us demonstrate our humanity."

Back in her suite after a successful evening, the Princess kicked off her shoes, and drank a bottle of fizzy water from the tray.

"Patrick, who the hell was that dreadful man who shouted out at me? He was horrid." Diana grimaced at the one black mark of the evening.

"You put him securely in his place, Ma'am. Try to forget about it. The rest of the evening was brilliant. Your speech was very well received. Congratulations once more on such a well-deserved award."

Diana examined the stunning crystal statuette, and placed it on the mahogany coffee table. She yawned.

"Thank you, Patrick. It was a splendid evening. I appreciate you getting me out of there before all those Americans could swarm all over me. I love their enthusiasm but at times, they surely can be a trifle pushy."

"Of course, Ma'am. You handled them all with your usual charm and grace." He paused. "Will there be anything else tonight, Ma'am?" Patrick waited to be dismissed.

Diana took a sip of water, smiled, and waved a manicured hand towards her private secretary. "No, nothing else, Patrick. See you in the morning."

"Very good, Ma'am." Patrick bowed his head, gave his careful smile, and left the Princess to contemplate her great success. Before he had shut the heavy double doors to her suite, she had picked up the phone to ring home and share the good news of her evening with her cherished friends.

Back in London a few days later, Diana picked away at a dinner tray in her sitting room, as she watched one of her favourite telly shows – *Coronation Street*. She rang Paul for some herbal tea, which he brought promptly.

"Anything else, Ma'am? You don't seem to be enjoying your dinner. Is anything wrong with the chicken?"

Diana shook her head no. "It's fine, Paul. I'm just feeling a little low. Do you have a few minutes to talk, or are you rushing home to Maria?" The Princess looked up at the butler with eyes brimming with tears.

"I'm always at your disposal, Ma'am. How can I help?"

Diana patted the sofa next to her. "Please sit down, Paul so we can have a proper chat."

This was a familiar exchange between boss and staff. Diana tended to push the boundaries to include Paul as more than a butler – at times she needed a listening ear, a confidante, a friend. As much as Paul valued this unique aspect of their relationship, he was resolute in maintaining the proper distance between the Princess of Wales and himself, and vowed never to overstep the mark.

"I'm more comfortable standing, Ma'am. Have you had some bad news?"

Diana sipped her chamomile tea. "No, nothing of that sort, Paul. Sometimes I find the highs and lows of my life are near impossible to manage. They adored me in New York. I danced to *Cheek to Cheek* with Colin Powell. He was no Fred Astaire," she joked. "But a smooth dancer, and I could tell he was tongue-tied to meet me.

Me! And then Henry Kissinger made such positive remarks about my work..."

Paul interrupted – a rare action on his part. "Didn't he say you were luminous, Ma'am? And that you are 'a princess in your own right who aligns yourself with the ill, the suffering and the downtrodden?' Surely that boosted your spirits, Ma'am?" The butler could see the Princess needed a little cheering.

"Exactly so, Paul. I hear wonderful compliments like that, all the famous celebrities gush over me, and I'm treated like a superstar. And then I come home to this." Her gaze took in the silent, empty room. "I'm eating dinner on a tray, watching chums having a pint in a pub on telly, whilst my boys are at school. How glamourous is this?" She sounded truly dejected.

Paul could see her point. Trying to manage the extremes between her professional and personal life seemed like an intolerable ambition. He truly didn't know how she did it – day in, day out, and year after year. It didn't help that it was a grey December evening, with a steady drizzle drowning out the London night.

"Well, let's not let ourselves feel too glum, Ma'am. You've had a marvelous success in New York, you wowed them in Argentina, and you astonished the whole world as a strong woman with your interview. Not bad for just over a month's work!" Paul endeavored to jostle his mistress into a better mood.

Diana rewarded him with a smile. "Yes, I suppose you're right, Paul. Sometimes I just wish the highs weren't so high, so the lows wouldn't be so low," she said, speaking from her intuitive self. "It's always been the same in the royal family. Whenever I would manage to do something right, no one ever said *well done* or *how clever of you*. It would have only taken a few small encouragements, and I could have kept going for years." Her tone was wistful. This had been a common theme throughout her fourteen years as Princess of Wales.

"Well, I think you do an incredible job, Ma'am. You should be immensely proud of yourself," said Paul with feeling. "Maybe you just need a break from this hectic diary. The holidays are coming in just a couple of weeks. Having the young princes back home is bound to lift your morale. I'm sure they're eager for Christmas."

"Yes, of course, you're right. Thank you so much, Paul. You've no idea how just listening to me, and allowing me think through issues out loud, really helps me. I guess it's my extraverted tendencies. I don't know what I'd do without you!" She beamed her beautiful smile at Paul. He flushed with pleasure. He truly had the best post in the world.

"Will there be anything else, tonight, Ma'am?" he posed as he did every night.

"No, Paul, just leave the tea things till the morning. And thank you again. You really are indispensable to me."

"Good night, Your Royal Highness. Sleep well." With that, he offered his usual head bow, and retreated.

1995 was ending on a bang. After her recent triumphs and her slight despondency about not spending all of the Christmas break with her boys, Diana was feeling she needed to settle one more score.

Since the separation in 1992, Charles had engaged the services of a nanny, to help with William and Harry when they were in his care. This infuriated Diana on many levels. Firstly, she didn't understand why Charles couldn't look after his own children himself. It's not as if they were still in nappies or needed constant watching. They were thirteen and eleven, bloody hell. Secondly, Diana couldn't help but feel jealous about all the time the boys spent with Tiggy Legge-Bourke. She was more a companion than nanny, and Diana seethed every time she saw photographs in the papers, showing the foursome fishing, hunting or hiking together looking too chummy for words. Thirty-two-year-old Tiggy was a sporty, fun-loving girl, and the boys adored her. This didn't help either.

The tabloids had been having a little fun at Diana's expense, hinting at a flirtation between Prince Charles and Tiggy. They had been captured sharing an innocent kiss whilst on a skiing trip with the boys, and it had been blown all out of proportion by the press. Tiggy had slimmed down dramatically from the outdoorsy girl she had been, and improved her wardrobe and style. All of this created a slow burn in the Princess.

At the St. James' palace staff Christmas party, Diana exacted her revenge. In front of the entire Wales' team, she boldly strode up to the nanny and said, "Hello, Tiggy, how are you? *So* sorry to hear about the baby."

The Princess had intimated that Tiggy had suffered a miscarriage, resultant from an affair with the Prince of Wales. The girl almost fainted, and fled the room in tears. Everyone was aghast that Diana could go so far. Diana tried to hide a smug grin.

But Diana hadn't counted on Tiggy's fury. She fought back. Her lawyer sent a letter to Diana's solicitors, accusing the Princess of circulating malicious lies that reflected very poorly on the nanny's character. Diana's own brother-in-law Robert Fellowes rebuked her by letter, telling her she had gotten the whole matter dreadfully wrong, and that the allegation was entirely unfounded. He pleaded with her to make things right.

Chastened, Diana took the advice of her lawyer, and settled. She knew she had gone too far, but had been unable to help herself. Sometimes when she was hurting, she lashed out to wound someone else. She never apologised to Tiggy or Charles – she rarely said she was sorry except for the most trivial things like being late – but she *was* contrite. Especially when she learned that Tiggy's drastic weight loss was due to the painful symptoms of celiac disease. But the damage had been done. She couldn't wait to turn the page, and fervently wished 1996 would be a better year. But a bitter blow was yet awaiting the beleaguered Princess.

CHAPTER FOUR

Charles, The X-File

Three weeks after the staggering *Panorama* interview, Diana received a letter from the Queen; a handwritten letter. She read it in dawning disbelief and pain.

It was addressed Dearest Diana, and signed With love from Mama, but the contents of the letter were far from pleasant. It had been hand-delivered by uniformed courier from Buckingham Palace, and handed to her by Paul. It was not a long letter, and clearly Her Majesty had received legal guidance, as the wording was formal and precise.

"The events of the last twelve months have been troubling, to say the least. The public airing of the difficulties in your marriage to the Prince of Wales were unnecessary, and distasteful to Papa and I. This latest BBC interview that you conducted, has now brought the issues to a stage that have constitutional effects.

We have been forced to consult with the Prime Minister and Archbishop of Canterbury to determine the best way ahead in this sad and complicated situation. You've given us no choice but to insist that you and Charles file for divorce, sooner versus later. The state of affairs has now become untenable.

We acknowledge that the fault in the breakdown of your marriage lies with Charles, equally as much as it does with you. It has been very distressing to see that the two of you have been unable to achieve a reconciliation.

The only option now is a final divorce which will resolve the matter permanently.

We are concerned with the impact to William and Harry, but are certain that divorce is the only way forward. It can't hurt them any further than the current separation. It is a regrettable circumstance, yet one that needs to be immediately rectified."

Diana re-read the letter twice, before picking up the telephone to ring Nora.

"Nora, I've had a letter from my mother-in-law, insisting upon a divorce. How dare she?" Diana had burst into tears when she heard her friend's voice.

Nora was also shocked. "Darling, whatever has happened? A letter from the Queen? When?"

"Just now. It was just delivered from Buck House. I can't believe she's interfered in my marriage like this. She's demanding a divorce. I never wanted a divorce! I even said so in the Bashir interview. How dare she?" The Princess repeated herself, clearly distraught, as she choked out the words amongst big, gulping sobs.

"Slow down, luv. What exactly did she say? Is she really demanding a divorce? Can she do that?" Nora was worried for the Princess. She knew that despite everything, Diana still cherished thoughts of a reconciliation with Prince Charles. She truly had never considered a divorce. It was too painful a reminder of her own troubled childhood.

"Yes, yes. She even said that she consulted with the Prime Minster and Archbishop of Canterbury – about *my* marriage! Without even speaking to me. So, John Major and George Carey know more about the future of my marriage than I do. I can't believe it, Nor." Diana was getting worked up to a proper state, and was gasping between hysterical weeping.

"Do you want me to come round, Duch?" asked Nora with concern. "I can be there in twenty minutes or so."

"No, it's alright, Nora. I need to call my mother-in-law, and speak to her straightaway. She can't just do this. How is this a constitutional crisis? It's my fucking life. And what about the boys? Has she thought what this will do to William and Harry?" The Princess was pacing the floor of her sitting room distractedly, trying to get control of herself. Paul could hear her downstairs in the butler's pantry, and knew trouble was brewing.

"Diana, I don't know what to say. She's the Queen. I suppose she can encourage you to finalise the separation permanently?" Nora felt helpless. She clutched the phone in her Belgravia flat, knowing how devastated this letter had made her dearest friend.

"Well, she may think so, but she doesn't know who she's dealing with. I'm a Spencer, and we Spencers fight for what we want. If and when Charles and I decide to divorce, it will be our decision, not the Queen's." It was hard to tell which emotion was overtaking her – anger or hurt. She was still crying between outbursts.

"Darling, please try to calm down. Go sit in the walled garden for thirty minutes. Or have Paul bring you a cup of herbal tea. Just settle down a bit before doing something you might regret." Nora knew in her current frame of mind, Diana might lash out – and with Her Majesty, Queen Elizabeth II, this could be very dangerous, indeed.

"I'm not going to settle down, Nora. I thought you would support me. If I can't rely on you in a crisis like this, well…I don't know. I must ring off now. I'll speak to you later." Diana slammed down the telephone.

"Diana, wait….!" cried Nora, but it was too late.

Just then, Paul knocked on the sitting room door and brought in tea. Diana looked up, as she pressed the buttons for Buckingham Palace on her phone.

"Ma'am, I thought you might like a calming refreshment," he offered discreetly.

"Paul, come in, come in," the Princess almost screeched, as she slammed down the telephone. Within a few moments, she had explained the situation, and even asked her butler to read the Queen's letter. As former footman to Her Majesty, he knew her moods and writing style well. "It's the only handwritten letter I've ever received from her," Diana sniffled.

He blanched as he read the formal note. This was indeed a serious development. He tried to caution the Princess against calling the Queen, but she wouldn't be dissuaded. She composed herself, and conducted a polite but brief conversation with her mother-in-law. She wanted to understand why the haste and hurry, and the Queen tried to calm her down, and reassured her there was no reason to rush into any decision.

Diana was not satisfied with her conversation with the Queen, and penned her own letter back, saying that she needed time. She would decide on a divorce on her own bloody schedule.

The next day, Diana received a similar letter from her husband. Charles. He too urged an immediate divorce, citing that the marriage was beyond repair. He claimed it to be a national and personal tragedy, and pleaded for the Princess' swift agreement that divorce was inevitable.

Diana's fury had not abated, and she fired back immediately, stating she was confused, and did not want a divorce.

Only a few days later, *The Sun* leaked the news of the Queen's letter. Buckingham Palace responded with a formal statement:

"After considering the present situation, the Queen wrote to both the Prince and Princess earlier this week, and gave them her view, supported by the Duke of Edinburgh, that an early divorce is desirable. The Prince of Wales also takes this view, and has made this known to the Princess of Wales since the letter.

The Queen and the Duke of Edinburgh will continue to do all they can to help and support the Prince and Princess of Wales, and most particularly their children, in this difficult period."

The next morning after her Harbour Club workout, Diana met with Richard Kay for coffee. Richard was a royal correspondent for *The Daily Mail* – the most sympathetic British paper to the Princess – and the two had struck up an unlikely friendship. Richard was a good-looking and affable young reporter, and had written several flattering pieces about Diana since the separation. Always in need of an empathetic supporter, Diana had thanked him for his loyalty by inviting him to lunch at KP. The pair got along famously, joking and laughing together. At times, Diana had rung her friend Richard, and leaked certain information she wanted known in the press, and he had usually complied willingly. So far, he had never let her down.

Naturally, they kept their friendship private. It would not have done for anyone to think she was colluding with the media – especially not the palace, nor any of Charles' people. He provided a friendly ear, that was all, and they both enjoyed their brief exchanges together.

Today, he listened as Diana recounted her anger over the letters from the Queen and Prince Charles. He was suitably dismayed on her behalf.

"Ma'am, I'm so sorry to hear of it. Has it come to that, then?" A divorce between the Prince and Princess of Wales was a severe measure. Even the separation had been somewhat of a surprise to many of the press and paparazzi. The façade of a happy marriage had been kept up for so long, that only friends and insiders had known how fractured it had become. After just three years, it looked as if the fairy tale was truly over. But Fleet Street was buzzing. Buckingham Palace, as usual, upheld a wall of stony silence. This type of press release was a powerful declaration of intent. Richard shook his head in sympathy.

"No, it's come to nothing," she snapped, as she took a sip of coffee. "I'll not be rushed or pushed into something – especially not by the Queen or the Prince. I've told him I don't want a divorce and I mean it. I want to stay married," she finished stubbornly.

Richard was taken aback. He had heard nothing but criticism of the Prince of Wales – and his mistress – ever since he had known the Princess. Perhaps her feelings ran deeper than she admitted.

"Well, you know best, Ma'am." Inside, Richard knew that the royal game was about to change forever. A divorced Prince of Wales? Would Charles still be able to take the throne as King one day? Would the Church of England uphold such a position? As mother to the future heir to the British crown, what could this mean for the Princess? These thoughts crowded Richard's mind, as he tried to assimilate this big news.

"Richard, don't look so concerned. It's going to be fine. And Charles just echoed what his mother's letter said. Surely someone from his St. James' Palace staff wrote it for him. It means nothing." In fact, Diana had noticed that her husband had used the same phrase - "sad and complicated situation" - that his mother had, so obviously, they had colluded on their one-two punch to the Princess. Diana was not amused. "You'll see, after the holidays, it will be onto something else. A painting trip to Italy or a ski holiday. Trust me, Richard." She beamed her beautiful smile at him. "And now – you can see – it's not my idea at all. The divorce, that is." She shrugged casually, but Richard wasn't fooled. He realised this was the reason for the coffee conversation. Diana wanted it known that the divorce wasn't *her* plan or suggestion. This exonerated her of blame, would draw public sympathy to her plight, and placed her in the best position to negotiate an advantageous settlement. He got it. Diana was a smart young woman, indeed.

"Quite so, Ma'am. I'm sure it's just a storm in a teacup. It will all blow over," Richard assured her. However, he felt just the opposite. The palace had made its first move, with the Queen's blessing. So, it was just a matter of time until proceedings would begin. In the meantime, Richard would keep close to the Princess, and be sure to print her side of the story – when she wanted to share it.

The pair parted wishing each other a Happy Christmas, and promised to meet up again in the new year.

Now Diana was even more thankful that she had refused the Queen's request for her presence at Sandringham for Christmas. It was impossible after both poison pen letters, to even consider spending time with the royal family. As a request from the Queen was in fact a command, Diana's flagrant refusal altered the relationship permanently from calm concern to icy politeness.

Diana spent Christmas Day alone at Kensington Palace, before jetting off to the Bahamas for a few days with a girlfriend. She had simply needed some time in the sun and surf to calm her jangled nerves. Like Scarlett in *Gone with the Wind*, she wanted to put aside her troubles, promising herself she'd "think about that tomorrow."

January 1996. A new year and a fresh beginning. Diana returned from her Caribbean trip tanned and rested. She spent a few days with the boys before they returned to school, and she took up her regular duties without missing a beat.

Early in the month, she had lunch with her old friend Carolyn Bartholomew at San Lorenzo's in Knightsbridge. The restaurant had been a preferred of Diana's for many years, and she was good friends with Mara, the owner. After a warm greeting between the two women, Diana sat down with her friend for a good natter.

"Caro, it's been too long since I've seen you. How is William? And my dear godson Jack? All well I hope, and you had a Happy Christmas?" Diana was dressed in a pink angora sweater and black trousers. She looked vibrant and fantastic.

"All just lovely. Albeit I think young Jack ate too many sweets over the holidays. He had a sore tummy more than once. He sends hugs and kisses to Auntie Diana. And how are you, Duch? Seems like the holiday did you some good." She smiled at her long-time chum.

Diana and Carolyn had known each other since West Heath Girls School. Carolyn had been one of Diana's room-mates at Coleherne Court when she had been dating the Prince. She had been part of the wild ride trying to hold back the onslaught of the press on the teenaged Diana. They had remained close throughout the years, and Carolyn had been one of the Princess' friends who had spoken to Andrew Morton for his biography: *Diana, Her True Story*. Carolyn was brown-haired and blue-eyed, with a calm and cheerful manner. Although an attractive woman, she paled in comparison to the exceptional charm and charisma of the Princess. But Carolyn wouldn't have it any other way. She was close enough to the fire constantly surrounding Diana, to stay far away from the flames. She liked her quiet life with her small family. But she also loved her cherished friend and supported her – no matter what.

"Poor pet," clucked Diana. "Too many Turkish delights?" Diana's eyes sparkled. She knew what treats tempted her godson.

"You know it, Duch. But's he's fine now. And you clearly enjoyed your time away. I know how much you love your vacations on the beach. You certainly look tanned and fit."

The women ordered lunch, and like old friends do, picked up right where they had left off in their last conversation. They chatted easily across a broad range of topics from their children to television show plotlines to details of their lives. Carolyn avoided the topic of the letters and divorce. She and Diana had discussed both endlessly over the phone, and were exhausted by it.

Diana reached out to touch her friend's hand, and leaned in. "Someone else has jumped ship. Patrick just resigned. My team is shrinking by the day." She sat back with a rueful look.

"Darling, why? He's been with you so long – five – six – years at least. What happened?" Carolyn was dismayed. She didn't want anything to set back the Princess during this trying time.

Diana shrugged nonchalantly. "He's claimed that I've shut him out of my decision-making. That I didn't tell him about the *Panorama* interview. That because of that, he wasn't able to smooth the way with the palace. That I don't trust him." She made a face. "I accepted his resignation, and wished him well. And he was with me for eight years," she corrected. "With all the stress in my life – especially now – I need to be surrounded by people who will lift me up, not drag me down. You understand, don't you?"

"Yes, I understand completely, darling. I always liked Patrick, but perhaps you've outgrown him. You're entering a new phase now and maybe a leaner, more focused team is what you really need." One thing Carolyn knew for sure, was that Diana had to have people around her who worked as hard as she did, were passionate about her interests, and were 100% dedicated to her. It was too bad about Patrick, though. He'd been marvelous managing her overseas trips, and made it look so easy. He had served Diana well, and stood by her in tough times.

"Yes, leaner and more focused. I like that," Diana mused. "Do you know that just two years ago I had an overblown staff of a private secretary, an equerry, two detectives, three secretaries, a butler, cook, chauffeurs, two hairdressers, a makeup artist, two dressers, and various ladies-in-waiting. And Anne, of course," she amended. "Now all I have is Paul, two secretaries, a cook, hairdresser, and a dresser. And Anne, of course," she giggled. "I seem to be shedding staff as quickly as I'm shedding husbands."

Carolyn also laughed. "Well, jolly good luck to Patrick, at any rate. But let's talk about the important bits. How is the new romance progressing?"

Diana blushed and giggled. "I think he missed me whilst was away. We've seen each other twice already since I've been back. I missed him too."

The Princess had met Dr. Hasnat Khan by sheer coincidence. She had been visiting Joe Toffolo, the husband of Oonagh Toffolo, her friend and acupuncturist. Joe was in serious condition, after having had triple-bypass surgery. She'd met Hasnat waiting for a lift, and had felt an instant connection. It was obvious he didn't have any idea who she was, and this thrilled her. He'd been totally distracted by his work and his patients, and this made him even more attractive.

At age thirty-eight, Dr. Hasnat Khan was not Diana's usual type. She usually went for urbane, rich, handsome, tall, and aristocratic men. Hasnat was different. Although tall and dark, he was slightly overweight, given his habit of buying takeaways for meals. He was Pakistani Muslim, and completely obsessed with his work. He had been born in Lahore, Pakistan, and was completing his doctoral studies at the West Brompton Hospital in London. He worked ninety-hour work weeks, and home was a tiny, cramped one-bedroom flat in Chelsea to which he paid almost no attention. He had no social life to speak of, and besides junk foods, he liked to drink and smoke to relax. Diana had him pegged as an Introvert – he was sparing with his words, but had lots of big ideas, so she wondered if perhaps he was more of an iNuitive than a Sensor.

What fascinated Diana about Hasnat was his compassion and dedication to his work as a heart surgeon. He really cared about helping his patients, and this was something he had in common with the Princess. They talked endlessly about helping others, and what more could be done for the sick and forgotten.

"So, is it getting serious with Mr. Wonderful then? You've only been seeing him a few months." Carolyn was thrilled beyond measure that perhaps, finally, her closest friend could be finding true love. But she also knew Diana. The Princess loved to be in love. Each new romance was "the one," and she threw herself into fresh relationships with wild abandon and high hopes. Carolyn supposed it was the effect of all the romance novels she had read as a teenager and young wife, that had shaped her unreasonable ideas about true romance. That, and being rejected by the only man she had ever truly loved - Prince Charles – had formed in her a deep hunger to love and be loved unconditionally. Carolyn hoped that this time, Hasnat truly was "the one," but she also wanted Diana to display some caution. Probably a vain hope, she thought ruefully.

"I know it's only been a few months, but we've been getting on splendidly. He insists on absolute privacy, which I've agreed to – for now – so it's our delicious little secret. Paul smuggles him into KP under a rug in the back seat for dinners, or sometimes I go to his Chelsea flat. What a jumble, Carolyn! Dirty dishes everywhere, I daren't even ask the last time the sheets were changed – but it's absolute heaven." Diana beamed. No one could doubt she was a woman in love – it was written all over her face.

"And between those dirty sheets – I hear doctors are amazing with their hands. Is it true?" Carolyn asked in a hushed whisper. They were onto coffee now.

Diana threw back her head, and laughed out loud. Luckily, they were in Mara's private dining room, so she startled no one.

"Well, a lady doesn't tell, Caro – but let's just say that the chemistry in that department is amazing. I know it sounds like silly schoolgirl talk, but I can't wait to see him. I feel giddy and nauseous. I have this happy glow inside me all the time – and when I see him, it's just ignited into something absolutely special. He has these dark-brown velvet eyes that you could just sink into..." Diana trailed off with a faraway smile.

"You *have* been struck by cupid's arrow. My goodness, he couldn't be more different from Charles, could he? Perhaps that's some of the attraction?" Carolyn probed her friend gently.

Diana's eyes turned a slightly icy blue. "Caro, leave off. I see what you're doing. Don't try to psychoanalyse me. Natty and I are having fun together, that's all. And I'm learning so much about physical healing. Heart surgery is fascinating, Caro. I'm even reading *Grey's Anatomy* to better understand how the human body works. Natty says I may get the chance to observe a heart surgery sometime." She had gotten excited again.

Carolyn could see all the signs of a princess in love. Incessant talking about her new man, developing a keen curiosity for his passions, feeling euphoric, ignoring any potential incompatibility warning signs – Carolyn had witnessed it all before. When Diana had been dating Prince Charles, she had feigned an interest in all things outdoorsy – fishing, hunting, horses, holidays at Balmoral – and this had been one of the factors that both the Prince and Queen had seen as validation that Lady Spencer was a good fit for the royal family. Once the wedding was over, Diana's indifference for the outdoors, and distaste for the Scottish holiday home, had come out in full force. The Windsors had been shocked with this about-face, none more so than Diana's husband Charles, who was bemused and bewildered by the switch-up of his new bride.

When Diana had been seeing Captain James Hewitt, she had shown a bizarre interest in riding horses – a pastime she had vigorously rejected since a bad childhood fall. But it had been a pathway to spending time with the handsome Captain, whilst he gave her and the boys riding lessons. That too, had dropped off after the initial pursuit.

And now this unexpected enthusiasm for all things medical. Yes, all the signs were there that Diana was in love. Carolyn hoped and prayed that this time it would work out. If her darling Duch could find her soulmate, nothing would make either of them happier.

Diana seemed not to notice Carolyn's inner reflections, and pressed on. "And I'm planning a trip to Pakistan next month. Ostensibly, I'm going to support the fund-raising campaign for Imran Khan's cancer hospital - Shaukat Khanum in Lahore. But I'm also going to visit Natty's family whilst I'm there. Isn't that exciting?"

"Imran Khan? Is that Jemima's husband?" queried Carolyn, who struggled to keep up with Diana's wide circle of friends.

"Yes, you know she married Imran last year. She's British, but has married outside her nationality *and* religion. And this interfaith couple is thriving. They spend time both in London and in Pakistan, and it's really working." Diana was soaking up as much information as she could from her new friend. Obviously, she was at least contemplating a serious relationship with Hasnat, if she was looking into the Pakistani lifestyle, thought Carolyn with worry.

"It sounds like it's going well, Duch. Of course, I don't know either of them, so who can say what really goes on inside a marriage? But I'm sure it's been a tremendous adjustment for them both, with ongoing compromise and deep understanding. And Jemima is not the Princess of Wales," she said with meaning. How did Diana think she was going to be the mother of the future King of England from far-away Pakistan?

"No, luckily, there's only one of me. In the event, it can't hurt to see what life is like there. And to meet Natty's parents. I can't wait. I'm going in late February after the boys' half-term break. I'm longing to spend time with them." As usual, Diana could switch from topic to topic at lightning speed. Luckily, Carolyn was used to this trait, and kept up admirably.

The two agreed to a kids' dinner at KP in mid-February. Diana promised chicken fingers and chips for the three boys, with a showing of the latest Indiana Jones video. Carolyn agreed, knowing Jack would love to spend time with his godmother and the two fun young princes.

The young moms embraced, and said their goodbyes after an agreeable lunch.

"Diana, it's such an energiser to spend time with you. I know how busy you are, and it means so much to me that you make an effort to see me. It sounds hackneyed, but you really do make my day."

"Oh Caro, it's you that lifts me up. You are such a dear friend. I can't talk to anyone the way I can speak to you. It's just so easy being around you." Diana smiled, and brought a finger to her lips. "And shhhh about the Pakistan trip. I don't want the press to catch wind of it."

"My lips are sealed, darling. You know that. Just please be careful. Don't get too ahead of yourself with Mr. Wonderful just yet. Take your time. Let the relationship develop naturally."

"Yes, Ma'am," replied the Princess smartly, with a mock salute. But Carolyn knew that she would do as she pleased, just like always. She sighed.

Since the Queen's correspondence in December, her mother-in-law had rung Diana a few times, and politely inquired about her position regarding the letter, and its request. Each time, Diana repeated that she didn't want a divorce, she still loved Charles, and she needed more time.

In the meantime, she continued to work with Anthony Julius, a powerhouse solicitor who was not associated with the palace or establishment. He set to work advising Diana, and began the protracted process of negotiating a divorce settlement. The Princess was determined to get herself a better deal than her pal, Fergie. Sarah had only managed a settlement of £500,000 provided by the Queen, for her to buy a new house for herself and her children, £1.4 million to set up trust funds for Princesses Beatrice and Eugenie, £350,000 in cash, an agreement that the Duke of York would pay his daughters' private school and university fees; and a modest monthly allowance which was based on the Duke of York's salary as a Royal Navy officer. Diana would not agree to such a paltry settlement. She was the mother of the future King of England, for Christ's sake!

On February 15th, the Queen invited Diana to Buckingham Palace to resolve the stalemate. They agreed on the most important point – that William and Harry's well-being was of the utmost priority.

"She couldn't have been more gracious about the boys," confided Diana to Paul, upon her return to KP. She had dressed carefully for the interview in a dove-gray woolen coat frock with black lapels; and understated jewelry and accessories. Diana had kicked off her black pumps, and sipped coffee with her butler in attendance. "You know I'm in a rather tricky position. Technically, the Queen has jurisdiction over how they are raised, which schools they attend, etc. I emphasized to her that I must still have a major role in their lives. That is non-negotiable. She reassured me, saying that nothing would change the fact that I am still their mother. And that she was concerned they'd been caught in a battleground with the rows and arguments during the separation. But that essentially nothing would change. What a massive relief!" Diana raised her arms in the air in victory.

"That's brilliant, Ma'am. I've always found Her Majesty to be more than fair, so I'm not surprised." Paul was loyal to both the Queen and the Princess.

Diana snorted. "Perhaps Paul – albeit only when it suits her, the Duke or Charles. Then I asked her about staying in KP. I reminded her it was the boys' home, and it was simpler to maintain security for them here. She acquiesced easily on that one. So, we're not going anywhere, Paul. I also asked her for a country home. She said she had to think about it."

"I'm relieved to hear it, Ma'am. It would be such an upheaval for the boys – and you – to find another residence. KP really is home – and you've done so much to make it warm and welcoming for the young princes."

"The next bit was unsettling, though," continued the Princess earnestly. "She stated as a matter of course, that I will lose my status as HRH after the divorce is final. She made it seem that this was pretty standard. However, the only ex that seems to have been stripped of the HRH title was Wallis Simpson after she married the Duke of Windsor. Albeit I guess she wasn't stripped of the title, since she never really had it. I'm not sure how I feel about this one, Paul. When she said it, I was so happy about the agreement over the boys' upbringing and keeping KP, that I readily agreed to this condition. Now I'm not so sure. She said it was more appropriate for me to be known as Diana, Princess of Wales." Diana had started chewing her fingernails.

"I'm not quite sure what to say, Ma'am. It does seem a small price to pay given the circumstances, yet is it really necessary?" In Paul's mind, he thought this act was a trifle petty, but he wouldn't dare say so.

"I just don't know, Paul. I've worked so hard all these years for the family as a senior royal, it just doesn't seem right to carry on without my title. I've certainly given enough blood, sweat and tears supporting them all this time. I suppose I'll have to give it some thought."

Paul rushed to restore her earlier euphoric mood. "I think you scored a tremendous victory today, Ma'am. Let's focus on that. Shall I crack open a bottle of champagne to mark the occasion?"

Diana laughed. "Why not, Paul? It's not often we have cause to celebrate. Let's have a glass of bubbly then."

"William, stop! Mummy, come and save me," shouted Harry. "He's locked me in again."

"Harry, don't be a prat. You're perfectly okay," laughed William, with an all-knowing big brother smirk.

The princes had been playing one of their favourite games. There was a dumbwaiter that carried food and supplies from the basement kitchen up to the second and third floors. It was just the right size to cram a small boy into, and to be hoisted up and down in some military game that was meaningful only to two brothers with vivid imaginations.

Diana was penning letters to distant friends when she heard the commotion. She smiled, put down her fountain pen, and rushed to find her two sons. Harry's cry had sounded a little more scared than the game seemed to warrant.

She found William peering up into the dumbwaiter shaft calling to his brother. "It's alright, Harry. Mummy's here." He turned to his Mum, and reported; "I think Harry is stuck between floors. I just noticed – he's scared, Mummy. Let's get him out straightaway." William was all concern now for his younger brother.

Diana peered up as well. "Don't worry, darling. We'll get you out, hold on tight." She turned away, and called to the butler, "Paul, come quickly. Harry is stuck in the dumbwaiter.

Seconds later, Paul came to the rescue, and freed Harry in no time. A scared, red-headed little boy was handed to his mama, who hugged him tight. He tried to be brave, but a few tears squeezed out. He tried to wipe them away quickly.

"Mummy, it was dark in there." A small sob escaped him.

"It's alright, darling. Hush now. It's alright," Diana repeated, as she comforted her youngest son.

"I'm terribly sorry, Harry. I thought you were just messing about. I didn't know you were really frightened." William patted his brother awkwardly on the shoulder. Diana hid a small smile to see her elder son cheer his brother. Perhaps she *was* having an impact on them to be caring and thoughtful. "Do you want to play with my new video game?" he offered.

Harry jumped up, his fear forgotten. "Oh yes, William, may I?" Diana gave a grateful grin to William over Harry's small head.

"And fish and chips for dinner, boys. With jam roly-poly for afters." The Princess called after the disappearing boys. Shrieks of joy wafted down the hallway.

"Ready, boys?" Diana called a few hours later. She was dressed in black jeans, trainers, navy blue winter jacket, and baseball cap.

Two noisy princes bounded down the KP staircase to meet their mother. They were similarly attired in dark clothes and matching caps.

She bustled William and Harry into the back seat of a dark town car. The princes' bodyguard sat in the front next to the chauffeur.

"Where are we going tonight, Mummy?" asked Harry, as he snuggled in beside her.

"The Great Ormond Street Hospital, darling," replied Diana. "There are loads of sick children there, and we're going to see if we can brighten their day for a little while.

"I've been there before right, Mummy?" asked William. "I remember the sick children in their beds, with machines and tubes coming out of them.

"Just so, William, and now it's Harry's turn."

When it came to charitable works, there were two Princesses of Wales. The glamorous Diana wore designer gowns and shoes, priceless jewelry, and walked red carpets to headline £5,000-a-plate gala events with celebrities, CEOs, and senior royalty. This was an essential part of her role – lending her support as a patron to underserved charities to draw attention to the plight of their constituents, whilst raising large amounts of money to fund new programmes, and thereby make a substantial difference in people's lives. Diana enjoyed this role – mostly – although she hated public speaking, so preferred to lend her name and not her voice. These work affairs were organised months, if not years in advance, with every detail planned to the letter. Having the Princess of Wales star at such events lent a magical quality and cache that attracted big names and bigger money. Any organisation was thrilled to bits when the Princess agreed to champion their cause. And she was always eager to help.

The second Diana operated under the cloak of darkness. She traded in her tiara for trainers, and snuck into the hospitals, hospices, sickrooms, alleyways, and backrooms wherever needy and desperate people needed a helping hand. For years, Diana had visited centres for HIV/AIDS, cancer and mental illness patients. She also called in to homeless shelters, rehabs, and hospitals for people suffering from alcoholism and drug abuse. She had even given money and clothes to street prostitutes, and spoken to lepers hidden away from the public view.

None of these visits were scheduled, and no luminaries welcomed the Princess with a live band or glass of champagne. Diana really had only one aim – to try to bring comfort to those unfortunates who needed it the most – the ignored, rejected, reviled, and sickest people in society.

Diana had brought her sons to these late-night outings before. She had first taken William to *The Passage*, a homeless shelter, a few years earlier. Nervous at first, he had behaved beautifully, and shown real compassion to those in need. He had come with her several times since then. Harry, too had joined in when he was old enough, and was showing a kindhearted spirit that made Diana proud.

She believed it was critically important that her boys understand that with great privilege, came tremendous responsibility. No one person was better than anyone else, and everyone needed to be treated with dignity and respect. William especially, needed to understand this lesson, and he had picked it up with gentleness and empathy. As future King, William would need to speak to everyone – on their level. He couldn't just sit remotely at Buckingham Palace, and imagine he knew what was on the minds of people. He would get loads of training about his royal duties – she felt that only she could teach him compassion and the common touch.

"Harry, you remember the rules. No staring, no laughing or pointing. It's alright to ask questions, but never make any of the children feel uncomfortable. Always look them in the eyes. And if you feel the urge, it's okay to touch the children...on the hand or face. Or give them a hug. But you must read the cues from them. If they are not comfortable or in any pain, don't force it. But I have found throughout all my visits, that most people long to be hugged and touched. Especially children. Trust your instincts boys, and you will never go wrong. Do you understand?" Diana turned her cobalt blue eyes to her sons.

They both nodded soberly.

"William, do you have any other advice for your brother?" prompted his Mum.

He paused for a moment. "You must ignore bad smells – no matter what. If a child has had an accident, or needs a bath, or even has bad breath from medicine – you mustn't flinch or comment. It makes them embarrassed, doesn't it, Mummy?"

"Quite so, William. And sometimes sick people have trouble controlling how they speak or move. Just treat everyone as normal, and try to speak to them about everyday things. You'll both do superbly, I have no doubt." She ruffled Harry's red hair as they pulled up to the entrance of the Great Ormond.

They were quickly welcomed, and ushered in by a senior hospital staffer. Diana was a familiar site at the children's hospital, so no one was star-struck to see her. Tonight, she asked to be taken to the ward with the sickest children – those with chronic diseases like cancer, leukemia, some awaiting transplants, and a few who were very close to death.

The ward was quiet, and many of the patients were asleep. Whirring noises from machines lent a buzzing sound to the atmosphere. Voices were hushed, and some exhausted parents were dozing in bedside chairs.

Diana approached the first bed with the boys close behind her. "Hello, Gina," she said softly to a Mum who was checking some tubes for her little girl. "How is Jessie doing tonight?" As she asked, she touched Gina's shoulder.

"Your Royal Highness," gasped Gina. "How kind of you to drop by." Her voice lowered. "We haven't had a good day. Jessie is just finishing her second round of chemo, and she's been quite sick ever since."

"You poor dear," clucked Diana sympathetically. "I see you're still awake, young Missy," she turned to the small figure on the bed. "Having trouble keeping down your dinner today? Was it rubbish beans on toast, Jessie?" Diana sat on the bed, and held the hand of the young girl. Jessie was seven years old and very tiny. She had big, brown eyes, and was wearing a knitted pink hat with bunny ears. This covered up her almost-bald head, and kept her warm. She had been diagnosed with lymphoma, and was undergoing intense chemotherapy treatments.

"Diana!" cried the little girl in a weak voice. "You promised you'd come back to visit and you're here! You look beautiful." She reached up a small hand to touch the Princess' cheek.

"Yes, and look who I've brought with me – my two handsome sons. I'm watching you though, Jessie – I don't want you running off with either one of them just yet." She giggled, and Jessie laughed, a welcome sound to her worried Mum.

"How do you do, Jessie?" asked William formally, as he sank to the opposite side of the bed. How was your treatment today?"

"Prince William," gushed the little girl in her whispery voice. "Is that Prince Harry too?"

"Yes, I'm here, little girl," he chirped. The small group broke out in laughter. Diana spent a few minutes conferring with Jessie's mum, whilst William and Harry amused Jessie with stories of first learning how to ride horses. The little family spent a good twenty minutes with Gina and Jessie. Diana could see some of the weariness lift from both their faces during the short respite.

For the next two hours, the Princess of Wales and her two sons moved from bed to bed, making small talk, asking about treatments and symptoms; and making jokes along the way. Diana never made anyone feel rushed, and she had a kind word for each family member. Sometimes she would joke about a show on the telly, or a new film coming out. For more serious cases, she listened intently as parents confided their deepest concerns and fears to the caring young woman. Diana and her boys hugged and touched suffering patients to make them feel loved and special. By the time they had visited each patient, the room was alive with laughter and a small measure of hopefulness.

"Ta ra, everyone," Diana waved, as she and the boys left the ward. "No bed switching after we leave now!" She bestowed one last, lingering smile and left with William and Harry trailing her.

"So, boys, did you see how just showing interest and focusing on one person at a time can make a real difference to those poor, sick children?"

"Yes, Mummy. Little Jacob seemed so happy to see us. I tried very hard not to stare at the big red mark on his cheek. He had ever so many bandages, didn't he

William?" Harry was the first to respond.

"He went through a bad fire and has terrible burns, Harry. He's going to be okay, isn't he, Mummy?" William turned hopeful eyes to his mother.

"I don't know," answered Diana truthfully. "He's awfully hurt. But you spoke to him ever so kindly, son," she praised William.

"Mummy, why do people like being around you so much? Everyone seemed to want your attention. You made them all smile." To Harry, Diana was just Mummy. He'd seen her on public occasions before, but was surprised to see how people were so drawn to her, even when she wasn't dressed up.

"I think it's a several things, Harry. Of course, they know I'm a Princess, and that seems to draw a lot of attention. But more importantly, true compassion and genuine caring will always capture peoples' hearts. Remember that, boys. That's the important lesson. Are you tired out? It's awfully late."

"Somehow I'm not sleepy, Mummy," responded William. "Talking to those children, and offering a hug or a smile has made me feel good, and I have more energy."

"Me too," echoed Harry with a yawn that belied his words.

Diana giggled. "That happens, William. Somehow giving back can fill you up with a feeling of goodness and hope. Try to hold onto that feeling. Now let's get the two of you home to bed. I'm very proud of you both. My little men did so well tonight. Now *you* deserve a hug." She tickled and hugged both her sons, to their delight.

All too soon, William and Harry were packed off back to boarding school. These separations were always difficult for all of them. Diana brought them breakfast in bed, and the three of them chatted over eggs, sausages, kippers, toast with jam, and juice before the final pack and go. They talked about their upcoming ski trip at the end of term. Diana commented on how tall William was getting, and that he would need new ski clothes and possibly ski boots and skis before the trip. As always, Diana joked and laughed with her two favourite men.

Once in their uniforms with cases packed into the car, Diana hugged and kissed her boys on the Kensington Palace courtyard. Harry fought back tears, and his Mum struggled to stay positive and upbeat.

"Goodbye, my darling boys. Always remember Mummy loves you best." They continued to wave at each other until the car was out of sight. The Princess walked slowly back into her empty, cheerless Palace.

CHAPTER FIVE

Everyone's Favourite Friend, Part II

"Lucia! Ciao, Bella. How are you?" Diana greeted her dear friend Lucia Flecha de Lima on the telephone. "It's been an age since we talked." Diana's voice was wreathed in smiles that transcended the phone lines from London to Washington, D.C.

"Darling Diana. I am just fine. But you – you are calling me from Pakistan, no? How is the heat?" Lucia smiled into her mobile phone from her luxurious Washington home, as she settled in for a chat with the Princess.

"Not too wretched actually, Lucia. I've had some Pakistani clothes made for me. They are cool and breathable. The embroideries are hand-sewn and absolutely lovely. And the fabrics are so colourful and soft. I've never been more comfortable at a public engagement." She giggled. "Perhaps I should wear a shalwar kameez to the next Trooping the Colour."

"Just so, my dear," smiled Lucia into the phone. "I'm pleased to hear you're in good spirits. Tell me, darling. What have you been doing in Lahore?" asked Lucia in her thick, Brasilian accent.

"As you know, darling, I'm here to support Imran and Jemima in fundraising for their new hospital. The situation is quite desperate, Lucia. I've toured a couple of the local hospitals, and the conditions are appalling! Patients spilling out into the hallways and common areas, deplorable lack of medications and treatment; and worst of all – the staff and doctors are exhausted and overwhelmed. I really need to do all I can to help." Diana sounded very serious. Indeed, she had been shocked and distressed at the state of health care here in Lahore, Pakistan. It seemed an impossible task to try to get it under any semblance of control.

"I'm very sorry, darling. I'm sure you will lend your name and status to raise as much money as possible. What else can you do?" Lucia knew that Diana took these types of needy situations completely to heart, and was willing to immediately help in any capacity, whatsoever.

"Imran and Jemima took me on a tour of their new cancer hospital – the one he built in memory of his mother, who died of cancer. It's splendid, really. Six hundred staff, all specialised equipment, and so on. And it's built and sustained totally on donations, can you imagine? No one is ever charged for doctor's services, and so they are constantly in financial crisis, trying to stay afloat. Imran has done miracles here.

Yesterday during the tour, I walked around all the wards visiting the patients. Lucia, it was ghastly, awful. I tried to meet as many as I could – especially the children and the most ill. Even if all I can do is touch them, give them a kind word or hug them. I feel helpless, but somehow even that little bit seems to help." Diana sounded tearful and distraught. "There was one little boy. His name was Ashraf Mohammed – I think he was about seven years old or so. He's dying of a brain tumour, Lucia. He only has a few weeks to live. He was so tiny and frail. I held him in my arms for the longest time, trying to will my strength into him. I cradled him as if he were my own child. I know it won't make him live any longer, Lucia, but perhaps he will feel a little more love. Sometimes I feel that's all I can do to help – and it's not enough. It's never enough." The Princess sounded somber.

Lucia tsked and tutted. "Darling, you do more help than you can possibly imagine. I really do think you have healing hands, you know. I'm sure the family were very grateful for all the time you spent with Ashraf."

Diana paused to consider the words of her friend. She found they soothed her.

Diana had met Lucia in 1991, when Lucia's husband, Paulo Tarso Flecha di Lima was appointed as British ambassador in London. The two women had been introduced by mutual acquaintances, and had clicked instantly. Although Lucia was twenty years older than the Princess, they had formed an immediate and long-lasting bond. She was one of Diana's few friends who dared to give her no-nonsense yet loving advice. Diana didn't always take it, but treasured the wisdom of her Brasilian friend. Diana had spent many happy weekends with Lucia and her big family, including five children, in their London home. Diana had been heartbroken when Paulo had been transferred to Washington in 1993, but the two women had maintained a close relationship, and travelled back and forth across the pond to see each other frequently. Diana considered Lucia to be a second mother to her, and basked in the feeling of always being welcomed into a large, loud, and loving Latin family.

Lucia was striking with shoulder length dark hair, flashing eyes, and warm smile. She was always dressed impeccably, and looked and acted every inch the diplomat's wife.

"And what else have you been up to, darling?" continued the older woman. "I know you – you always pack so many activities into your overseas tours. Did you meet any other interesting Pakistanis?" she teased.

Diana pretended to ignore the meaning of her friend's question. "The fundraising banquet was last night. I think it was a tremendous success. I'm not sure yet how much money was raised, but I think it was loads. And they announced at dinner that I would be signing autographs at a table afterwards, and I was proper mobbed." Diana's characteristic giggle returned. "Imagine hundreds of people wanting my autograph!"

"Darling, those signatures will be treasured possessions for these people for years - no decades - to come. You always underestimate the impact you have on people."

"I suppose so," replied Diana doubtfully. "If it can help raise funds for the cancer hospital and make a few people happy, then I've done my job."

Lucia laughed. "And besides the banquet? Any other special visits planned in the diary?"

Diana laughed too. "Lucia, you know I'm meeting Natty's parents later. I'm trying not to be nervous, but I really want to make a good impression – not as the Princess of Wales, but just me – Diana."

"And I'm sure you will, darling," responded Lucia warmly. "Just be yourself. They can't help but love you."

"Thanks for the reassurance, Lucia, but I'm not so sure. The culture here is so different. Within Natty's family – and all the Muslim community here, I think – arranged marriages are the done thing. Even though Natty is far away in London, his parents still have an incredible influence on his decisions, his life, and well – everything, really. If I don't make a good impression, I don't know if he'll ever consider a serious relationship with me." Diana sounded worried.

"It is a lot to overcome; you are right about that. Hasnat comes from an old and esteemed family, and as the eldest son, he is expected to marry well, and to his parents' choosing. They must be concerned that he's not married yet."

Diana sighed. "Yes, well that actually gives me some hope. At thirty-eight, he is certainly showing them that he is his own man. Doing his doctoral medical studies in

London, for example. But I agree with you that Mama's influence reaches far across those kilometres." She sighed again.

"Well, darling, I'm sure you will dazzle them with your kindness and beauty. Your authenticity always shines through." Lucia reassured her insecure friend.

"Thank you, Lucia, you always boost my spirits. I must dash now, though. I have a few more calls to make, and then the hairdresser is coming. I'm not certain how they will get on with this power cutting in and out all the time, though. It's a bit primitive even in this luxury," she laughed.

"Goodbye, Bella. Ring me later with all the news. I love you dearly."

"Goodbye, Lucia." Diana rang off.

The Princess made a few more calls – to Nora, Carolyn, and her sister Sarah, before the hairdresser arrived. Miraculously, the power stayed on, so Diana could get her hair styled before she dressed carefully for the evening ahead.

"I'm not sure they liked me," Diana said in a small voice, a few hours later.

She had returned to the sumptuous sitting room of the rented house where she was staying in Lahore, with Imran and Jemima Khan. She and Jemima sipped cool drinks in the heat of the late night.

"What makes you say that, Diana?" asked Jemima seriously.

"Well, the entire family greeted me nicely, including Appa, Natty's grandmother – but I never really got the chance to speak to his parents privately. The huge family were very kind to me and fed me scrummy foods, but it still felt somewhat forced. Not that I was on trial, exactly, but that everyone was observing me. I don't think I did anything wrong, really. But nothing too tremendously right, either."

As usual, Diana was sitting on a low cushion, with her long legs curled up under her. She was still wearing the rose and ivory Pakistani traditional dress she'd worn to the Khan's home. She looked lovely, but a trifle pale.

"You mustn't read too much into it, Diana. At least not yet. For one thing, things move very slowly here – much more unhurriedly than you are used to in Britain. They were appraising you for the first time, that's all."

"Do you really think so?" asked Diana, her incredible blue eyes looking directly at Jemima." I really wanted to make a good impression."

"And I'm sure you did," reassured Jemima, with a gentle touch on Diana's arm. "How could they not love you?"

Diana smiled slightly. "Well, you are slightly biased, but thank you. "How long did it take Imran's family to accept you?"

Now it was Jemima's turn to sigh. "I'm not sure they do yet. As you know, we married in Richmond at the registry office with no family in attendance, after our Islam ceremony in Paris. Now that I'm expecting a baby, I feel more hopeful that we'll all come together as a family. But being a white Englishwoman marrying into a Muslim Pakistani family is not trouble-free, Diana."

Jemima Khan had been Jemima Goldsmith – the eldest daughter of Lady Annabel Vane-Tempest-Stewart and multi-millionaire and financier Sir James Goldsmith. She was a British journalist, who had fallen in love with Imran Khan, a former cricketer and now philanthropist. Jemima had converted to Islam before the wedding, and had taken up many Pakistani customs, including dress. She now lived in Lahore with Imran, as they awaited the birth of their first child later in the year.

Diana had met them both in London, and was fascinated by their love story – all the more now that she was in love with a Pakistani man herself.

"I fully understand and respect it," replied Diana fervently. "I would never want to change Natty or anything about his culture or family. It's part of what makes me admire him so much. Tell me more about how you fit into Imran's family."

This was one of the Princess' pet topics of conversation. She was throwing herself into the Asian culture, and wanted to soak up anything that would help her understand Natty's family and their ways.

"As you know, Diana – family is everything in the Pakistani culture. They all live together – grandparents, husbands and wives, and all the children. Sometimes a son is boarded out to an uncle's family for a time, but this just gives him another whole family to love as he is the 'special one' in the new home. When a man marries, he brings his wife to the family home, and they all live together under one roof. Of course, all are expected to follow the family rules, and respecting elders is a critical element of this. Mothers play a very key role, and it's not an exaggeration to say that many full-grown, married men with their own families are in love with their mothers in a strange way. Mother's word is law, and no one will gainsay her.

There is so much love in the family, though, Diana, that it is well worth it. Each person is cherished and treasured for their own self. Everyone helps to raise the children, and guests are always welcomed warmly. No one is ever turned away, and a guest's visit might easily turn into a three-month stay. It is an enchanting way to live." Jemima was clearly happy in her choice of marrying into such a culture.

"That's what I crave so much, Jemima. To be loved and accepted for myself – always. And to be part of a big, loving family. As you know, my own fractured when I was only six years old, and my childhood was very awkward. It was not the warm and welcoming home environment that you see here. I long to be part of it!" Diana spoke quickly in her excitement to get the words out. She clasped her hands together, her bangle bracelets jangled, and looked out the open window into the humid night. "I sensed all of what you said at Natty's house tonight. You could see that everyone belonged. Everyone had a place, even in such a large household."

"Yes, it's always that way. It seems the bigger the family, the more welcoming and giving they become. So, tell me, how did Mr. and Mrs. Khan treat you?" Jemima asked curiously.

"Well, when I arrived, there was a large group of people – Natty's aunts and uncles and their families. And of course, Appa was there." Diana smiled in remembrance. "You know I've been corresponding with her for the last year or so. We send each other letters and little gifts. She is such a kind woman, and so wise. It was wonderful to meet Natty's granny. She smiled, took my hands into hers, and kissed them. We hugged like old friends. Then the power cut, and we all had to go outside on the lawn to wait for the food to be served. What a wait, Jemima!" Diana giggled.

"Yes, that's something else to get accustomed to here. Food always takes hours to prepare and serve – especially with unreliable power and the resulting interruptions. But it's beautifully presented – and delicious – when it finally arrives." Jemima offered.

"Everything tasted wonderful. We had lamb and lentil stew with rice, so many vegetables and fruits I'd never seen before. And they pressed so many sweets on me!" Diana gushed.

"I hope you ate everything, as I advised in advance, Diana," asked Jemima in a slightly ominous tone.

"I did my best," answered her friend. "I know it's an insult not to eat the food – especially after being prepared so lovingly." Diana looked thoughtful. "Then they took me over to meet Rasheed and Naheed – Natty's parents. They were very nice to me. We sat on the porch and discussed my work, Imran's hospital, and so on. But nothing personal at all. I found them very hard to read."

Jemima nodded knowingly. "They were probably quite overwhelmed to meet you, Diana. The Princess of Wales in the Khan home! My goodness. I don't know if they see you as a serious prospect as a wife to their son – it's just too soon to tell. But it shows them respect and deference that you were willing to come all this way to meet them – even without Hasnat being present. Whether they can accept a white woman, let alone a Princess of the realm as a daughter-in-law – only time can tell, dear."

"Natty and I have never talked about marriage, Jem. This was just a friendly visit to meet Appa and Natty's family. Nothing more. But I *do* hope they liked me. His family was wonderful." She paused for a moment. "Maybe we'll never have bacon or sausage again at this rate!" Diana roared with laughter, and Jemima joined in. She had already given up pork as a newly-converted Muslim. She thought to herself that bacon wouldn't be the only thing Diana would have to give up, were the romance with dishy Dr. Khan to progress to the next level.

The two friends talked long into the night about the joys and challenges of a mixed marriage between Muslim Pakistani men and white Christian women. It was not the first nor would it be the last time that Diana sought the counsel of Jemima in this matter.

After she returned to London, Diana was summoned to Buckingham Palace to meet with the Queen and Prince

Charles. Although nervous, Diana was grateful for the opportunity to present her own case to her husband and the monarch directly. Prince Philip was not in attendance.

After the formalities had been attended to, the Queen got to the matter-at-hand.

"Charles, Diana. I've called you here today to urge you in the strongest terms, to proceed with the divorce at once. The Duke and I are saddened that the situation has come to this, but it has, and it's time to finalise the divorce. It's in the best interests of everyone, particularly the boys." Her Majesty, Queen Elizabeth II made her statements calmly and with an air of finality.

"But, Mama. I don't want a divorce. None of what's happened is my fault, surely you see that." Diana pleaded with her mother-in-law.

Charles stood by silently, with his hands behind his back. At age forty-eight, the heir to the British throne was still a good-looking man. His hair was greying quite visibly, and he might not have been as lean as he once was, but his piercing blue eyes were as mesmerizing as ever. And although he seemed quite agitated, he still exuded that sense of manliness and courtliness that had always appealed to the Princess. He fidgeted with his cufflinks, and said nothing, waiting for his mother to respond.

"Diana, I think discussing or apportioning blame at this point is inconsequential, and bears no fruit. You've both done and said some distasteful things – particularly in the public eye – that make it impossible to follow any other course of action." She gazed in the direction of her son.

"Hmmph," he paused, looking towards the fireplace. "I agree with Her Majesty, Diana. Let's end this crisis, and proceed with the divorce straightaway. Please don't make this harder than it already is."

"Harder than it is?" repeated Diana incredulously.

"Charles, you're the one who couldn't leave his mistress alone for the entire length of our marriage. You don't think that was hard for me?"

"Diana, please..." the Prince spread out his arms in a useless gesture. "The time for all that acrimony is over. Please," he repeated. He refused to be drawn into another futile row – especially in front of the Queen of England.

Diana turned to the monarch. "Does this mean Charles will be re-marrying, Mama?" she posed in an outraged tone.

The Queen looked straight at her daughter-in-law. "I should think that's very unlikely," she replied quietly.

Diana fought to keep her tears at bay. "I want you both to know that I never wanted a divorce. I thought we had come to terms on an arrangement that works – for the palace, for us, and most especially for William and Harry. An amicable separation with proper roles for Charles and myself. I see now that it's impossible," the Princess acknowledged in defeat.

"Thank you, Diana. I believe what we're all in perfect accord about is to minimise the impact on the boys. You are their mother, and that will never change. You will always be in their lives. You have my word." The Queen quickly summarised the agreement.

"Thank you, Mama," Diana managed to squeak out without bursting into tears.

The Queen rose, signifying the end of the interview. "We'll be sending you papers to finalise arrangements very soon. Again, I must repeat that the Duke and I couldn't be more disappointed to see the union as it has."

The audience had lasted twenty-one minutes.

The Princess was inconsolable that night. She cried until there were no more tears. Paul attempted to soothe her as best as he could. Diana rang up all her dearest friends, sharing her trauma and distress. All provided support, none could change anything.

Jane Atkinson, the Princess' new press secretary, reluctantly issued a statement that night – without the approval of Buckingham Palace. It stated that her client had 'agreed to Prince Charles' request for a divorce.' Diana wanted it known that she had arranged to remain at Kensington Palace, that she would 'continue to be involved in all decisions' about Prince William, thirteen and Prince Harry, eleven; and that she would not leave the marriage without the title of Diana, Princess of Wales – albeit she was losing her status of Her Royal Highness.

Nora had tried to talk her out of this press release. "Darling, please think this through. At least sleep on it. There's no need to issue this today. Please consider what this might do to your negotiating position. You don't want anything to impede your access to the boys." Nora was flabbergasted that Diana was considering such a rash deed.

Diana peered at her friend, with red-rimmed eyes. "I must make the first move here, Nora, don't you see? If I wait, the palace will announce terms as if they are agreed-upon, and then I'll be forced into a corner. I must state my position loudly and clearly. Look what happened to poor Fergie."

Both women nodded, soberly recalling the poor treatment the Duchess of York had received – including an immediate cutoff, and a very modest settlement.

In the end, Diana prevailed. As Nora knew she would. When the Princess was determined on a course of action, there was no stopping her.

Buckingham Palace retaliated in a rare public move by issuing their own statement—contradicting Diana's account—asserting that 'all details on these matters, including titles, remain to be discussed and settled.' And the Princess' lawyer, Anthony Julius, would say only that those discussions between lawyers were still pending.

Diana called Ludgrove School to break the news to

Harry. She made a swift visit to Eton College to advise William in person. Both were short and cheerless meetings.

Events were moving towards their inexorable conclusion.

It was February 28, 1996.

"Diana, it's marvelous to see you. You look lovely, as ever." Countess Raine Spencer rose from the afternoon tea table at the Connaught Hotel to greet her step-daughter.

"Raine, it's brilliant to see you as well. You never age. You always look so stunning."

The two women kissed and hugged warmly, before sitting down to a discreet table in the famous Mayfair restaurant. Elegant patrons pretended not to stare at the famous pair – the Princess of Wales with her one-time enemy, her father's second wife.

Raine was clad in an immaculate chocolate-coloured fitted suit – tailored jacket and skirt – set off by a teal chiffon scarf at her neck. Her hair looked fresh from the beauty salon, although Diana knew that she always looked as flawless as she did at this moment – whether for a special date such as this, or an informal coffee at her townhouse. As usual, she was elaborately made up, and glittered with expensive diamonds – earrings, brooch, and a matching bracelet. Diana noted with a small smile that Raine also carried a matching handbag and white gloves. She'll never change, Diana thought fondly.

The Princess was dressed in a navy-blue pantsuit – fitted with double columns of large gold buttons evoking a military uniform. She matched these with her much-loved gold hoop earrings, and a slim, gold watch. She was carelessly elegant.

A waiter hovered unobtrusively.

"I'll have the afternoon tea, please. With Darjeeling tea," Raine ordered efficiently. She turned to Diana. "Will you have a glass of champagne, darling?" She raised a perfectly sculpted eyebrow.

"Not for me, thank you. But please go ahead. I'll have the tea as well, with hmmm, mint tea, I think. It's chilly out there today." Diana smiled, as she handed her menu to the waiter, who bowed and retreated.

Raine turned expectantly to her step-daughter. "How are you doing, Diana? And the boys? It's been an age since I've seen them." Raine smiled graciously.

"I've just had to send them back to school after the half-term holiday. It's always such a wrench for me." Diana fiddled with her napkin, and sighed. "You know, Raine, Mummy used to cry whenever she had to put us back on the train to Daddy's house in the country. Now I understand how she felt. No matter how many times I've had to say goodbye to William and Harry, it's always a difficult farewell. I have to fight back the tears, just so I don't embarrass them."

"Don't dwell on it, dear," replied Raine briskly. She didn't want their lovely tea to be spoiled by a tearful Princess. "It's the way of the aristocracy – and the royals – to have to part with our children for their own best interests. I consoled myself with that, whenever I had to send off my own children to a new school term. Did you have a chance to get away at all with the boys?"

Diana smiled at the Countess' expert change of topic. "Yes, we skied at Lech again. It's a beautiful spot. Albeit the bloody photographers practically stalked us the whole time." Diana frowned.

"Yes, I saw the papers," tutted Raine. "I don't know how you could even manage a good ski run with them constantly chasing you. It seemed they were grasping for any photographs they could take. How ghastly for you and the princes."

Diana shook her head. "It's extraordinarily difficult to try to ignore them. I do my best, but it wears me out. And I hate to see the boys affected. William absolutely detests them. I'm not sure how he's going to cope with a whole lifetime of dealing with the vultures." She paused for a moment, as the tea tray was brought to them. "I even walked up to them asking for some space. But it came to naught, as usual." Diana rolled her eyes, and reached for a cucumber sandwich.

"You tried, Diana. That's what's important. Your boys know you are fighting for their privacy. Even if the despicable press is relentless." The Countess daintily served herself an egg and mayonnaise sandwich, and a scone with a miniscule amount of jam and clotted cream.

Diana nodded, as she took a sip of tea and nibbled on a strawberry. "I always think of Daddy when we ski there. That's where I received the dreadful news that he had died." Her vibrant blue eyes clouded over at the memory. She reached for Raine's hand. "You know I would never have gone on holiday with Charles, had I known Daddy was so near to death. I had just seen him the day before we left. And the doctors reassured me that he would recover from the pneumonia. I still feel so badly I wasn't there for him at the end." Her lip quivered.

"Nonsense, Diana. We've discussed this before. There was no way you could have known. Even I wasn't there…" she faltered and looked down at her plate. "I had left to go home for the night, when they called me back saying he had passed. My poor Johnnie. He was alone at the end. No one at his side." She was close to tears herself. "But we mustn't indulge ourselves in painful lookbacks, darling. Your daddy wouldn't have wanted us to feel sad. He had a good, long life, and his daughter was the Princess of Wales. He was so proud of you, Diana." Raine smiled encouragingly at her step-daughter.

Diana returned a watery smile. "I do miss him so, Raine. Each and every day. And I know you do, too. When Daddy had his stroke, you were with him, and willed him back to life. I'm forever grateful that you clung to him so tightly, and fought for him."

Raine tried to look modest. "Thank you, darling. It was a horrid time in all our lives. But I loved Johnnie so much, and I was determined not to lose him." She made a small face. "Albeit I felt I was fighting all of you, too."

Diana gazed intently into Raine's eyes. "We were ghastly to you. All of us – Sarah, Jane, Charles, and I – we never gave you a chance. I don't know how you muddled through all those years. We were unspeakably rude and disrespectful to you. I'm so very sorry for my part." Diana reached out her hand to touch her step-mother on the arm again.

It was not the first time that Diana had apologised for the atrocious behaviour of her youth.

"Hush, Diana. There's no need to revisit those days. I'm just so delighted that you and I have been able to move past them. Your father would be so pleased to see us having tea together." Raine didn't hold a grudge, albeit she certainly could have.

Although Earl Spencer had been divorced from their mother, Frances before he met his new wife, all four children had taken an instant dislike to the usurper in the Spencer family. Raine had been married to Lord Dartmouth, borne and raised four children, and was very active in local politics. She was a force to be reckoned with, and Johnnie Spencer had fallen in love with her vibrant and strong personality.

Unfortunately, the Spencer children had not. They called her 'Acid Raine,' and chanted 'Raine, Raine go away' to her. They were rude and ill-mannered – either ignoring her entirely, or playing cruel tricks on her like taunting or disobeying her. Early on, Diana's older sister

Jane had deliberately not spoken to the new Countess Spencer for two years – ignoring her whenever their paths crossed.

In addition to thinking no one was good enough for their father, the children resented all the changes that Raine made to the Althorp estate. Johnnie had been left with overwhelming death taxes when he inherited the Earldom from his father, and drastic measures had to be taken to save the centuries-old great house. This included selling valuable and precious works of art. Although the children blamed Raine for these radical decisions – including gaudy redecoration of their ancestral home – this was not fair, as clearly their father was in accord with these decisions. However, Raine bore the brunt of this fury.

Matters weren't helped when, in 1978, the Earl suffered a serious stroke. At first, his hold on life was tenuous, but after a number of weeks, he pulled through. Throughout this difficult time, Raine was his biggest champion, never leaving his side, and even ordered an experimental drug to be tried upon her husband. He eventually recovered, albeit never to his former booming health. During his illness, Raine limited visits by the then almost-grown up Spencer children, which almost caused an all-out war. The Earl convalesced at Althorp, but the children rarely came to visit. Sarah, Jane, Diana, and Charles couldn't abide the countess' company, or the travesty she had wrought upon their home, so they stayed away. This saddened the Earl very much. He loved his children and his wife, and longed for more family visits.

When he died, the Spencer children immediately kicked Raine out of Althorp – putting her expensive belongings into dustbin bags and leaving them in the courtyard. Raine was heartbroken, but not surprised to be treated this way by her step-children.

At the funeral, Diana was distraught, and refused to be comforted by her husband. Afterwards, she approached Raine, and offered her condolences. It was seen as a tentative olive branch, which the older woman eagerly seized. Since then, Raine and Diana had cultivated a tentative friendship – meeting occasionally like this for tea or luncheon. The Princess had even invited Raine for lunch at KP. Raine had been delighted to get reacquainted not only with Diana, but with William and Harry as well.

The other Spencer children still held ill feelings for their step-mother. They thought Diana disloyal for striking up a friendship with her, but Diana was determined to let bygones be bygones.

Raine had married a French Count after Johnnie's death, but it had been a short-lived relationship. They divorced after only two years. The sixty-seven-year-old woman now lived a quiet life in her Mayfair townhouse. She cherished her bond with the Princess of Wales.

Diana sipped her tea, and spoke quietly. "You are very gracious, Raine. Truly." Her ruminations were making her a bit sad, so she briskly changed the subject. "And how is your dear mother? Still going strong?" Diana smiled.

Raine grimaced. "Yes, Mother is still giving press interviews, if you can believe it! At her age."

Raine's mother was the famous Barbara Cartland, author of over seven hundred books, including many romance novels. Diana herself had been a huge reader of her books as a teenager, and many of her beliefs about *happily ever after* stemmed from the unrealistic, but captivating stories penned by Cartland.

"How lovely," responded Diana as she sipped her mint tea. Both Raine and Barbara were larger-than-life characters with poofed hair, over the top makeup, and impossibly frilly clothes. Cartland habitually wore pink, and instilled in her daughter the need to always be impeccably groomed.

"Please give her my love. Perhaps we should visit her one day together. Would she like that?" Diana smiled.

"Oh yes, she would love it, Diana. With your feverish schedule, I don't know how you could manage it, but if you could – Mother would be thrilled. She treasures every note you send her. She still takes credit for your marriage to Prince Charles, you know." Raine smiled ruefully.

The Princess laughed. "Well, she can take all the credit she wants. The marriage is over, and he was no fairy-tale Prince. But I always loved her books." Diana sighed.

Raine's laugh tinkled throughout the restaurant. "I think you were one of her biggest customers, Diana. How many have you read?"

Diana made a silly face, and crossed her eyes. "Who knows? Remember you used to give me a stack every time I would visit Althorp? Perhaps fifty? I finally realised that my Prince was not my hero, and wouldn't be rescuing me." She gazed off unseeing out the window of the Connaught.

Raine tsked over her sad step-daughter. "Don't fret, Diana." She patted her hand. "A woman as beautiful, as kind, as loving as you – you're bound to find someone to love and treasure you. He just hasn't found you yet." She smiled encouragingly. More than anything, Raine wanted to put that smile back on the face of the Princess, and for her to be happy – at last.

Diana kept her private thoughts to herself. "I really hope so, Raine. Is it too much to ask for a man to love and care for me as deeply as I would him?" She laughed shortly. "But who would take me on?" She paused, and waved a hand at the army of press, photographers, and dozens of gawkers who just wanted a glimpse of the glamorous Princess just waiting outside the doors of the hotel. "Who would take *this* on?"

"Someone strong, self-confident, and very, very lucky," replied Raine firmly. She glanced down at her expensive Cartier watch. "Oh, my dear, I must dash. I have a meeting with my solicitor. But I've so enjoyed our lunch. Please, can we do it again soon?"

"Of course, Raine," replied Diana, with her winning smile. "I have an appointment myself. But let's have lunch again at KP very soon. I'll ring you." The two women embraced, kissed on both cheeks, and parted – both feeling warmed and energised by the companionable encounter.

The glow from the tea stayed with Diana the short distance back to her KP home. It was true she had an appointment for a massage, but she an hour before her masseuse arrived.

"Hullo, Paul," she greeted her butler, as he opened the front door.

"Hello Ma'am," he smiled in returned, as he performed his customary head bow. "How did you find Countess Spencer?" He took his mistress' coat, as she bounded into the hallway and up the stairs.

"Just fine, Paul. We had a splendid tea. I think I'll write a few letters before Anton comes."

Paul was pleased to see the Princess in such good spirits. She had been quite low about the impending divorce over the last few weeks. "Would you like coffee or something cold to drink, Ma'am?" he called after her.

"No thank you, Paul. Just come and collect me ten minutes before Anton is to arrive.

Diana went to her desk, and pulled out a fresh piece of KP writing paper, picked up her fountain pen, dipped it into her Quink jar, and sat, poised.

She was an avid letter-writer, not only standard thank-you notes, but also keeping up correspondences with many friends and acquaintances. Thinking about the past with Raine had made her think of her early years in London. She had adored working in the Young Kindergarten Centre, when she shared her Coleherne flat with Carolyn, Ann and Virginia.

Diana nibbled the well-worn end of her pen, as she thought back to those carefree days. The wonderful freedom she'd had back then, driving and biking all around London – her biggest worry was being on time for work, or not forgetting to pick up the takeaway for dinner. What she would give for that freedom now, she sighed to herself. To be able to walk the streets of London without being recognised, mobbed, and photographed – it would be a dream come true.

The last year of her freedom – at the age of eighteen – she had also worked as a part-time nanny for an American family called the Robertsons. She had looked after baby Patrick two days a week, and formed a strong bond with him and his mother – Mary Robertson. She'd invited Mary and her husband Pat to her 1981 wedding, and had kept in touch ever since – even when the family had moved back to America. Diana had been very sad to see Mary and her beloved Patrick go, and had been delighted to meet up with the family in Washington a few years later. Patrick was a young boy then and didn't remember her, but she still hugged and kissed him as if he were her own child. She ached for those simpler days. She sighed again, and started writing furiously.

"Dear Mrs. Robertson,

I just now returned from afternoon tea with my step-mother, Raine. Yes, you read that right! We've become the most unlikely of friends, but somehow it works. I think she's very lonely without Daddy, and you know I can never ignore someone in pain. I see now that she's been putting up a front for so many years and behind that, she's suffering. I can't forgive myself for being so rude and thoughtless to her years ago. Do you remember all the times I avoided weekends at Althorp, so I wouldn't have to spend any time with her? What I would give now for just one of these weekends back to spend with Daddy. Jane and especially Sarah think I'm the ultimate traitor for being friends with Raine, but they can just rot. It doesn't serve anyone any good to hold onto all those old, negative feelings.

Enough of that! How is my dear Patrick and his sister Caroline? I miss you all dreadfully. I can't believe Patrick is now a sixteen-year-old young man! The last snaps you sent were so lovely – thank you so much. I can still see the shadow of his baby face in that serious young man. Is he enjoying high school? (I think that's what you call it in America???) Is it too soon for him to think of university? It's hard to imagine my William will soon be in that phase. I can't even abide him being away at Eton. I surely hope he chooses a university close to London. Although his grandparents will have some say, about that, I'm sure!

Harry is a rascal as usual, but I adore that little scamp, no matter his scrapes and adventures. Those innocent blue eyes and impish grin gets him out of trouble every time. Do you know his last exeat, when he changed out of his uniform, he had a two-day old piece of cake stuffed in his coat pocket? What a horrid mess that was! He claimed he was bringing it for me, but I rather think he meant it for himself on the way home, and simply forgot he had nicked it. He couldn't understand why he couldn't still eat it after his joyful discovery – all crumbly and falling apart. How could I refuse him a fairy cake instead?

I suppose by now, you may have read that Charles and I will be getting a divorce soon. Albeit goodness knows it's no one's business but our own! I still can't fathom why so many people are so interested in my life, but there it is. I have to be on my best behaviour all the time, poor me!

It's a sad time. I'm crushed that my mother-in-law is insisting that we divorce. I NEVER wanted to divorce Charles. I thought we could come to an agreement we could both live with. Surprisingly, Charles and I are getting on much better since the separation, and I'm more at peace with the choices he's made. The boys seem to be adjusting pretty well, and thriving with their studies, and various sporting pursuits.

Mrs. Robertson, you remember how certain I was to marry Charles and never, ever get divorced? I didn't want for my children the unhappy childhood that I suffered myself. And yet, it seems this is exactly what's happening. It's horrifying. And I shudder to think that Charles may marry Camilla some day! She acts as his wife in all but name now, serving as hostess at Highgrove, vacationing with him, inviting his friends for dinner parties. But to think of him marrying her – and that she would one day be Queen – I simply can't bear it.

But the divorce is truly happening, and I'm managing as best as I can. I don't know when all the legal arrangements will be finalised. I have a very good solicitor who is protecting my interests. I must ensure I maintain control of my precious boys. As it is, it's heartbreaking to think how they will get sucked into the royal family even more now, without me there to help them make sense of it all. I can only enjoy every precious moment I have with them, and create fun and lasting childhood memories for them. They are my life, now more than ever.

I see Paul hovering politely at the door, so I'll have to finish up before my next appointment. I think of you often, and the commonsense advice you always give me. Please tell me you'll be coming to London soon. I'd love to have you at KP for lunch or dinner. All my love to you, Pat, Caroline, and of course, my darling Patrick. Lots of love from, Diana xx"

CHAPTER SIX

The Most Amazing Mum

"Mummy, I'm so excited. Are we really going to meet Ethan Hunt tonight?" Harry's young face was eager with anticipation.

Diana ruffled his hair. "Well, darling, you're going to meet the actor who *plays* Ethan Hunt – Tom Cruise - at the Mission Impossible premiere. Isn't this a splendid treat?" She smiled indulgently at her youngest son.

"Thank you ever so much, Mummy. I want to see him shooting up all the bad guys." Harry was hopping from one foot to the other.

"Well, you realise all that shooting is just pretend, Harry," admonished his mother. "I don't want you getting frightened, or we shall have to leave the theatre."

"I'm not a baby, Mummy. I'm almost twelve, you know!" Harry looked slightly put out.

"I know, darling. You're my big lad now. How silly of me."

"Why are you silly, Mummy?" William entered the nursery sitting room, dressed in wool trousers, a crisp white shirt, and sports coat. At almost-fourteen, he could very nearly look his mother in the eye. He is impossibly fine-looking, Diana thought to herself. And every inch a Spencer. She said nothing, knowing it would embarrass her teenaged son, and cause his now-famous blush to appear. She wanted to keep the evening light and fun for her boys.

"I was just going to tell Harry a joke. Why are leopards so bad at playing hide and seek?" Diana paused for effect.

"I dunno, Mummy, why?" asked Harry.

"I know, Mummy," replied William with a grin. "Because they're always spotted!" He and his mother delivered the punchline together. Diana threw back her head, and laughed.

"Mummy, you have the best jokes," sighed Harry contentedly.

Good thing he hasn't heard any of my more risqué jokes, thought Diana. Charles would pitch a fit. He was always so serious!

The Princess eyed her two sons closely. "All right, men, ready for inspection?"

Both boys saluted and smiled. Harry was also dressed in his work clothes – freshly-pressed trousers, and a shirt with a sports coat. His hair looked a little sticky from a recent encounter with some type of food substance, but otherwise he passed muster.

"Harry, aren't you forgetting something?" his mother asked, trying to appear stern, whilst she hid a grin.

Harry felt his shoulders, arms, and legs. "Mummy you said we didn't need a necktie." He seemed bewildered.

"Harry where's your shoes?" asked his older brother. He shared a knowing glance with his Mum.

"Oh bother, I've left them in my bedroom. I'll be back straightaway, Mummy. Don't leave without me."

"We'll meet you downstairs by the front door. Race you, William!" Diana dared her oldest boy, as Harry ran in the other direction.

"You're on, Mummy," replied William, as he sprinted towards the door. Two tall blonde-headed figures dashed down the stairs, laughing the whole time. William got to the bottom of the landing just a moment before his mum.

"You beat me fair and square, William. Well done, you." Diana couldn't resist giving him a quick squeeze, which he wriggled out of in adolescent dismay.

"Does that mean I may have whatever sweets I want at the cinema?" he asked his mother with big, blue, innocent eyes.

"Perhaps not whatever you like, but certainly yes, you may have some candy or popcorn." She turned to face the staircase. "Harry, come on. We don't want to be late."

Diana looked terrific in a caramel-coloured wool pantsuit, and navy silk blouse. Her skin had a lovely golden glow from her sessions on the tanning bed. She wore diamond stud earrings, a heart-shaped diamond necklace, and now towered over her children with high-heeled nude pumps.

Paul opened the door for the trio, as Harry joined them, proper shoes intact. The butler handed them their coats, as Diana scooped up her bag. "Have a wonderful time, Ma'am. And you too, boys." He waved them off to the waiting car, as the three chatted easily.

"So, what is Tom Cruise like, Mummy?" asked William. You've met him before?"

"Yes, Papa and I met him a few years back at the premiere of *Far and Away* in 1992, I think. He has the most dazzling smile, and is so friendly and charming. You'll adore him. He was with his wife Nicole Kidman – she also starred in the film. She is gorg! I don't think she's joining him tonight. But we'll be at the same Leicester Square Theatre. How about that?"

"Will he do any stunts for us, Mummy?" asked Harry seriously. "Like drop in from a helicopter, or turn his shoe into a gun?"

William answered on his mother's behalf. "Harry don't be a prat. He'll be dressed up in a suit and tie for the red carpet, won't he, Mummy?" Two sets of blue eyes bore into their mother's for assurance.

"Well, you never know, William. He may have a spectacular entrance planned. We'll just have to wait and see." Diana smiled. She couldn't be happier to be spending an evening with her two boys. Her world just felt right when the three were together.

"Will there be lots of photographers there?" Harry persisted.

"You and your questions, Harry!" chided Diana in good humour. "I'm sure there will be loads of press, including photographers and reporters. It is a red-carpet event after all. So, remember to smile nicely – no tongue sticking out – and shake hands with whoever we meet."

Diana thought ruefully of the time when Harry was four years old, and the press had teased him by sticking out their tongues at him. Naturally any small boy would mimic it back. Which he did. And, of course, that had been captured on film, and printed in the papers, calling Harry cheeky and rude. It still made Diana livid how her young son had been manipulated. But she knew that the media were watching all of them, all the time, so they had to constantly be on their best behaviour. And manners were very important for all children, especially royal ones, so she made sure to remind them to behave as grown-up as possible.

The car pulled up to the theatre a short while later, and the three Wales' emerged smiling. Diana shook the hand of the official greeter, and the boys did the same, once introduced. As always, there a large crowd calling "Diana, Wills and Harry" to try to capture their attention. Luckily, they were contained behind metal barricades to keep them back. And the light bulbs popped all around them like strikes of lightning. The princes kept their composure, which made the Princess inordinately proud of her sons. They walked the red carpet into the theatre to meet the cast in a formal receiving line.

They shook hands, and made small talk with the movie's director Brian De Palma, and some of the other actors from the film – Jon Voight, Kristen Thomas Scott, and others. Finally, Tom Cruise waited to greet the royals at the end of the line.

"Your Royal Highness, how lovely to see you again." Tom bowed, and bestowed his famous smile on the little family. "I'm so happy you could make it tonight – and your sons too."

Diana giggled, being a little star struck, even though she'd met this iconic film star before. "It's marvelous to see you again, Tom. These are my sons, William and Harry. They have been so eager to meet you." She pushed them forward.

William reached out his hand, and said formally. "How do you do, Sir?"

Tom grinned, as he shook William's hand. "I'm doing great. And please call me Tom. And Harry, nice to meet you, too. Are you looking forward to the movie?" He also shook the hand of the younger boy.

Harry just nodded, speechless. Tom certainly had the star quality shining through in grand effect tonight.

"I think they were hoping you'd jump out of the ceiling, or be brandishing a weapon," Diana joked.

Tom looked at the two princes intently. "I hope you boys won't be disappointed. There's a lot of surprises coming your way in the movie. You'd better sit tight."

Diana loved the way the star addressed the boys directly, and didn't just focus on her. Tom had a way of making every person feel important when he spoke to them.

"And how is your lovely wife? I'm sorry we won't be seeing Nicole tonight." Diana was slightly tongue-tied herself. This was one gorgeous hunk of man!

"She sends her regrets, Ma'am. She's at home with our two little ones – Connor and Isabella. They're not quite old enough for a movie like this are they, Harry?"

Harry shook his head no, having not a clue what his idol was talking about.

Diana stepped in. "They are just toddlers aren't they, Tom?"

"Yes, Isabella is four, and Connor is two. They are quite a handful. I can only imagine what a mess they would create let loose in a place like this." Tom laughed.

"I understand, Tom. I can't picture these two rascals at a theatre event like this at that age. Harry would probably be climbing the furniture, with William chasing him. Luckily, we're past that stage – I think." Diana laughed too.

They spoke for a few more minutes before the lights started to dim, signaling the film was about to begin.

Two hours later, a pair of young men left the theatre with their mother, spellbound by all the stunts and action they had seen. Diana had wanted them to slip out a tad early, so that Tom and the cast could enjoy the adulation and attention they deserved, without the spotlight being put on her.

"Mummy, did you see Ethan, I mean Tom, hanging over the floor? And racing in the speedboat?" Harry was tripping over his tongue remembering all the action scenes.

"And how he climbed up the side of the building? And what about when that huge building blew up? I just loved every minute of it, Mummy. Didn't you?" William was just as chuffed.

"I don't know how he did all those dangerous stunts. I heard he insisted on doing a lot of them himself. He was amazing, I agree. It was rather frightening at times, though. I was certainly glad to have my two strong men there with me." Diana hugged them both.

"I wish we could have stayed longer to talk to him. He's just brilliant. Smashing." William was flushed with the thrill of it all.

"Mummy, didn't it seem like he was taller in the film than in person?" Harry was curious.

"That often happens with film stars, darling. They seem larger than life on the screen, so when you meet them, they always look smaller." Diana smiled to herself in the dark. In her high heels, she had towered over the famous Tom, but found him charming and irresistible, nonetheless.

"And you mustn't ever say anything so rude to him in person," scolded William.

"William, I never would!" protested his brother. "I'm just saying between us, that's all."

As the car pulled past the guards at KP and up to the front door, Diana felt that all in all, it had been a wonderful outing. She knew she was lucky indeed to be able to provide such glamorous events for her sons. It almost balanced out the ongoing harassment by the press - almost, but not near enough.

"Darling, you look rather fetching. That scarf is lovely with your colouring." Diana greeted her elder sister Jane with a kiss on either cheek.

"Duch, you are stunning as always." Jane smiled. She was dressed in casual blue trousers, an aqua silk shirt, and a patterned silk scarf that picked up both colours. "And thank you. Robert gave it to me for my last birthday."

Diana giggled. "He'd better up his game next year. Isn't it the big 4-0, as the Americans say?" Diana was casually elegant in black denims, a purple cashmere sweater, and black suede boots. "How is dear Robert?" she asked with just a note of irony. As private secretary to the Queen, Robert's allegiance to the crown was unwavering. He loved his unpredictable sister-in-law, but they had an uneasy relationship at best. Robert had felt completely blindsided by the Morton book, and had been mortified by the Panorama interview. With current volatile divorce proceedings underway, Diana and Robert were barely on speaking terms. By a tacit, unspoken agreement, the two sisters did not delve into these matters, but kept their relationship topics to family, and lighter topics.

"Diana, I've barely turned thirty-nine. Don't push me over the top just yet." Jane playfully punched her sister on the arm. "And Robert is just fine. Too busy as always. He sends his love."

Diana raised an eyebrow, and was about to make a comment, when the third Spencer sister made her timely appearance.

Sarah McCorquodale was the eldest Spencer daughter, and Diana's favourite. She was bright, outspoken, and lively. Diana had always envied her elder sister's self-assurance and breezy confidence. She had the Spencer red hair and fiery temper to go along with it. Today, however, she was smiling. She was dressed in an emerald green pants suit, set off by a bright scarf of many hues.

"Hello ducks," she exclaimed. "Don't we all look lovely?" Hugs and kisses all around were the next order of the day – although rather perfunctorily. Diana had inherited most of the warmth in the family. The others were more like their mother Frances, who didn't always show affection with ease.

The three met at Spencer House in the heart of London. Although the famous historical mansion was currently let out for business purposes, it was still owned by her brother, Earl Spencer. Diana adored it, and arranged for a private dinner there with her siblings once or twice a year. They had come through to the magnificent library for pre-dinner drinks. One of the most elegant rooms in the entire property, the Spencer House library, was furnished in rich mahogany with gilded trim, and boasted many first editions.

Built by the first Earl John Spencer in 1756, the classically designed Spencer House had been conceived by the Earl as a London townhouse for his new bride and himself – away from their country estate of Althorp. Designed by the famous architect John Vardy, it boasted white Greek columns and neoclassical details that made an imposing presence overlooking Green Park. The Ritz Hotel was a stone's throw away from the magnificent estate. John and Georgiana Spencer had loved their London home, and gave many lavish parties and receptions to cement their social status amongst the town's elite.

In addition to a dozen or so bedrooms and full servant's quarters, the main floor was a showpiece that included a grand Dining Room, Music Room, Great Room, and Diana's favourite – the Palm Room.

"Don't you just love it here? I can feel the spirits of our ancestors gliding through the halls. I can almost hear Georgiana's skirts rustling through the doorways, as she greeted her guests." Diana studied the room with a dreamy expression on her face. She loved Spencer House, and it had been her idea to dine here tonight. She found the romantic story of the first Earl and his wife enthralling.

Sarah snorted. "Diana, will you never cease to have starry-eyed ideas? That was centuries ago. This old relic is alright, I suppose. But it's just a house, after all."

"Sod off, Sarah," chided Jane good-naturedly. "It is a grand old place, and one of the only remaining eighteenth century aristocratic homes left in London. I agree with

Diana. I'm proud it's in the Spencer family." Jane was ever the peacemaker.

She and Sarah sipped on Pimms, whilst Diana helped herself to coffee from the tea tray.

Diana carried on, without seeming to have noticed Sarah's barbed remark.

"It's simply a lovely old place. Remember the stories Grandmother Spencer used to tell us about how during the Blitz in World War II, all the precious paintings and sculptures were moved to Althorp for safekeeping? Even the doorframes and fireplace marble were dismantled and sent. It's looking much better since the recent restoration – truly glorious." The Princess smiled.

"I suppose that's one thing we can thank our illustrious stepmother for," said Sarah drily. "When she ransacked Althorp, and sold off our precious paintings to the highest bidder, Spencer House was eager to buy back some of these priceless *objets d'art*. So that's something, I suppose." She sniffed, and took a sip of her drink.

"And how is Raine?" asked Jane. "I thought I saw a photograph of the two of you having lunch together recently."

"It was tea, and she's fine. And there's no use trying to start wrangling about her. I've made peace with her, and that's that." Diana's cornflower eyes took on a hint of blue steel. Jane and Sarah exchanged glances. They knew that look, and decided not to pursue the touchy topic.

"How are the boys, Diana? William doing well at Eton?" Jane turned to her younger sister.

Immediately Diana's face softened. "Going from strength to strength, Jane. His academics are wonderful – thank heaven he didn't get his dim brain from me! And he's thrown himself into the sports as well. Rugby, especially. And he's taken up water polo. I think he's trying to please both Charles and I – swimming for me, and polo for his father. He's rather competitive."

"I wonder where he gets that from?" Sarah laughed. "Remember when you came in first at the Mother's Day Race at Wetherby? Even then, you had to win. Was that William or Harry's Sports Day?"

Diana grimaced. "William's. I only came in third at Harry's. But I can't help it." She shrugged. "When I want something, I go after it. We all learned that at boarding school. Jane, I remember you were captain at field hockey, amongst your other achievements."

All three women laughed. You could see the Spencer similarities between them. Although Diana was the only blonde, they all shared tall, lithe frames, with blue eyes and ready smiles. Their brother, Charles also sported the Spencer ginger hair and fair complexion, albeit he was far away in South Africa.

"And Harry, is he rather the big cheese now at Ludgrove on his own? Or feeling at a loose end?" They were all protective of the younger lad. As the spare to William the Heir, they wanted to ensure he received his fair share of attention.

"Loving it," declared Diana proudly. "I was afraid he might feel lonely without William there, but he's blossomed. "They grow up so fast," she sighed. "KP is so quiet without them. It's like living in a morgue."

"Dinner is served," announced the butler.

The three women strode through the Music Room and Great Room, through to the Palm Room where Diana had arranged for a small table to be set up. It was exquisitely set with heirloom Spencer plate and silver. Winter flowers adorned the centre of the antique table.

The splendid room was designed after the King's Bedchamber at Greenwich Palace. White columns were decorated with carved and gilded palm trees. The pale green walls featured inlays with Greek statues, and the wood floor gleamed with polish. Palm trees had been chosen as a symbol of marital fertility for the young

Spencer couple. The frieze of griffins was a nod to the heraldic supporter of the Spencer arms. The room was warm and welcoming.

"Diana, this *was* a good choice. I never understood why you always bypass the formal dining room for our dinners, but this is much nicer." Jane approved.

"It always makes me think of Grandmother. She loved sitting here in the late afternoon sun overlooking the gardens. I miss her so much."

Countess Cynthia Spencer had been the seventh Earl's wife. Genteel and elegant, she had been a positive influence on the young Diana, who had spent holidays with her here in her youth. She had sat at her grandmother's knee, begging to hear the stories of Spencer romance in the eighteenth century. Many people commented that Diana bore a certain likeness to her grandmother. This made Diana inordinately proud. She had been devastated when her grandmother had died of a brain tumour, at age seventy-five. The Princess believed that Cynthia watched out for her in the spirit world, and sometimes Diana could feel her presence – or thought she did. She had been to see a medium a few years earlier, who confirmed that Cynthia's spirit was never far away. But she would never confide this to her no-nonsense older sisters. Still, Diana was proud of her family's noble history and rich heritage. Spencers were a grand and distinguished British family.

The sisters dined on salad, steamed fish, and vegetables. All three had developed lifetime habits of eating sparingly to maintain their figures – a lesson learned from their still-slim mother. They chatted about the other Spencer children – Sarah and Jane each having three.

"I can't bear the thought of sending Colin away to boarding school next year," murmured Sarah with a frown. "What is this barbaric custom of aristocratic British families sending their sons away from home at the tender age of eight? Perhaps it's because he's the baby, but it seems like it will be more of a wrench than when George went four years ago. I suppose he'll adjust. Somehow they all do."

"Yes, it seems like an age since Alex went off to boarding school," commented Jane. "But I agree with you, Diana. The empty house feels a treat straightaway, but becomes desolate after a time. Who knew we'd be longing to hear from our children – remember when they were climbing all over us, and we couldn't wait to have Nanny take them off to the nursery for their baths?"

Both Sarah and Diana nodded, but the Princess really didn't agree. She had always hated every moment she had been separated from her boys – starting from the overseas trip to Canada that she and Charles had made in 1983, when they missed William's first birthday.

"Bloody hell, we're getting all maudlin, aren't we? Let's be happy our children have somehow turned out so well-adjusted – especially with us as mothers!" Leave it to Sarah to lighten the mood.

"Speaking of Alex, I have a birthday gift for him," interjected Diana with a smile. She had barely touched her food, and nodded to the butler to clear. "William recommended the latest Nintendo game for him. I couldn't honestly tell you the name, but apparently, it's just the thing. Remind me to give it to you when we leave."

"Diana, thank you ever so much. You never forget a birthday or anniversary. How do you do it?"

"An excellent private secretary, that's how," Diana giggled. But they all knew how personal dates meant the world to the busy Princess. "And speaking of birthdays, isn't that why we're here? To celebrate yours, dear sis?"

On cue, the butler brought in a small birthday cake.

"Diana, you always think of everything," cried Sarah. "But I thought we decided not to celebrate birthdays after thirty?" She paused. "But I hope it's a Madeira cake?"

"Of course, it is," responded her sister. "I know what you like." She turned to the butler. "Can you please serve it with tea and coffee in the Painted Room?"

This was another of Diana's treasured places at Spencer House. The theme of the room was a celebration of the Triumph of Love, in honour of Lord and Lady Spencer's own happy marriage. Music, drinking and dancing nymphs were depicted in the decorations on the walls and ceiling. It too was painted green, with matching couches dotted around the room. It was here that the sisters enjoyed their coffee and cake, whilst Sarah opened small gifts from Jane and Diana.

"Who has spoken to Mother lately?" asked Jane.

Diana curled up her legs under her on the antique sofa. "I spoke to her Thursday last," she replied. "She didn't have much good to say, though. She wants me to leave my marriage without a fuss. Not bloody likely!" Diana held up her teacup, and made a face.

"How is that going, Duch," asked Sarah. Jane pointedly stared at her cake dish, and said nothing. She would not be drawn into this conversation.

"As well as can be expected, Sarah. The negotiations are slow going. But truly, I don't even want a divorce. It's Charles and the Queen pushing. I thought we could have a formal separation, and make it work. But apparently not." She slammed down her cup into her saucer.

"Isn't it rather flogging a dead horse at this point, Diana? You are leading separate lives in different homes. Why not just put an end to it, and get on with your life?" Sarah was slightly exasperated. Why couldn't her sister see what was obvious to all? The marriage was over, dead. Diana should pluck up her courage, and take Charles for all she could get.

"You two should understand this better than anyone! I never wanted a divorce. I never wanted my children to go through what we all did when Mummy and Daddy split. This is my worst nightmare coming true." Diana wiped away a tear.

"Chin up, darling. The boys are doing splendidly. And isn't it better for William and Harry to see their parents happy for a change? Even if not together? Remember how awful it was when we saw Mummy and Daddy rowing at Park House? It was dreadful." Sarah had used these arguments before, but hoped it might sink in this time.

"I suppose you're right, Sarah," replied Diana in a small voice. "I just hate to fail. And after all I've given to this fucking family. Years of sacrifice and doing everything their way. It's always their bloody way."

"Charles rang me yesterday. Our brother and Victoria are finding it heavenly without the media attention in Cape Town, but still missing London. He sends his love." Jane interjected a new topic rather abruptly. "They're delighted with little Louis – a son finally, to take up Althorp as the Earl someday." Jane stood up. "Well, I hate to break up this little party, but I need to be getting back to the Old Barracks. It's been lovely girls, and Happy Birthday, dear Sarah." Jane made a hasty departure.

"Alright, then. If you must. I'm going to stay with Diana here for a bit. We want to plan a cousins' visit to Althorp this summer. I'll ring you with the details."

The women kissed and hugged, as they said their goodbyes.

"She couldn't have gotten out of here any faster, could she?" Diana had returned to the sofa. "More coffee, Sarah?"

"Yes, please. One more cup and then I must fly, too. I'm just in town for the night, you know. Back to Lincolnshire tomorrow." She paused. "Duch, you mustn't

138

blame Jane for rushing out like that. She's in an impossible position. She can't possibly comment on any matters that involve Her Majesty. It would just compromise her husband. She couldn't do that."

"Oh, that old stuffed shirt. Robert is a fussy, old woman. Why she is so loyal to that prat, I don't know. Jane knows what that family has put me through!"

"Of course, she's loyal to her husband, don't be a cow, Diana," replied Sarah sharply. "And Robert is a trusted secretary to the Queen. So that's that. Don't put Jane in a position to choose – she'll always side with her husband and Her Majesty."

"Just like everyone else," sulked Diana.

"Stop grousing, darling," chided Sarah. "You have millions of people on your side. And you're in a tremendous position to do well for yourself. I assume you have a good solicitor?" Sarah's tone was brisk. She didn't have much patience for Diana's tears or moods.

"Yes, of course I do. I just can't believe it's all come to this. You know, this summer we will have been married fifteen years. Hard to believe it's now a load of rubbish." Diana was feeling a bit wobbly again.

"I can see you're getting yourself into a bit of state, darling. My turn to leave. Try to see the best of the situation. Stiff upper lip and all that. You have your health and your incredible sons. You'll be a wealthy woman in your own right; you have a tremendous impact in the world. And you're beautiful too! All you need now is a new chap, and the future could not be brighter for you. Take a moment and be thankful." Sarah stood up, and smiled kindly to soften her words. "Thank you for the birthday dinner and Harrod's bag. I love it...and you." Sarah pecked her sister on the cheek, as she started to walk through the halls of Spencer House. "And ring me tomorrow. I'm taking the 2:17 train. Perhaps we can talk about our summer plans before that."

"Of course, darling," replied Diana as she attempted a smile. It was lovely to see you. Hugs and kisses to Neil and the children. And yes, I'll ring you in the morning after I get back from the gym." In a cloud of expensive perfume, Sarah was gone.

Although by now it was quite dark, Diana returned to the Palm Room to stare out the window. Grandmother, where are you when I need you? How can I get through this bloody mess on my own?

"Hullo, Paul," Diana greeted her butler a short time later. "Any calls?"

Paul immediately noticed her subdued mood. "A few, Ma'am. I've left them in your sitting room. How was the birthday dinner? You found your sisters well, I hope?" He smoothly took Diana's coat and bag, as she walked slowly into the foyer.

"Well enough. I don't know why I bother confiding in them about anything. They just tell me to get on with it, or just change the subject. Just like Mummy. I wish Daddy was still alive. He always listened to me."

Paul could see that his mistress was worked up. "Shall I bring you some herbal tea, Ma'am? Anyone I can reach for you on the phone?"

"No thanks, Paul, I'm coffee-logged at the moment. I will ring Nora shortly, but I think I can manage to operate the telephone myself."

Paul looked sheepish.

"I know you're only trying to help, Paul," the Princess replied softly. She wound her way up the staircase without the usual bounce in her step.

"You're *not* a rotten Mum. Far from it. Give yourself a shake, girl!" Nora had been listening to Diana's account of the Spencer evening, and was determined to cheer up her best mate. "Why ever would you think otherwise?"

Diana had dismissed Paul for the evening, changed into a long dressing gown, washed off her makeup, and pulled back her hair into an alice band. As usual, she was sitting on the sofa in her sitting room, with a pillow on her lap, and the phone in her hand.

"Because I'm getting a bloody divorce, that's why. My sisters want me to just get over it, and get on with life. But it's just not that simple. I never wanted my boys to suffer through a divorce – living in two different homes, being teased at school, embarrassed at social functions as everyone is so awkward – all of it. I hate it, Nora. I loathe it all."

Nora paused to consider her words. "I don't often agree with Sarah and Jane, but perhaps they have a point." She rushed to explain, as Diana let out a sharp cry in protest. "Wait – all I meant is that it's time for *you* to take charge. Don't be a victim, darling. That's letting them win. Show them you are made of sterner stuff. Do this on your terms."

"What do you mean?" asked her friend doubtfully.

"Go on as you have done. Haven't you always led from the heart, knowing you were doing the right thing – even when the family disagreed? It started even with naming William, remember that?"

"Yes, Charles wanted to name him Arthur or Albert. How horrid! But I didn't relent. I knew his name was William. And I had to thrash it out with him to have the baby born in the hospital, and not at home like the rest of the Windsors."

"Exactly so. And didn't you choose a more modern nanny for him? Barbara Barnes, wasn't it? Someone younger, less stuffy?" Nora was warming to a theme.

"Yes, do you remember – Charles wanted his old nanny Mabel Anderson to look after William? Can you fancy that? She was ancient by then. But I put my foot down."

"Yes, you did, "replied Nora with enthusiasm. "And didn't you also insist that the boys go to nursery school instead of being tutored at home?"

"Yes, that was my idea, too! I knew William needed to be around other children, if he were to have any kind of normal life. And he was better behaved after that. Remember when they used to call him *Basher* for hitting the   other   children?"

"Your instincts have always been spot on, Diana," encouraged Nora. "And just think how young you were! When William went to nursery, you were only in your early twenties! That was brave."

"I suppose I've always known what's best for my boys," mused the Princess. "I insisted on them wearing casual clothes when not at school – not the Victorian dress that Charles would have had them in. I recognise they can't have a normal life like everyone else, but I've really tried to give them experiences so they can see what it's like for other people, and so they can let down their hair too."

"And don't you take them to McDonalds and the cinema, and make them stand in the queue and pay like everyone else? And how many other royal children have gone to theme parks and rented go-karts?" Nora prompted her friend.

"None that I know of," giggled Diana. "I really feel for them, Nor, – especially William. I know what a life of royal duty is like – torture at times, simply dull as ditchwater at others. I can't take that away – but I can help them prepare for it. And I can certainly show them some fun, too. Heaven knows, they need it," she responded fervently.

"What about Disneyland? I still hear Harry talking about the roller coasters and rides. And you've always taken them skiing each winter. They really are very lucky young princes, Diana."

"Thank you, Nora. I've really tried. William and Harry are my world, truly." Diana said softly.

"And what thirteen-year-old boy comes home from school, and finds the world's top three supermodels waiting for him at the top of the stairs?" Nora laughed.

"What a picture William's face was that day! He'd put up posters of Cindy Crawford, Christy Turlington, and Naomi Campbell on his wall – just like any other teenage boy. I knew he was in love with them – puppy love. So, I arranged for them to come to tea one day – as a surprise. William turned so red. I don't know if he was more embarrassed or excited! It was hilarious." Diana was laughing so hard she could hardly speak.

"Was he chuffed to see them?" asked Nora

"Completely tongue-tied. They were so gracious, naturally, and kept up a cheerful banter. He hardly uttered a word, poor boy. But I'm sure he'll never forget that day."

"See what I mean, Duch. You may have the means that other mothers don't have – but you use them to make special moments and memories like that for your children. As you say, William will never forget it. That's a good mum."

"I must balance what The Firm and palace do on the other side. The royals can suck you up like a Hoover, Nora. And the boys love hunting, shooting, and fishing at Balmoral. They love being outdoors with their father. And Charles *is* a good father. His interests are very different than mine, but one can't argue that a good, healthy outdoor lifestyle is also good for William and Harry."

"Yesss… in moderation. Although, being shut away for weeks at a time in Scotland with your royal grandparents and a houseful of staff is not normal life. I agree – it's a good holiday for them, but William and Harry know that KP is home."

"I hope so, Nora. I really do. I want them to feel they have a strong home base here. And don't forget – I know what lies ahead for them both. I've never tried to keep them away from their Granny or royal duties. Especially William – we've had so many long talks about what's ahead, how he should handle himself, his worries and fears. No one talks to him the way I do – letting him express his feelings, and not bottling them up like that bloody family of emotionless Germans. They wouldn't know a feeling if it came up and bonked them on the head." Diana giggled again.

"That's why you are so important to those boys. You let them have lots of fun and normal adventures, yes. But you always ensure they know their manners, treat people right, and are as prepared as they can possibly be for their lives ahead. And on top of that, you also take them to homeless shelters, AIDS centres, hospitals, and hospices to understand the truly needy of this world. That's just brilliant, Diana."

"Being remote from the people you serve won't help William when it's his turn to become King. He needs to be in touch with them, understand them, relate to them. And it's not just palaces and movie premieres, and Scottish holidays. It's representing people of all walks of life. And it gladdens my heart so, Nora, to see how they both take to these excursions. William, especially – he truly cares about these people down on their luck – alcoholics, criminals, homeless people. He wants to listen, and understand their problems. That's the first step to helping solve them – awareness and understanding. Harry is learning fast, too. He's young, but his spirit is giving and loving. I couldn't be prouder of the two of them." Nora could hear her friend smiling down the telephone line.

"And I couldn't be prouder of you, Diana. Sure, Charles has an impact. And he is a good father, I agree. But what makes those young men who they are – that's all you. They know you love them. You're an amazing mum."

"I just follow my instincts. They've never set me on the wrong path," replied the Princess humbly. "I started talking to each of them in the womb – telling them I love them. And I'm always hugging them, touching them, looking them straight in the eye when I speak to them. All the things I wished I'd gotten from my own parents. It's amazing, isn't it, Nora? Some people are just doomed to repeat the mistakes of their parents in the next generation. I see it all the time with drugs, abuse, and neglect. But somehow, others can rise above and do something completely different – but absolutely right for their children. I guess I'm one of the lucky ones who could see past my own experiences to make better lives for my boys. I've never really thought about that before, Nor. I just *know* what to do, even against the most tremendous opposition. And I'll never stop fighting for them. Not till my last day on earth. I just hope it's enough to help them navigate the hard life ahead." Diana finished quietly.

"You know, you're right, darling. Even for myself, when I'm scolding Clemmy, or getting impatient with her, I can see I'm sounding just like my own Mum. I don't really question how I was raised, or if I should do anything different. You're even helping me to become a better mum. How about that?"

"Jolly good, Nor. I'll just add you to my list of people who need me. And gladly so. You've stopped smacking her since we talked last, right?" Diana was stern.

"Yes, I have, Diana. I've been doing what you said. Getting down to her level, looking her in the eye, staying calm, and trying to reason with her. It doesn't always work, but mostly it does! And we don't both walk away feeling bad about what happened. But there's a good example – my Mum used to give me a good whack from time-to-time, and see how I've turned out? Not too badly, I hope?"

Diana smiled to herself. "Not too rubbish at all, darling. You're the dearest friend I could ever have. Your mum must have taught you how to be a great listener. It's one of your most sterling qualities. And one that I test too often, I fear." Diana heard a downstairs clock chime midnight. "Oh dear, here I've kept you again far too long. But thank you, Nora. You make me believe that somehow this disaster is going to turn out right, after all.

"And it will, darling. Keep on trusting that golden instinct of yours. Don't let your sisters get you down by playing back all the old tapes. Believe in yourself. And don't take yourself too seriously."

"Oh, that reminds me, Nor. Have you heard this joke?

She: 'You are the worst lover I have ever been with!'

He: 'How can you tell that in only ten seconds?'

Diana cackled like a hyena.

Nora laughed. "Diana, I don't know where you pick up these jokes. That's a good one! But I won't tell my husband. Men are sensitive about things like that."

"Goodnight, Nora. And thank you again. I'll ring you tomorrow."

"Goodnight, darling. Sleep well."

CHAPTER SEVEN

The Heart Surgeon

"Paul, is everything set? Is it perfect?" Diana fluttered around the butler's pantry of Kensington Palace.

The Princess looked spectacular. Her skin glowed from a vigorous workout, and late morning facial. Her makeup was naturally elegant, and her newly-highlighted and styled hair was fabulous. She'd had a fresh manicure today, and her nails were a glossy baby pink. She was dressed in a red sweater than clung to her curves, and was cinched at the waist with a thick black belt over a long, narrow black leather skirt, and tall boots. She looked sleek and confident.

"Yes, Ma'am. The drawing room table is set for two. There's cold lager in the refrigerator, and two chicken dinners are here ready for the microwave. Will there be anything else?" Paul looked expectantly at the Princess.

Diana stopped and smiled. "Of course, everything is just right, Paul. No, I think the only thing we need now is our guest. He's working late again at the hospital. He works so hard, you know!"

Paul smiled in return. "Yes, Ma'am. Just let me know when you want me to collect him." He gave his traditional head bow, and went to check on the flowers.

Just then, Diana's mobile rang. She'd been holding it in her hands, and snatched it up to her ear quickly. "Hello. Yes, hello, Natty." She sank to one of the stools in the pantry. "Was it awful? Poor you. It's been a horribly long day for you, then. Yes, I'm waiting for you with a glass of beer, and warm company." She giggled. "Alright, Paul will come for you at the hospital. Around the back entrance, just to be sure. You never know where the paparazzi will be lurking. See you soon, darling!" She hung up the phone, and turned her dazzling smile on the butler. "Paul, Paul.... he's waiting for you."

The Princess waited alone in her sitting room. It was early evening in March of 1996. Paul had gone to collect her new love, Dr. Hasnat Khan, and Diana simmered with excitement to see him. She paced the sitting room eagerly, peeked through the curtains to the KP garden, and straightened an already-perfect pillow cushion. Finally, she sat down to allow herself the luxury of thinking about her new man.

They'd met about six months ago, and two things had struck her immediately when she'd met Dr. Khan. One was that he was completely unaware of who she was, and the other was that he had magnificent brown eyes. He'd nodded politely when they met, but didn't show he was aware that he'd just been introduced to the Princess of Wales. This had been wildly exciting for Diana. And a challenge. She'd felt an immediate spark, an undeniable chemistry. She'd described it to her healer Simone Simmons as love at first sight, but even that could barely describe the impact that meeting the doctor had kindled in her.

She'd contrived to "run into" the tall, dark-haired doctor at every chance she could get. Oonagh and her recovering husband had been surprised – and delighted – that the Princess was able to spare so much time at the sickbed. She chanced upon Hasnat, whilst waiting for the lift or on the hospital stairs. He was unfailingly polite, but distracted and dashed back to his patients. Diana sighed, thinking of those early days.

Dr. Hasnat Khan was a thirty-eight-year-old Pakistani heart surgeon, currently working alongside the world-renowned Professor Sir Magdi Yacoub, whilst studying for his PhD. He was tall, dark, and handsome but from there, Diana's vision of an ideal man ended. Hasnat was overweight, with a penchant for takeaway foods – especially greasy fried chicken. He smoked fairly heavily, enjoyed his Carlsberg beer, and never exercised. He was a workaholic who gave all his energy and attention to his heart patients. He came from a traditional Muslim background, with a large family supporting him back in Lahore, Pakistan. He lived alone in London in a small, Chelsea flat to which he paid almost no attention. Working routine fourteen to eighteen-hour days, Hasnat had no time for anything but his work – and the Princess of Wales.

It was difficult for Diana to sort her jumbled thoughts into a cohesive pattern. She knew that her relationship was unorthodox, to say the least. She and Natty came from different backgrounds, and hardly shared any common interests. But there was a bond that constantly pulled them together, despite the odds - the connection of helping others in need. It was intoxicating to Diana to see the lengths that Hasnat would go to for a patient, saving actual lives, and bringing hope to distressed families. The two would talk for hours about the work that was yet to be done in the world to help the sick and afflicted. Diana had never met anyone like her *Mr. Wonderful,* and it scared her at times. She was falling deeply in love with this compassionate man, and yet it was difficult to see how they could have a real future together. Diana bit her lower lip, thinking of the challenges ahead. For starters, the religious differences. Could the mother of a future King of England marry a strict Muslim man? And where would they live? Would he want to go back to Pakistan after he'd finished his doctorate? Could she ever leave England?

A car door banged, interrupted her jangled thoughts. Diana glanced in the mirror to fluff her hair, examined her perfect lipstick, and ran lightly down the stairs. All of those disquieting questions could wait. Tonight, she would simply enjoy being with the man she loved.

"Diana, it's most indecent that I arrive here hidden under a rug in the back seat of Paul's car. Must we go through these pretenses?" Hasnat entered the foyer in an irritable mood. His dignity was severely injured by these clandestine arrangements, made to keep their relationship secret, and thought that it unmanned him. He was a famous heart surgeon – both here and in Pakistan.

Diana rushed to greet him. "Darling, I'm sorry but you know it's for the best. The longer we can keep our relationship a secret, the better. Do you want the press and photographers hounding you day and night like they do me? Now, come and give us a proper kiss." Diana reached up and put her arms around Hasnat's neck, and pulled him in for a lingering embrace. "Mmm, now isn't that much better?" she asked in a husky voice.

"Yes, Diana you are glorious. And you smell fantastic." Hasnat smiled as he pulled her closer. "And of course, I don't want the paparazzi stalking me as they do you. I don't know how you do it. I just don't like this cloak and dagger rubbish."

"You're here now," soothed the Princess. "And you haven't even told me if I look alright," she pouted. She stood back so that Hasnat could take in the full effect.

He gave a low whistle and stared. "I think you'll do for a night in." He smiled. Hasnat was a man of few words. A deep thinker, he spent many hours in reflection and prayer. If Diana went asking for compliments, she'd be sorely disappointed. But the expression in his eyes told her everything, and she had to be satisfied with that.

"Come on, then. I've poured you a lager and put out the ashtray, so you can relax after your long day. Come on up and tell me all about it." She linked arms with him, and started up the stairs. At the landing, she turned back and called to Paul, waiting discreetly in the butler's pantry. "Paul, that's all for tonight. You can go home to Maria and the boys. See you tomorrow." With long days that often stretched into the late evening as his working norm, Paul was delighted to have a night with his family. He checked on the food one last time, said a prayer that the Princess wouldn't burn anything, and promptly took his leave.

Hasnat sat on the sofa, sipping his beer. He had kicked off his shoes, and was lounging comfortably with the Princess who sipped a lemon water.

"Tell me about your cases today, Natty. How did the surgery go with Mr. Pettit?" Diana had taken a great interest in the medical field since starting to date Hasnat. She wanted to know all the details of his cases, and was working her way through the textbook *Grey's Anatomy* to learn about how the heart and human body worked. It was hard going, but she was determined to get closer to her lover's world.

"Luckily, it was a pretty straightforward case of angioplasty. The patient had a blocked artery that was causing angina. Once I got in there, I had to also implant a stent to decrease the chance of another blockage. He should be alright, but his age and lifestyle don't help him. He's sixty-two and rather overweight. I've had to be quite stern with him about stopping the alcohol, and losing weight. But with the proper care and taking my advice, he should enjoy a good long life." He took a sip of his beer, and lit a cigarette.

"Natty, look at you. Talking about a healthy lifestyle whilst you're puffing away. Why don't you take your own advice?" This was a common refrain from the Princess. As she fell deeper in love with the handsome doctor, she wanted him to embrace the wholesome choices that she valued. She hoped as their relationship deepened, that she'd convince him to give up the smoking, drink less, and eat healthier. She'd invited him to play tennis once or twice, and he had just laughed. He simply didn't care.

"Diana, my work consumes me. For every Mr. Pettit that I save, there are hundreds – no thousands – of other patients who need my help. There are not enough hours in the day as it is. My work simply comes first." And to Hasnat, that was that.

Diana knew not to push the point. She felt that if they ever got to a point of seriously considering marriage, she would be able to influence him in a positive direction. Any step-father to her boys would need to be an impeccable role model.

"And your work is vitally important Natty, dear. You know how much I respect what you do. I can't thank you enough for letting me observe that recent heart operation. It was so fascinating to see a live heart beating, and to see you repair that poor woman's internal damages."

Diana had begged Hasnat to let her watch him at work, and he had finally relented. He hadn't known, however, that she would be bringing a camera crew with her. He'd been quite furious about that. She'd explained it was to help bring awareness to the problems of heart disease, but he hadn't been convinced.

"Diana, you're welcome in the operating theatre anytime – alone. I was pleased you weren't more squeamish. Not many people can observe all that blood, and not be affected."

"I've seen more than my fair share of hurt and injured people, darling. In fact, I don't even see the blood or wounds or scars on people anymore. I just see the humanity that shines through. And it leaves me with an aching need to help – somehow, anyway possible." She wrinkled her brow. "Why does the media always dig for an ulterior motive? Reporting that I shouldn't have been allowed to wear mascara in the observation deck was just ridiculous. I should know by now, they'll always find the most horrid image, and splash it across the headlines."

"I just don't understand why that rubbish gets published all the time. There are so many more important global issues – AIDS, cancer, poverty, and so on. Sorry, darling, but what you wear to a gala just seems insignificant next to all the want in the world." He took another sip of his beer, and sat back.

"I couldn't agree with you more, darling," replied Diana as she rose, trying to maintain her good mood. "But can I help what they print about me? It's relentless how they hound me. There's simply nothing I can do about it." She grabbed his hand. "Now let's have some dinner. We can talk more about the Trust that we could set up together. I had some ideas about fund-raising for a new type of treatment centre that we discussed….."

The two trailed into the drawing room for a late supper of chicken and salad. Hasnat protested that the chicken was steamed and not fried, but otherwise, ate without comment. Diana heaved a sigh of relief that the microwaved chicken and broccoli turned out alright – she was a dreadful cook.

They returned to the sitting room where they remained immersed in conversation – two heads close together in intimate conversation. Diana felt she had never met anyone who *got her* the way Hasnat did. It was intoxicating how they spoke of helping the sick and needy together. And those limpid brown eyes. Diana could drown in them.

After a while, Hasnat knelt in front of her. He began to slowly unzip one black leather boot, and lovingly removed it. Diana smiled as he took her foot in his hand and started to rub it. He moved to touch her leg, and touched the smooth calf and thigh. He unzipped the other boot, and gave her other foot the same treatment. Slow and methodical, he locked eyes with hers, as his hands moved slowly up under her skirt. Diana leaned back, closed her eyes and enjoyed the sensations shimmering all over her body.

She felt his lips on hers as he murmured, "I've been wanting to do that all night." She lay back on the sofa as Hasnat laid on top of her, kissing her softly, yet urgently. She could taste the beer and cigarettes on his breath, but it just added to her excitement.

"Let's go to the bedroom," suggested Hasnat thickly. "I want to take off all your clothes."

Diana simply nodded in a haze of pleasure, as she led him down the hall. They fell on the bed together. Diana tried to unbutton his shirt, but he shook his head no. He wanted to make this encounter last and last. He made love to her slowly, bringing her body exquisite pleasure before taking his own. Diana was in absolute heaven.

"Well, one doesn't kiss and tell, does one?" asked Diana of her friend and healer Simone the next day.

"When one looks as glowing and happy as you do, one doesn't need to!" replied Simone with a chuckle. "You look like the proverbial cat that swallowed the cream," she added lightly.

"He does make me want to purr, that's a fact," giggled Diana. "And it's true what they say about surgeons – what Natty can do with those hands! Glorious, simply glorious."

The two women sat in Simone's London flat, surrounded by mystic objects and fragrant candles that gave the small place a positive energy. Simone's three cats roamed the place, and one landed in its owner's lap, waiting to be petted. Simone gladly accommodated. Diana normally called her energy healer to KP at least twice a week, but today she had decided on a whim to stop by Simone's on her way to an acupuncture appointment. As always, the healer was at the Princess' disposal.

"Mint tea, Diana?" she asked. Diana nodded, as the red-haired Simone put the kettle on. "So, if you don't want to kiss and tell, why else have you dropped by? I know there's something on your mind."

"Of course, you do, Simone. I can never fool you. Well, here it is. I'm thinking of a course of action, and want your advice." Diana seemed slightly nervous.

Simone sat back down on a comfy armchair, scooped up the cat again, and smiled. "Let's hear it. But be warned, I'll give you my honest opinion, Princess or not."

"That's what I love about you, Simone. You don't tell me what I want to hear – at least not always. So, there's really two things here. You know I'm going back to Pakistan next month to help Imran and Jemima with the cancer hospital? I was so moved by the enormity of what they are trying to accomplish, I simply must help."

Simone raised an eyebrow. "And is there another reason you're going? Visiting a certain Pakistani family again, perhaps?"

"Perhaps," replied Diana enigmatically. "I'm starting to have real feelings for Natty, you see, and I must explore how we could have a life together. It can't hurt to meet with his parents, to try and understand his way of life better, can it?"

Simone rose to tend the tea. She returned with two mismatched cups, and a plate of store-bought shortbread biscuits. She handed Diana a mug unapologetically.

"Hmm, the fact that you're asking yourself if this is a good idea should tell you something, Diana. You must suspect it's not the right thing to do. What does Hasnat think?"

Diana sipped her tea and looked down. "I haven't told him, Simone." She put up her hand to stop Simone from jumping in. "The visit itself to the hospital is the important thing, you see. I'm just *considering* a side trip to the Khan family. And I'm planning to stop into Cape Town to see my brother and his family. So, it's a legitimate trip, you see."

"I see everything," replied Simone, in her slow, halting voice. I see you're going behind the back of the man you say you love to try and win over his family, before he's even asked you to marry him. I see you're trying to work out a life with him, and not even doing him the honour of consulting him. I think it's dangerous, Diana. Hasnat is a mature man – thirty-eight. He knows what he wants, and he won't thank you for interfering with his family and culture – and his own future."

Diana frowned. "It's not like that, Simone, Not at all. I'm simply trying to test the waters, see if they've warmed up to me at all. And to seriously look around and determine if I could ever live there."

Simone gasped. "Live in Pakistan! Diana, darling, you are daft. Besides the obvious religious and cultural differences, how do you reckon you could take two royal princes out of England to live in a place like Pakistan? It's unimaginable."

Diana slammed down her cup. "I know, I know. I'm just trying to examine all options, Simone. With the money I'm hoping to get from Charles, I shall have enough funds to choose where I want to live. Surely there's a solution here?"

"Are you also considering a move to South Africa, like your brother?"

"Not really, Simone but...maybe?" Diana raised troubled eyes to her friend and counsellor.

"I really can't comment on where you could live, Diana. But certainly, before you start considering a move outside the UK, you should consult the man who's most affected? Why do you even need to leave London? His work is here. Your work is here. You have a life with the boys at KP. Why would you need to leave Britain?" Simone was slightly bewildered with the ramblings of the Princess.

"Think, Simone. Please. Look at the bloody press. They never leave me alone. Ever. Remember what happened with those photos they took of me at my gym a few years ago? I'm not safe anywhere. Hasnat will never accept that intrusion into his life. He's as much as said so." Tears began to mist her clear blue eyes.

"That was an absolute invasion of privacy beyond the pale, Diana. I'm so proud of you for taking them to court."

Diana waved her hand. "That's just one example of many, Simone. Too fucking many! Hasnat won't stand for a life like that, with photographers shoving cameras in his face all the time. And so far, they don't even know about him. When he really experiences the daily onslaught, he'll go running back to Pakistan, or somewhere else." Diana was fighting the tears now.

"Diana, you're working yourself into a state about something that hasn't even happened yet. All I can say is that you should definitely talk to him about your visit before you go, that's all. Now you said there were two things. What's the other one?"

"Hmm, I'm not sure I should tell you now," Diana's tone was a bit sulky. "You're supposed to help and support me, not bite my head off."

"I'm not biting your head off, Diana. You asked for my advice, and I've given it. It's up to you whether to take it. If you don't want to share anything else, that's fine with me." She smiled encouragingly. "I'm here to help you, Diana. You know that."

"It's nothing much, really. I was just hoping you'd be pleased that I'm going to visit my brother. Mending fences and all that."

"I think it's marvelous that you want to build a bridge back to your brother. Tell me more about it."

"As you know, Simone – Charles and I haven't been speaking for the last couple of years. Ever since the incident about the Garden House at Althorp." Diana took another sip of mint tea. "You remember - after the separation, he offered me the house on the Althorp grounds? I was at the end of my tether at the time – so distraught about the separation, and desperately looking for a bolt-hole – a place to get away with the boys. Charles offered me the Garden House – and it was just perfect. Far enough away from the main house to give his family privacy. And remote enough to keep the press away. I had toured it with William and Harry – they were so excited. I had even engaged Dudley Poplack to redesign it. You remember him, he helped me with KP after the separation? And then, suddenly, Charles changed his mind. He said that the place wasn't secure enough, that people could still intrude, and his family wouldn't be safe. Simone, I was heartbroken, just destroyed, that my own brother would do this to me!"

"I remember, Diana. You had such high hopes for starting anew at your childhood country home. Did he ever give you any more explanation than that?"

Diana stood up and began to pace the small room. "No. I sent him a letter sharing my disappointment and anger. I poured out my heart to him, Simone. I *knew* if he read it, and understood my side of things, he'd change his mind. But the letter was returned to me, *unopened!* He said if he ever read it, our relationship would be permanently damaged. As if this isn't enough harm!" As always when the Princess began to relive a distressing time in her life, she was brought back to those same childhood feelings of betrayal and abandonment. "I thought then I would never forgive him. But time does heal all wounds. I realise now that he's my only brother. I looked after him when it was just the two of us as children. So, I'm going to South Africa to spend time with him and the children. I haven't seen my nieces and nephew in more than two years. Surely, family is more important than a bloody house?" She stopped to gaze pleadingly at Simone.

"Diana, I couldn't be more gratified to hear you say that. The spiritual work you've been doing on yourself in the last few years is helping you to overcome these bad, familiar feelings. And family *is* more important than any old house. I think you'll reflect back on this decision, and be very proud of yourself. Enough people in your life have let you down, Diana. Let your brother back in."

Diana was starting to recapture some of the good feelings she had brought with her to this impromptu visit today. When others affirmed her and her decisions, it buoyed her up no end.

The two women chatted for another quarter of an hour before the Princess had to leave. She thanked her healer for helping to give her peace of mind, and received a blessing from Simone.

After she left, Simone blew out the candles she had lit, and snuffed the incense burning brightly around the room. There's something that girl didn't tell me, she thought to herself. She can bluff all she likes. She tidied up the tea things. All in good time, though. All in Diana's good time.

Diana remained thoughtful as she bustled about her busy day. There *was* something else she'd wanted to discuss with her healer. A plan she was considering. But something had held her back.

Natty was such an amazing surgeon but he was thinking too small. He was all-consumed by his London practice. Diana knew she could help him make even more of an impact on the world. She had contacted her friend, Dr. Christian Barnard – world famous South African surgeon. She planned to meet with him when she visited her brother in a few short weeks. She was certain she could convince him to offer Hasnat a position in Cape Town. She had thought it through, and mentally ticked off the boxes for a new life in South Africa.

Firstly, because of the historic ties to Great Britain, the Queen couldn't possibly object to the princes spending parts of the year there – even just school holidays. Secondly, the climate was pretty good with loads of cultural and educational opportunities – for all of them.

Next, there was a large Muslim community there – surely that would be a selling point for the handsome doctor? And working with Dr. Barnard would be an incredible career opportunity for Natty – and he could expand his helping influence in a needy corner of the world.

Lastly, she would be closer to her Spencer family – Charles, Victoria and the children – so they could help her and the boys adjust to a new way of life. All good points in her favour!

Contacting Dr. Barnard had been a stroke of genius in Diana's mind. He was eminent in his field, and had been the first heart surgeon to perform a heart transplant back in the early 1960's. Diana thought he would be the perfect person to convince Natty to relocate to Cape Town to continue his career, with Diana at his side.

She allowed herself to daydream about the future. Mrs. Hasnat Khan. She liked the sound of it, although giving up the title of Princess did give her a slight pang. She shook her head. Being the wife of a famous heart surgeon would be a fair trade. She longed for another child – a daughter. And Natty could give her that little girl. She would be so beautiful with Hasnat's dark colouring and big, brown eyes. Perhaps even two girls, she thought recklessly.

Diana knew in her mind that she was getting ahead of herself. It had only been a few months. Goodness, Natty hadn't even met the boys. They'd not yet had to brave the public and media scrutiny that was sure to envelop them all. But she knew Natty was *the one*. She could see herself with him for always and forever. She'd even given up on her soon-to-be ex-husband. Surely that was proof positive that she was over Charles, and ready to move on with Hasnat? She even wished Charles well with Camilla. With the expansive happiness of a woman newly in love, she only desired that everyone around her was equally as happy.

Diana had been in love before, but had been badly hurt. First by Charles, then the massive public humiliation by James Hewitt. Even the rejection by the married Oliver Hoare had scarred her heart. It wasn't lost on the beautiful Princess that now a doctor, a surgeon, wanted to love her and repair her broken heart. This must be her luck in love, turning finally. Didn't she deserve it? She was about to turn thirty-five this summer. Had love found her….at last?

CHAPTER EIGHT

End of the Fairytale

In the event, Diana's plan went horribly wrong. The start of her trip to South Africa unfolded as planned. Her reconciliation with her brother had been uneasy, but left Diana feeling hopeful about a satisfactory relationship in the future. They had tacitly agreed to leave the past behind them, and focus on the present and future. Diana loved meeting her nephew Louis, who was the spitting image of his father, and rekindling relationships with her three older nieces. She had sensed some tension between Charles and Victoria, but every marriage had their ups and downs, didn't they?

By great good luck, the press did not track the Princess to her brother's home. Brilliant!

Her meeting with Dr. Barnard also went rather well. He promised nothing in terms of a position for Hasnat, but would help him if approached. Diana was chuffed that she was planting seeds to grow for the future.

The visit to Pakistan cemented Diana's love for the family culture, but she didn't feel she had advanced her cause at all. The family welcomed her warmly enough, but seemed standoffish. Truly, they appeared perplexed as to why she was even there. In her own mind, she just wanted to be around Natty's family more, and learn about his traditions and background. Somehow, it was awkward and uncomfortable all around.

The trouble began when Diana returned to London. She had ignored Simone's advice, and not told Natty she was spending two days in Pakistan. He thought she was only going to South Africa to meet her brother. To say he was furious that she had visited his family without even advising him, was a severe understatement. He was livid.

"Diana, what did you think you were doing?" he asked with icy calm. Natty never raised his voice. "How could you dare presume to visit my family and my parents, without even telling – no, asking - me? What are you playing at?"

He had come to KP unannounced on a Friday morning, disheveled, with messy hair, and a few days beard growth. His shirt was coffee-stained, wrinkled, and untucked. And he was very, very angry.

"I meant nothing by it, Natty. There was no evil master plan. Quite simply, I just wanted to pay my respects to your family, and learn a little more about you. I wasn't even sure I was going to make a stop there, until a few days before I left. There was nothing to tell." It sounded lame even to her own ears.

"Diana, you're asking me to believe that you just dropped in to see my family on your way back from South Africa? That's eight thousand kilometres. Your overseas tours are organised with military precision. You planned it out as surely as the royal calendar. Do you think I'm daft?" Hasnat stood in the foyer, having refused to even come to the sitting room.

"Well, of course it was planned. I was helping Imran and Jemima with their cancer hospital. It's a cause worthy of support. And if I can use my ridiculous fame to draw attention to these needs, why shouldn't I?" Diana sputtered, as she tried to regain the upper hand.

"Diana, stop. You don't have to convince me that you can shine a spotlight on a cancer hospital. That's not what this is about. At least own it. You made me look like a fool. Imagine my mother calling me, asking why you were visiting her, and I didn't even know you were there? And to see your photograph plastered across the tabloids, dressed in Pakistani clothes? What were you thinking?" His tone was shocked and recriminatory.

"Natty," she started. He stared at her. "Hasnat," she amended in the face of his fury. "I'm sorry. Please come and have some coffee. I can explain."

She was successful in getting him to the sitting room. Now, she just had to talk her way out of this. She concentrated her steady blue gaze on his face, and looked deep into his chocolate eyes. She tried to grab his hands, but he shook her off.

"Darling, let me explain," she repeated. "My intentions were nothing but honourable. I wanted to see your family, to explore if I could live in your world. That's all. I had no hidden motives. I just want them to like me." Her voice broke.

Hasnat hated to see her cry, but stayed strong. "Diana, we're enjoying each other. Very much. I like spending time with you. But we've never spoken of making a life together, or you becoming a part of my world. Bloody hell, Diana. We've barely ever left this sitting room." He sounded totally exasperated.

"You're right, Natty. Utterly right," she placated. "I promise I will never do anything like that again. And I'm truly sorry if I embarrassed you and your family in any way. Should I ring to apologise?" Diana was now eager to make amends. She was starting to panic.

"NO! Don't ring anyone. Especially not my mother. Leave well enough bloody alone." He started to run out of steam.

"Natty, I swear I won't. Please don't be cross with me." She stopped, as she had an idea how to get back on track with her lover. "Listen, I have something else to tell you. Something splendid! Whilst I was in South Africa, I met with Dr. Christian Barnard about creating a position for you in Cape Town. He said he would be happy to meet with you to discuss it." Diana looked expectantly at Hasnat, certain he would be pleased with her efforts on his behalf.

"You did WHAT?" he exploded as he jumped to his feet. "You spoke to a world-renowned surgeon about a job for me? Diana, you have gone too far. You have interfered in my private life, now you're meddling with my livelihood. You don't understand me, if you think you've been helpful. You've actually damaged my reputation. I don't need your help. Now. Or ever. I don't need the fucking Princess of Wales to sort my life for me."

"Hasnat, wait, please." Diana tried to clutch his arm, but he shook her off again.

"Do not say another word. I'm leaving now. That's it. Don't ring me. Don't come over. I need to be alone."

"For how long?" wailed the Princess.

"I have no idea," he replied tersely, as he left the room.

Diana broke down in sobs, and collapsed on the sofa.

For weeks, Hasnat would not take her calls. She left countless messages on his mobile, and at the West Brompton Hospital. She waited hours for him at his flat, but he never showed up. She sent him letters, pleading for his forgiveness. She asked Paul to meet him at his local pub, but Hasnat wouldn't speak with the butler either.

Finally, he showed up one night at KP. He presented himself at the guard's gate, and asked to see the Princess. She welcomed him with open arms and wept as he held her and stroked her hair.

"Diana, I can't stop thinking about you. Believe me, I've tried. I've fought against myself for hours, aching to see you. Dammit." He ran his fingers through disheveled hair, and looked as if he hadn't slept in days. "We can only get past this if you promise never to do anything like that again. Promise me." He was kissing her eyelids, her cheeks, her lips. He was desperate, starved for her.

"Never again, Natty. I promise," Diana whispered, as she clung to him in relief and amazement at his love for her. She gave him a tremulous smile through her tears. The romance was back on.

The Duchess of York came for lunch the next day. Fergie and Diana had been in constant contact over the last few months. The Wicked Wives of Windsor were locked in simultaneous divorce negotiations. The two were inseparable, asking one another for advice, sharing legal proceedings and developments, and crying more tears than they thought possible.

Sarah's divorce was final on May 30, 1996. She appeared in the doorway of the sitting room with red-rimmed eyes. She rushed into Diana's arms.

"I knew it was coming, Diana. But I never thought I would feel as awful as I do, when I actually saw the divorce papers. Pages and pages of lawyer-talk ending ten years of marriage in cold black and white. How did we end up here?"

"I know, darling. It's them. All of them. The Firm, the men in gray, the establishment, the press. Everyone crowds into our marriages, until we get squeezed out. After we've provided the needed heirs, of course," Diana finished bitterly.

"But I still love Andrew," cried Sarah. "He's always been my best mate. He's the first person I called after I signed the papers. Isn't that ridiculous?" Her sister-in-law was sobbing openly now.

Diana enfolded her in a big hug. "Shhhh," she comforted as if soothing Harry after a scraped knee. "It's all for the best. You'll see.

"How?" wailed Sarah. "Out of the family, half access to my daughters, and the papers always out to crush me. What did I do wrong?"

"Sarah, stop. You did nothing wrong. We all make mistakes, but you can't blame yourself for everything. Wasn't Andrew out to sea for most of your marriage? Didn't you live a lonely life at Sunninghill without him, bringing up the girls? How is that a cheery marriage?"

"You're right, you're right," Fergie sniffled. "I have to stop crying over something that can't be changed. I must be strong for Beatrice and Eugenie. It's done now. But you know what's so ironic, Diana? The person that has treated me the most decently in all this nightmare is my ex-husband. Why couldn't we have loved each other better when we were married?"

"I wish I knew, Sarah. I've stopped asking myself that. Now, tea or wine?"

"Oh, a glass of wine wouldn't go amiss, Duch. Aren't we celebrating after all?" She gave Diana a wan smile, as Paul magically appeared.

A couple of hours later, the Duchess left. The sisters-in-law had reminisced about the good old days back when they had been young and hopeful. And so stupidly naïve to think two young and silly girls could take on the monarchy – just by loving their husbands.

"Paul, I feel so for Fergie. She really got caught up in the royal machinery. But I have to land myself a better arrangement. My sons' future depends upon it. Thankfully, I engaged a better solicitor." Diana was fatigued, and slightly panicky. "Poor Sarah. Besides the girls being looked after for school and trust funds, she's only getting a small allowance from Andy's naval salary.

And a tiny amount of money from the Queen. It's shameful she was treated that way."

"Ma'am, didn't she also get a settlement for a new home to purchase for herself and the princesses?" Paul asked.

"Yes, that's true, Paul. But all that is a pittance when you remember what she's sacrificed for the Germans. They're basically tossing her out on her arse. Appalling. They're not going to get away with that with me. That, I can assure you."

"Quite so, Ma'am. You do have an excellent solicitor. And if I may say, your position is much stronger than the Duchess'. You've never put a foot wrong in almost fourteen years of royal service. As lovely and fun as the Duchess of York is, she has made some gaffes from time to time."

"Go on, Paul. Gaining weight and saying foolish things once in a while is hardly a crime." Paul started to open his mouth in protest, but she raised her hand. "I know her past is a bit checkered. Having an affair, and getting caught on film was stupid. I think she's rather a lost soul, actually. I truly hope she finds what she's looking for." Diana's voice trailed off. Her trusty butler couldn't help wondering if the Princess was talking about her sister-in-law – or herself.

"How are the negotiations coming along?" Paul had been her steadfast supporter, and listening post over the last few months. There had been innumerable meetings with her solicitor, Anthony Julius, and his team. After each one, the Princess was either jubilant or downcast, depending on the points covered. Mostly, she was exhausted with the process, and longing for it to end.

"Slowly but making progress, Paul. I can't tell you how helpful it is for me to talk things through with you after these grueling sessions. I admit I don't understand all the legal talk, but being able to sort it all through with you is soooo helpful. I'm ever so grateful."

"Stop, Ma'am. No need to thank me. Ever. It's a privilege to help in any way I can," Paul reassured.

"Well, bring us a coffee then, so I can tell you the latest."

"Of course, Ma'am. Straightaway."

As Diana waited for Paul to return, she fussed around the sitting room, picking up a framed photograph of her father, putting it down, then picking up a photo of herself as she greeted her two sons aboard Britannia with open arms, many years ago. It was one of her favourite images of her and the boys – she joyful and delighted at the reunion, and they equally thrilled to see their mum. She'd loved that black and red checked suit too, she mused. I suppose all the family photos will now be like this – either me with the boys, or Charles and them fishing and shooting at Balmoral. Never again a family of four.

"Here we are then, Ma'am." Paul bustled in efficiently, and served the Princess coffee. At her wave, he served himself as well.

"I think we're almost there when it comes to the financial settlement, Paul. I don't want to say until it's finalised, but I'm pretty confident on that score. And keeping this place is all but signed off on. I'm losing my office at St. James Palace, but I suppose that's somewhat understandable. The men in grey don't want me or my supporters anywhere near the Prince or his staff. What a joke. As if I'm any kind of threat!" Paul made soothing noises, and Diana continued. "We'll have to set up a makeshift office of sorts here at KP soon, Paul." He nodded. "For our tiny staff." This bit was true. The staff was now skinnied down to Paul, Anne, her personal assistant Victoria, a chef, household staff, and a driver. A sorry lot compared to the vast household she used to run.

"Very well, Ma'am. That's not a problem. We'll convert one of the main room floors, I expect. You can let me know your wishes, and I'll take care of it."

"Yes, Paul. And let's ensure we do another sweep for bugs when the new furniture and equipment is installed. I don't want anyone to overhear my conversations, or read my correspondence." Paul nodded. Over the years, the Princess had become almost fanatical in her insistence that Buckingham Palace was watching and recording her every move. Regular sweeps had never detected any evidence of this bugging, but she was sure her instincts were right. Who could blame her with the constant scrutiny surrounding her and her actions?

"The Queen is letting me keep my jewelry," the Princess continued with a sigh. "Albeit I must give it up to William and Harry's wives when they marry. It's hard to imagine my little boys being husbands, but I'm sure that will be happening in the blink of an eye. I tell them both, especially William, that he must take his time, and marry for love only. I don't want him making the same mistake that his father and I did. He mustn't rush into anything. As the future King of England, it's crucial that he selects the right young woman for the job. And most importantly, they must be madly and truly in love."

"He seems to have a good head on his shoulders, Ma'am. I've known him since he was a young boy. He's thoughtful, kind, and very protective of his brother. Luckily, he has you to guide him, to steer him in the right direction."

Diana smiled a rueful grin. "The royal family is hopeless at preparing anyone for life in a fishbowl. They just turn away, and talk horses and dogs. But I never stop speaking to both princes about the life ahead – not just the responsibilities, but also how lucky they are, and how they must try to live as normally as possible. Hopefully some of that will take root. But teenagers! Who knows what William really takes on board?" She giggled.

"I think he listens to you very carefully, Ma'am. You speak to him often, and speak about everything. That surely will have an impact on how he treats people in the future. I know with my own boys – you are never quite certain if they're paying any attention whatsoever. You just do what you think is right, and hope for the best."

"Too true, Paul. So, the only real sticking point with the agreement now is my title." She put down her coffee cup, and looked directly at Paul. "You know when I met with the Queen in February, my number one concern was continuing to have access to the boys. Being their full-time mum. Nothing is more important to me than that! My mother-in-law was so reassuring about that matter, that I didn't push hard when she mentioned she'd need to consider my future title. She said she would talk to Charles about me being known as Diana, the Princess of Wales, and I acquiesced. To be honest, I was so relieved I didn't have to fight for my boys, that I didn't think to consider about the title, so I said nothing.

But now that a few months have gone by, and we've been in such a tug-of-war about every nitty thing in this settlement, I'm rather changing my mind. Why should I have to give up my status as Your Royal Highness? I haven't changed. I'm still the mother of the future King of England. I never wanted this divorce, remember? Why should I have to give up my title?" As usual when this topic arose, Diana couldn't keep her emotions in check. The tears began to fall, and the Princess impatiently wiped them away.

"I suppose it's protocol, Ma'am," offered Paul rather helplessly. "The Queen is very particular about precedents, and doing things just the right way."

"I know, Paul, but it's not fair. After all I've done for this bloody family. It's the final insult. Is she not thinking of the impact to her grandsons? Do you know I'll have to curtsey to The Duke and Duchess of Gloucester, Princess Alexandra, and technically even my own sons? It's a proper insult!" Diana was weeping openly now, and Paul handed her a handkerchief."

"I'm so sorry, Ma'am. Taking away your HRH title does seem rather petty. Is it Her Majesty, the Queen or His Royal Highness, Prince Charles behind this move?"

"I'm not really sure, Paul," said the Princess through her tears. "I suspect it's Charles – he doesn't want a royal ex-wife around. It messes up his plans for a future with *her*, I'm sure. But as neither he nor Mama will speak to me directly, I just can't say for certain." This brought on another flood of tears. "Should I fight for this? I don't want to jeopardise my access to the boys."

"I can't advise you, Ma'am. But if they've conceded everything else, perhaps you should consider how important the title is in the grand scheme of things? People will still adore you, as they do now. Maybe more."

"It's not about that. It's about what's right. Maybe I'll ring my brother-in-law Robert, to see if he'll ask the Queen for it on my behalf. It's just not fair. Charles doesn't have to give up anything, why should I?"

Both Paul and the Princess knew this was simply not reasonable. The power was all in the hands of the Windsors. And Diana was all too familiar with this hard truth.

Later that afternoon, Diana spoke to William on the telephone.

"Hello darling," she started, her voice slightly wobbly.

"Mummy, what's wrong?" asked her son with great concern. "You've been crying. What's happened?"

William had a very strong bond with his mother, and knew instantly when she was upset about something.

"Oh William. I hate to burden you with this. But I've been talking to Paul. And then I called Lucia and Nora. But now I'm in a proper state."

"Mummy, what is it? Is Harry alright?" William was starting to get truly frightened.

"Oh yes, he's fine. It's not that, William. It's just that I've been having a bit of a howl about losing my HRH title with the divorce. It may seem silly, but it's something I've worked so hard for. All these years of royal engagements, supporting important causes, and raising millions of dollars for so many charities. And all of this as Her Royal Highness, the Princess of Wales. It feels awful to have it taken away from me, just because your father and I can't get on."

"Mummy, I'm sorry, but don't worry. I'll give it back to you when I am King," William tried to comfort his mother, but it only made her cry harder.

"I haven't seen you since the annual Parents Day at William's school in May, darling. How did it go? I know you were frightfully concerned about seeing Charles, with all this bitter back-and-forth with the divorce going on." Rosa and Diana were having tea at Rosa's London home. Diana had called her dear friend, and invited herself over, ostensibly to see her god-daughter Domenica. But Rosa knew that her chum needed a kindly face amid the divorce proceedings.

Diana smiled a touch guiltily. "Well, I *was* nervous, Rosa. You're right. Not just seeing Charles, but also the Knatchbulls and Romseys." Diana named some of the couples in Charles' inner circle, who were also parents of Eton boys. "I had requested to travel with Charles – to put on a front for William, you know. Teenagers are already so self-conscious, and with all the press – I just wanted it to be easy for him. Of course, that request was denied." The Princess' tone was sharp. "They all ignored me when I got there, just froze me out. But I am my mother's daughter. I put on a smile and a brave face for William and the cameras. I'm such an idiot, but I can't help it. I always must get on with the show. I chatted and talked it up with everyone during the pre-luncheon drinks. Then it was time to be seated for lunch. I really wanted to sit next to Charles, but they had put me beside the provost. And Charles next to his wife. I wasn't having any of that, I'll tell you!

I marched right up to the provost's wife, and very nicely asked her if I could exchange places, so I could sit next to my husband." Diana smiled.

Rosa clucked. "Diana, you didn't!" she exclaimed. "Was there a fuss?"

"Yes, I did, and no there wasn't," she replied gleefully. "The woman could hardly refuse, so there we were together. Charles was none too pleased, but something in me just made me do it. Sometimes you have to choose the right place to stand up for yourself."

"I saw the photos in the paper of you kissing Charles on the cheek. I mean, you couldn't miss that – it was a national headline – *A Kiss is just a Kiss* – what was that all about, darling?" Rosa knew that Diana couldn't resist grabbing headlines for herself from time-to-time, but didn't understand the motivation for this specific incident.

"Rosa, I just wanted Camilla to know what it feels like to be on the receiving end, for once. I knew she'd see that photograph and grasp that no matter what, I'm still William's mother. Technically, I'm still Charles' wife, but that won't be for long. I suppose it was my final shot at her. Not very mature, I'm afraid. But I still hope it gave her a pang or two." Diana looked rather triumphant with her small act of defiance.

"I certainly upstaged my husband," she continued. "He was rather spluttery and awkward – but that's Charles, isn't it?" Diana giggled.

Rosa winced slightly. "Darling, you know best of course, but is it really necessary to show him up in public like that? No man likes to be humiliated, let alone the Prince of Wales. Won't it threaten your position with the divorce?"

"No, that's almost final. And Rosa, think of all the times he's humiliated me? Going on national television and admitting adultery? How about that for 'showing me up?'" Diana bristled at the criticism.

"Hush, Diana. I was only saying, be careful. You've learned enough by now, that sometimes these shows of independence can backfire." Rosa was prudent not to mention the Morton book, or Diana's own *Panorama* interview, neither of which had brought her any closer to her famous in-laws.

"True enough. But it's done now. And like almost any other decision I make in life, it's captured forever in the tabloids. Do you think once I'm no longer married to Charles, that the public attention about me will finally desist? Or at least decline?" she asked hopefully.

Rosa shook her dark head ruefully. "I'd like to believe it will stop, Diana but let's face it. You're getting all this publicity and attention for you, and what you're doing. So why would that stop? You're still going to be doing charity work, aren't you? And you're still William and Harry's mum."

Just then Rosa's nanny entered the cozy sitting room with one-year old Domenica in her arms. She stood by the door, waiting to be noticed.

Diana jumped up immediately, and took the slowly-wakening baby from her nanny's arms.

"Oh, little love, how precious you are. So sweet, so cute." She covered her god-daughter's face in kisses. Domenica smiled sweetly at her.

"Diana, must you carry on so with her? You'll spoil her rotten," Rosa objected.

"But she's just such a pet. And with the gentlest temperament. Look, she smiled at me! She knows her Auntie Diana!" The Princess held the baby close, and took in her sweet smell.

"Of course, she knows you, silly. You're one of her favourite people – after me, Daddy and Savannah. But you really must stop buying her extravagant gifts. That giant stuffed panda was unnecessary. You're too good to both my girls, darling."

Diana ignored the comment, as she continued to coo and make silly faces at Domenica.

"It looks like she's gotten another tooth. I hope it wasn't too painful." Diana sat in a chair with the little girl, and bounced her up and down. "I'd sing to you sweetie, but my voice is dreadful. Shall we play pattycake instead?"

Rosa sighed, knowing it was useless to chastise her friend. Diana was always generous to those she loved. Not just the girls, but Rosa herself.

"You are so good with babies and children, Diana. William and Harry are lucky to have you as a mum," she said sincerely.

Diana finally looked up from the baby. "Well, I'm lucky to *be* their mum. And yes, I adore little angels like this one. How I'd love to have a daughter. Do you think I'm too old, Rosa?" she asked, cocking her head slightly to one side.

"Hmm, let's see. You're about to turn the decrepit old age of thirty-five. You're in amazing shape and very healthy. And you've already had two safe pregnancies and live births." Rosa's voice faltered, as she thought of her own stillborn child buried at KP. "So why couldn't you have a little girl? All you need now is a suitable candidate to father the baby." Rosa quickly recovered her composure.

Diana gave her friend a sympathetic look. "I certainly have enough suitors lined up take my pick. From politicians to entrepreneurs to film stars to rich businessmen – they all seem to be circling, waiting to pounce once I'm officially back on the market again." She laughed.

"Isn't there a certain DDG that might object to this line of suitors?" teased Rosa. She giggled to think of the serious Dr. Khan as Drop-Dead-Gorgeous.

"Yes, I suppose he might," mused Diana. "But I must have a good look-round before deciding on the right man. Do I want a little girl with blonde hair and blue eyes? Or curly brown hair and matching eyes? Or another ginger that resembles the Spencers? I guess we'll have to wait and see. But I'm rather leaning towards big brown eyes and silky dark hair. Wouldn't that be a beautiful combination in a little girl?"

Domenica opened her mouth as if in protest. She made a small howl.

Diana quickly cradled and rocked her. "There, there, pet. No one can take your place. You're my little love, aren't you?" The baby stopped crying, and Diana gave Rosa a smile over the baby's head, as if to say *see? I've still got it.*

"Speaking of dark-haired men, did you hear the one about the two sailors on leave in Malta?" Diana began a joke.

"Shh, darling. Not in front of the baby." Rosa picked up her child, as the two women laughed.

August 28, 1996. Four years separated, fifteen years of marriage, and two children; and the divorce was final. Diana had fought hard for and won a generous settlement for herself and her sons. She was awarded a reputed seventeen-million-pound lump sum payment, plus a business allowance. She could keep her home at Kensington Palace, although a country home had been refused by the palace. Charles would continue to pay for all the boys' school fees, clothes, medical, and other expenses. Custody was to be shared equally amongst the parents. Lastly, she would lose her status as HRH – Her Royal Highness, and now be styled as Diana, Princess of Wales.

Diana bounced down the stairs on this momentous day, and bestowed a dazzling smile on her faithful butler.

"Well, that's it, then. It's finally over, and I didn't do too badly, did I?" she breezed. "It's a new chapter for us, now, Paul. We must embrace it, and not linger in the past. Remember – I still love my husband."

"Quite right, Your Royal Highness," greeted the butler with his customary bow.

"But Paul, I'm not HRH anymore," she objected.

Paul shook his head stubbornly. "You will always be Your Royal Highness, the Princess of Wales to me, Ma'am. As such, I will greet you this way every morning, just as I always have."

Diana patted him on the arm. "Alright, Paul. If you insist. Now where's my coffee? Let's have a look at the papers. I'm sure they're full of the divorce news."

The Princess was determined to turn the page, and set forth in a new direction. Paul was relieved and delighted to see her in such an upbeat mood. He had expected a flood of emotion. He did notice that she was still wearing her engagement and wedding rings, but politely made no comment. When she was ready, she'd remove them.

The previous month, after the terms of the settlement had become public, Diana had taken an enormous step by quitting her patronage of over one hundred charities. Some saw it as an act of spite, in exchange for the removal of her HRH status. In writing to the heads of the charities, Diana clarified that she wanted her former charities to be free to seek another royal patron, now that she was technically no longer a member of the Royal family. In truth, she was stung, and extremely hurt about the title issue. She didn't see why she needed to carry a full load of duties and responsibilities, when they had essentially cut her out of the family tree.

She had decided to cut ties with all but six of her most cherished charities: the Centrepoint charity, which provided shelter for the homeless, the English National Ballet, the Leprosy Mission linked with Mother Teresa, the National Aids Trust, Great Ormond Street Hospital for Sick Children, and the Royal Marsden Hospital in London, which specialised in cancer research and treatment. She would now focus her full attention on just these six, and hopefully make an even greater impact.

The reaction to this announcement was one of dismay and abject disappointment. The Princess of Wales was a huge calling card for these charities. Just having her name associated with one guaranteed higher attendance and donations. Her appearance at an event or fundraiser substantially increased contributions. This was a huge blow to ninety-four important charities.

Diana had discussed this decision with many of her closest friends and family: William, Nora, Simone, Rosa, Lucia, and others. They all supported her decision, and need for time and space. But now what?

Nora had visited KP after her summer holiday with the family. After an early morning roller blade around KP, a half-hour on her tanning bed, and a colonic irrigation session, the Princess was eager to see her gal pal for lunch.

"Darling!" she greeted the tiny Nora in the front foyer. "How was Italy? Did you have a fabulous time?" The two friends hugged and kissed, and headed up automatically to the sitting room. Diana sat on the sofa, whilst Nora plopped down on the huge hippo.

"Italy was wonderful. We had a brilliant time, and I've gained a stone, I'm sure. No one can make pasta like the Italians. And you, darling? How are you bearing up – with things being all official now?"

Diana shrugged. "It's been a long time coming, so I suppose I should say I'm just fine. But it still hurts, Nor. I remember when Fergie said that a couple of months ago, and it's true. As much as it's a great relief, there's such a sadness that goes along with it. The fairy tale is over. Not that it ever was truly one." Diana bit her lower lip.

"Are you sleeping any better, darling?" Nora asked hopefully. The stresses had taken their toll on the lovely Princess over the last few months, and she'd begun swallowing a couple of sleeping tablets every night in order to get any rest.

Diana shrugged again. "Slightly better, I suppose. Especially when Natty stays over," she gave a small smile. "Otherwise when I'm all alone here, and the boys are at school, I just can't help going through everything in my mind over and over again, wondering what I could have done differently. I don't like being alone, Nora," she stated unnecessarily.

"Have you seen Charles at all?" Nora asked quietly.

Diana perked up visibly. "You won't believe it. A few days before my birthday, he dropped in unexpectedly. He was taking the helicopter to an engagement, but was a bit early. I was ever so shocked to see him. It was rather awkward at first and then..."

"And then you made a joke?" finished Nora.

"Too right, Nor. I asked if he had come to take the furniture away. He laughed uncomfortably, but that broke the ice. He came up here and we had tea. It was all very civilised, yet strange. We had a good chat about the boys, Harry starting at Eton, and so on. It felt familiar but still different."

"Did you feel anything for him?" asked her friend curiously. "Did you want him to throw you down on the carpet, and take you right here?"

"Hardly," Diana responded shortly. "I'll always love Charles, and he is the father of my children, but that spark is gone. Not that he would ever throw me down on the carpet. Not his style at all! Although, perhaps if he had more often, we wouldn't be divorced. I could have fancied a little more cave man in the romance department." Diana smiled wistfully. "I'm just hoping, Nor, it's the start of a truce for us. A new way for us to get along, and sort out the boys when needed. I'm actually hoping we could be friends, if that doesn't sound too daft."

"Maybe not daft, but perhaps a little premature. I'm thrilled you got on with him without rowing, but the friendship thing might take a little time. What else happened whilst I was gone?"

"You'll never guess who called me from Hollywood?" Diana changed gears quickly.

"It could be anyone. Steven Spielberg, Tom Cruise, Elizabeth Taylor, who?" Nora replied. "You have quite an impressive address book."

"Leave off, Nora," joked Diana. "It was Kevin Costner. Remember how dishy he was in *Bull Durham?*"

"I sure do. He could put his slippers next to my bed anytime. Whatever did Kevin Costner want with you?" Nora was all ears.

"He wants me to be in a film with him," shrieked Diana. "Do you remember *The Bodyguard* with Whitney Houston? Where he protected her from an obsessive stalker? Well, he wants to make a sequel called *The Bodyguard II,* with me as the star. Can you imagine?"

"But, you're not an actress or a singer," spluttered Nora. "How would you make that work?"

"I would actually debate you that I'm the greatest actress of all time. What do you think it takes to try and be interested in some head of state at a stodgy dinner for three hours? Or try to seem enthralled during a dull speech about the environment? But of course, I'm not trained as an actress. And I told Kevin I can't sing." Nora could tell her friend was excited at this new prospect.

"So, would you actually do it?" asked Nora wide-eyed. "What would the Queen think?"

"I don't really care what she thinks. I'm not part of the royal family anymore, so I can do as I like." She tossed her head. "William thinks it's a brilliant idea."

"I see," said Nora. "Well, if *William* has given his blessing, by all means, go ahead," she joked with her chum.

Diana tossed a throw pillow at her. "Sod off. In the event, nothing has been decided. I've asked Kevin to send me the script. I'll read through it, and then decide. It's a big proposition – being in America for a number of weeks, learning my lines, trying not to look foolish. But it's exciting to be wanted, Nor "

"It certainly is. My goodness, that would be a new chapter for you. Never a dull moment with you, darling."

Diana giggled. "Speaking of new chapters, I have something I must show you. Stay right here." She jumped up lightly, and ran down the hall as she called to the butler. "Paul, kindly bring Nora a glass of wine. I'll be right back."

Ten minutes later, a striking brunette entered the room. She had long brown hair, large glasses, and was dressed in jeans and a casual sweater.

"Diana is that you?" hooted Nora, as she sipped her white wine. "Whatever in heaven's name are you doing?"

Diana bent over double laughing. "It's my new disguise. Paul bought me the wig and glasses on Kensington High Street. Can you recognise me?"

"Barely, darling. If it wasn't for your height, and the fact that I knew it was you, I'd never have known it was the Princess of Wales. Astonishing."

"Goody!" replied Diana, clapping her hands. "With a little unique makeup and a cockney accent, I think I can just about pull it off. Buy me a pint, luv?" she quipped.

"When are you going to use it, Diana?" asked Nora, slightly dazed. "Where does the most famous woman in the world want to go unrecognised?"

"On a date," her friend replied. "With Natty. I dreamed up the whole idea to get us out of KP once in a while. We're still trying to keep our relationship under wraps – at least for the present. He loves jazz clubs, and has been wanting to take me to one for quite some time. We could never think how to do it, until I came up with this perfect plan."

She twirled around. It really was quite astounding. It hardly looked like her. The wig and glasses made a huge difference. Maybe she could really pull this off. If she could tone down her star power.

"I think it's a smashing idea, Duch. Have you tried it out yet?"

"No, we're going to give it a trial tonight. Maybe you can help me pick out an outfit after lunch that's not too posh? Nora, you know how I long to live a normal life. Maybe with this disguise, I can have a chance at it. I can't wait."

"I'd love to, darling. But speaking of lunch....?" Nora raised an eyebrow, along with an empty wine glass.

"Of course, Nor. I'm sure Paul is holding it for us. Now what kind of a name should I pick to go with the new look? Ruth? Betty? Eileen?"

"How about good old Elsie?"

"Elsie is perfect. Suits you to a T," said Nora.

The two mates laughed together, as they went into the dining room for lunch.

A few hours later, Nora received a call on her mobile phone.

"Nora, it's me Elsie. 'Ow are ya, luv?" whispered Diana into the phone.

"Where are you, Els?" asked Nora with a smile.

"We're in a queue at Ronnie Scott's in Soho. Can you believe it, we've been waiting over forty minutes? Isn't that wonderful?" Diana sounded very happy.

"Diana, only you could be chuffed about standing in a queue for forty minutes. Elsie, I mean."

"And we've been talking to the most interesting people. I'm having a real laugh. And Natty thinks the disguise is very sexy. How about that?"

"I think that's wonderful, Elsie. Have a lovely time and call me later... I mean tomorrow. You may be busy later." Nora chuckled as she rang off.

"Ta, Nora. Bye."

Diana and Hasnat enjoyed their first night out together, and no one ever knew it was the Princess of Wales having drinks, and listening to jazz in a London club that night. Diana thrilled to sit unmolested at a table with her love, and didn't even mind the smoky bar. Natty tried to explain the finer points of jazz music to her, but she just sipped her wine, and enjoyed the whole experience. She knew it was probably just the novelty of it, but she thought she could really get used to this normal, anonymous life.

Natty smiled at her.

"You look lovely tonight, darling. "Those leather pants are smashing. And I really like the way you've done your hair," he teased.

The Princess of Wales smiled at the heart doctor. "Just let me know when you're ready to take me home, darling."

CHAPTER NINE

A New Direction

"Umm, a helicopter pilot. Or maybe a curator of a museum – perhaps The National Gallery? And King, of course." The second-in-line to the British throne grinned, showing his shiny braces to his mum.

"A helicopter pilot? That sounds interesting, William," smiled Diana. "In the army?" she asked curiously. The two were enjoying the late summer afternoon sun in the KP gardens, and Diana had asked her son his thoughts about his future. The Princess was basking in the precious company of her boys. Harry was playing inside with a school chum, whilst she and William soaked up the sun. She was well aware the clock was ticking inexorably towards the time when the princes would leave for their annual Balmoral trip with their father. She hated the wrench of her sons being taken away from her – as she considered it – and being further indoctrinated into the royal family and their traditions. It helped her to know that they both loved it there – the fishing, hunting, and shooting as well as the rest of the outdoor pursuits that enthralled young men, not to mention being spoiled by the rest of the royal family. However, she hated being out of touch with them, and the influence that the Windsors had over William and Harry. She gave her head a mental shake. Enjoy the moment, Diana. They're here now. Stay present.

"I'm not quite sure, Mummy. Perhaps the army. Albeit as you know, the Windsors are naval men. However, I don't want to fly just for the sake of flying. I want to help people. But how?" This last syllable squeaked a bit as William's fourteen-year-old voice broke. He turned red, but Diana chose to ignore his embarrassment.

"Darling, what about an air ambulance or rescue pilot? I'm not quite certain how it all works, but I've seen medical teams on telly who fly helicopters to rescue stranded mountain climbers and such. You'd definitely be able to combine flying with helping," Diana beamed, as the two stretched out their long legs on garden chaise lounges.

William sat up, looking excited. "Really, Mum? That sounds brilliant. I would love to help rescue people in need." He paused, and his brow furrowed. "But would Granny let me?" he asked worriedly. "I'm afraid I wouldn't be allowed." William was quite aware that as heir to the throne after his father, his safety was of paramount importance to the sovereign.

"I don't know, William. It might be considered too dangerous for you. However, all those girls coming to gawk at you at a museum or art gallery might be even more hazardous." She giggled. "But you must always pursue your dreams, William. If Granny is against you becoming a helicopter pilot, we'll need to fight to find a way. If that's what you truly want." She looked deeply into her son's blue eyes. "Will you be able to manage all that, while also being King?" A smile tugged at her lips.

"Oh Mummy, I won't be King for years and years. Granny will be Queen for a long time to come, and then it's Papa's turn. But I can't just sit around waiting and doing nothing. I must be useful," he said vehemently.

Diana sighed, and ruffled her son's hair. "You are very privileged William, and I'm heartened to hear you understand you have responsibilities that are unimaginable to most people. Being useful will help ground you, and put to good use the incredible position you have, for enormous value." Diana's eyes glistened with pride in her eldest son.

"Just like you, Mum," her son countered simply. "The example you've set for me and Harry has clearly shown us how important it is to help those less fortunate – no matter who they are, or where they live. You've helped so many people – I just want to carry on this work when I get the chance."

"William, it makes me so proud to hear you say this. And remember your father too, is making a tremendous impact with his Prince's Trust foundation. For me, it's almost like I fell into the charity work that I do now. I didn't want to carry on with plaque ceremonies, and spading at tree plantings. I was called to do more. It's difficult to explain, darling. But I believe you understand, don't you?"

"I think I do, Mummy. It's like this ache, this pull to try to make things better for others – be they sick, sad, or homeless. Even if we can just take their pain away for a little while, somehow it seems to help." William struggled to put his feelings into words.

Diana nodded, and hugged him. He didn't try to squirm away as he had taken to in the last couple of years, and for this his Mum was grateful.

"I know Papa and everyone in the family works rather diligently on behalf of so many charities. But I still think what you do is extraordinary, Mum. Especially all those nights you go down to homeless shelters and hospitals to give hope to the hopeless. I don't know how you do it. But I promise I will always try to live up to your standard." William's tone was awestruck and fervent.

"Oh William, don't put me so high up on a pedestal," Diana tried to laugh him off. "Yes, I've helped some ill people. But I've also made some dreadful mistakes. I go by instincts, mostly. Usually, it doesn't steer me wrong." She sighed. "But look what's happening now, William. I'm trying so hard to find a new role for myself – you boys are almost grown, and my royal duties have dwindled to almost nothing. Yet the palace keeps refusing my requests to become a roving ambassador for Britain. I don't know what to do." Diana was careful not to criticise the Queen – William's grandmother - but a tone of irritation had crept into her voice.

"I'm sorry, Mum," William sympathised. "I wish I could help."

"Thank you, darling. I don't think there's anything you can do. It's all part of me moving on to this new chapter in my life, I suppose. I shall have to feel my way around as always, until I get it right. I *do* think I could bring vast press attention to such important causes – to raise awareness and loads of money. The Red Cross still wants to work with me – and so many other prestigious organisations. What could be wrong with that? Even the Prime Minister John Major believes there is a role for me. And the people and press outside of England are so much less vicious in their attacks on me. Ever so grateful for any support I can give them. It's just so frustrating, William! I'm only trying to help!"

"I know, Mum. What are you planning next?"

"Well, my friend Simone has been telling me about the alarming effects of landmines in some war-torn countries. Civilians who are trying to get about their own lives have their arms and legs blown off by stray landmines left behind. She showed me some photographs, and the impacts are horrible. I asked the Foreign Office for permission to visit Cambodia – one of the worst countries for landmine casualties - but I was refused. Too dangerous. Too political," she said with disgust. "Me, political? What a joke. They just want me to put on a fancy gown and borrowed jewels, and open another film premiere. Just so they can plaster my bloody picture across all the papers the next day, and make loads more money."

"Well, Mum you do look smashing when you're all dressed up," offered William loyally.

"Thank you, darling," the Princess replied absently. "But after fifteen years serving the monarchy and royal family, surely, I can do more than dress up in a designer gown, collect flowers, and shake hands. I don't even wear most of those hideous old frocks anymore."

Suddenly William clapped his hands. "Mummy, I have a brilliant idea. Why don't you take all your gowns – especially all the old poofy ones that you never wear anymore – and auction them off for charity? That will make people sit up and notice. Just think how much money you could raise – for AIDS, the homeless, even the Red Cross!" The fourteen-year-old Prince was delighted with his own suggestion.

"Are you serious, William? Sell off my wardrobe?" Diana asked slowly.

"Not your entire wardrobe, Mum. Just your ballgowns. You know – the fancy ones that you hardly ever wear? How many do you have? Don't you have a whole roomful of them?"

Diana started to get excited. "You're right, darling. I do have heaps of gruesome old dresses. I would never put most of them on again. Why not sell them for charity? William, you *are* brilliant." She resisted the urge to hug her son, but bestowed her luminous smile upon him. "Paul, Paul," she called excitedly.

The butler came running quickly to aid his mistress.

"Yes, Ma'am. Is everything alright?" he asked with concern.

"Yes, yes, Paul, everything is more than alright. William has had a wonderful idea. To auction off my old gowns for charity. Isn't that splendid?" Diana jumped to her feet.

Paul called upon his royal training to retain his reserve.

"Yes, Ma'am. That does seem a marvelous concept. How may I be of assistance?"

"Come on William, Paul, let's have a look at the gowns and start choosing some for the auction." She grabbed her son's hand, and ran into the first-floor wardrobe room. Paul strode hard to keep up with the Princess.

She started flinging open the rows of cupboards, revealing dozens of carefully preserved gowns dating back to the early 1980's. They were colour-coded starting from white at one end, working up to black at the other, with a rainbow of colours in-between.

"Just look at all these dresses! How many ballgowns do you think there are in this room?" she cried, looking at her butler. She began counting the lovely frocks on their velvet hangers. "Sixty-two here alone – and upstairs there are even more. Each one is a memory, and a dear friend. But now is the time to sell them all."

William and Paul smiled at each other, overjoyed to see Diana so enthusiastic for this new project. Two of the Princess' favourite men would do almost anything to see Diana happy.

The next couple of hours were spent picking out dresses, and reminiscing.

"Ah, my *Gone with the Wind* dress," she exclaimed with a flourish, as she held up an off-the-shoulder floral print dress. "And my John Travolta gown." The dark blue velvet frock was held up to be admired. Dozens more were selected, stories told, and items were either chosen for the auction, or left behind in the wardrobe – too precious to part with. Paul carried up the chosen gowns to a disused room on the second floor.

Thus, began an endeavor that was to last until June of the following year when, ultimately, seventy-nine dresses were chosen to be sold at Christie's in New York. Visitors to KP during the interval were duly asked about which gowns to add to the collection pile. Nora, Rosa, Carolyn, Fergie, Simone, Frances, even Lucia in Washington were all consulted, and many an afternoon ended in giggles as Diana was persuaded to put on a frilly and frothy monstrosity from her early years as Princess of Wales. Diana changed her mind on many occasions, and William ruthlessly helped her to weed through and select the ones that would fetch the best prices. She decided the beneficiaries of the auction would be the Royal Marsden Hospital Cancer Fund and AIDS Crisis Fund, and engaged with Christie's Auction House to manage the sale. Diana bragged shamelessly to her friends and other guests about how William's idea would both free her from the chains of her past (physically and emotionally), and that it all been his idea. The tall, handsome blonde Prince smiled sheepishly, but was secretly delighted to have inspired his Mum to embrace the project, and the new phase in all their lives.

"Ma'am, it's the Duchess of York on the line again. Are you at home?"

It was several weeks later. William and Harry were at Balmoral with Charles, and the royal family. Diana was grateful to her son that she was distracted with dress-sorting, but was still feeling at a loose end without her boys at home.

The Princess sat at her desk, catching up with her correspondence. She peered up from her letters, and frowned at her butler.

"No, I'm not. I wish she would stop ringing. I'm not going to speak to that bitch again." Diana's voice was calm but steely.

"Very good Ma'am. I'll advise her that you're not at home. May I bring you anything?"

"Yes, Paul. Some herbal tea would be lovely." She bent her head to her letter, and chewed the end of her pen as she searched for a word.

Paul bowed his head, dispatched the phone call, and returned promptly with the tea tray.

"What did Fergie have to say?" asked the Princess.

Paul smiled inwardly, knowing his mistress couldn't resist asking about her once-close sister-in-law, no matter what front she hid behind.

"She begged to speak with you – anytime day or night. She said to tell you she's so sorry if you're cross with her, and she's desperate to make things right with you." Paul kept his voice neutral as he poured the tea.

"Ha. She should have thought of that before she started running her mouth with her biography, and press interviews," Diana said with disgust.

Sarah, the Duchess of York had written a memoir called *My Story*, detailing her less-than-fairytale life behind palace walls. Provocatively, she had posed for the book cover barefoot, perhaps a tongue-in-cheek nod to the toe-sucking photographs of her and Texas oilman Steve Wyatt. Diana considered it vulgar. She also thought the book was a rather forlorn version of the York's marriage and breakdown. But what had infuriated her most was a reference to a time that Diana had borrowed a pair of her sister-in-law's shoes, and Fergie then contracted a planter's wart. This was unforgivable to Diana.

"If she wants to write a sordid little story of her royal life, that's her right, I suppose." Diana shrugged. "But slagging me, and then doing nothing but speak of *me* in all her interviews – especially in America - is just too much. I used to feel sorry for poor Fergie, but not anymore. She's cooked her own goose."

Paul nodded sympathetically, knowing his boss was immovable on this subject. Sarah had been ringing, writing letters, and even showing up at the KP gates unannounced, in a despairing attempt to reconcile with her ex-sister-in-law. But to no avail. Paul had tried to comfort the hysterical Duchess who wanted her old chum back. He really hoped that with time, Diana would relent, and end the freeze-out as she had with others. The two had been the greatest of friends throughout their years as the Wicked Wives of Windsor, and Paul himself had a soft spot for the once-cheerful redhead. Only time would tell, he thought to himself.

One of the Princess' less-endearing qualities was her practice of freezing out people that she deemed to have been disloyal, or betrayed her in some way. She sometimes jumped to conclusions about their motives and actions, and quite simply cut them out of her life. Paul had seen it countless times with staff, and even close friends and family members. She would refuse to speak to the offender, and ignore pleas to explain or apologise. In some cases, she would inexplicably forgive and ring the person weeks later to pick up the conversation where it had been left off, but many relationships were permanently severed. In fact, some staff were forced to resign, when Diana refused to speak to them for weeks on end. Paul himself had been on the receiving end of these deep freezes from time-to-time, but had luckily been forgiven, and all had been forgotten. So, he knew from personal experience how perplexing and heartbreaking these silences could be.

The latest and high-profile freeze outs were Elton John and Gianni Versace. The famous singer had acted as a go-between the Princess and the famous designer. Versace had sent Diana many clothes throughout the years, and she had agreed to write the forward to a new book he had written called *Rock and Royalty*. When the proofs for the book had arrived, Diana had been shocked to see racy photographs of famous people, next to more sedate images of members of the royal family – including her and the boys. The Princess did not think the Queen would be amused with her endorsement of such suggestive photographs, so she pulled out of the project. And had refused to speak to either the singer or designer since.

"Paul, do I look alright?" fussed the lovely Princess. It was fall of 1996, and Diana had the boys for a weekend school exeat. They had enjoyed a fun day of lounging about and shopping; and the chef had even prepared a picnic for them to eat whilst watching telly. It had been relaxed, and Diana had cherished every moment.

But now she was nervous. She had invited Hasnat over for an after-dinner drink, to meet William and Harry for the first time. She had spoken to them about the surgeon in the most general of terms, and had recently casually mentioned that she was dating the heroic doctor. She had asked them if they wanted to meet Dr. Khan. In the ways of young men, they had shrugged and agreed nonchalantly, and Diana had duly organised this evening. This was the first time she had ever introduced the boys to any man she had dated since the divorce. It had to go smoothly!

"You look smashing as always, Ma'am," replied Paul. And she did. Diana was wearing tight black leggings, an oversize red jumper, and black flats. Her makeup and jewelry were minimal as befitting a day at home, but Paul could still tell she had taken great care over her hair and toilette. Her blue eyes sparkled, but he could tell by her restlessness that she was apprehensive.

"Thank you, Paul. You've got the drinks tray ready? And treats for the boys?" She had already double-checked this earlier, but Paul just smiled and nodded. He knew how important this evening was to his boss.

She waited in her sitting room for Natty for a painful thirty minutes, whilst the boys played videogames in their nursery playroom. She paced the room, checked her watch endlessly, and finally rang Nora to calm her nerves.

"I hope I'm doing the right thing, Nor, and that it's not too soon," she fretted.

"Diana, I'm sure it's not too soon. You've been dating him a year now. It is getting rather serious, isn't it? It's best to see if you can mix your two worlds together." Nora attempted to soothe her.

"It's just that Natty is not really into children, I fear. He's so wrapped up in his career, he hardly has time for me. I don't know how he will get on with the boys."

"Give him some credit, darling. He sits at the bedsides of strangers every day – he knows how to talk to people. And William and Harry don't have to love him – they have their own father. And God knows a whole, bloody family of Windsors. Hasnat doesn't need to be taking them out playing football, or talking to them about girls," reassured Nora with a smile in her voice.

Diana laughed. "Yes, I suppose you're right. William and Harry already have lots of family – including the Spencers too, don't forget. I just want them to like him, that's all. If we were to get married someday, they'd all be together often enough. I couldn't bear it if they didn't adore him, Nora. I'd have to give him up, I really would. But I do love him so. I just hope it all works out," she finished breathlessly.

"Do you really think marriage is in the cards, darling?" asked her friend. She had heard this before, but the relationship was surely progressing if Diana was talking about marriage; and now the boys were meeting the famous heart surgeon. She too, fervently hoped it would all work out. Privately she had her doubts. She felt that Hasnat and Diana came from such distant worlds, with opposite beliefs and values in many ways. She also knew the two were desperately in love, and melted into each other's arms whenever they could steal time together.

Nora could hear the shrug in her friend's voice. "I don't know, Nora. I mean, this has to lead somewhere, doesn't it? Otherwise, what are we playing at? The obstacles seem insurmountable at times. Where could we live? America? Australia? Somewhere where an airplane ride could reunite me with the boys as often as possible. I just don't know. But love conquers all, doesn't it?" Diana's voice held a note of desperation.

Nora sighed. Despite all her heartbreak and letdown in love – with Prince Charles, James Hewitt, and others – Diana still believed in happily ever after. "Australia?" she repeated. "That's an awfully long way from William and Harry, darling. And you know they must be brought up in England. Could you bear to be so far away from them?"

"I know it is, Nor but I'm just looking for options. They love me in Australia, and it is a commonwealth country. I'm visiting there in a fortnight's time. I plan to really take a hard look at it, and see if it might suit. I certainly have the money for lots of plane trips, thanks to Charles."

"I hope so, Diana, because I couldn't bear to be so far apart from you. I couldn't imagine not seeing you every week. And Clemmy would miss you terribly. Not to mention all your other friends and family, your charity works here in the UK…" her voice trailed off.

"Yes, and the media and photographers stalking and hounding me daily here in the UK," she parroted. "I can't stay holed up here in KP all the time, Nora. I have to craft a life for myself that's somewhat normal."

Nora clucked and sympathised. She knew how much Diana craved an ordinary existence. Would it ever be possible for the superstar Princess of Wales?

"Right, I must go, Nor. He's here – finally. Wish me luck, and I'll ring you later!" Excitement had crept back into her friend's voice. Nora knew she really did have deep feelings for the sensitive and caring Hasnat.

"Of course, darling. Best foot forward. And no racy jokes in front of the boys." The two rang off, and Diana bounced down the stairs. She had heard the knock at the door, and quickly fluffed her hair on the way down to meet her love.

"Darling," she exclaimed, as she met him in the foyer. She gave Hasnat a quick, hard hug as Paul took his overcoat. "Have you had a perfectly awful day?" She kissed him gently on the mouth, and he kissed her back.

"Not too terrible," he replied with a smile, as he looked deeply into her eyes. She adored this – when he was with her, he was very present and attentive. Unfortunately, he was often late, distracted, or in a rush to get back to the hospital. But for now, his dark brown eyes looked admiringly at the striking tall blonde. "No surgeries today, but I had to follow up with an older patient whose blood pressure has been spiking after surgery. I may have to go back in tomorrow to repair a valve."

The pair sauntered arm-in-arm up the staircase. Hasnat made to enter her sitting room where they spent most of their time together, but Diana steered him towards the formal drawing room.

"I have everything set up in here, darling," she explained. "I thought it more of a neutral ground for you to meet the boys." Despite her smile, she was a bit jumpy and Hasnat put a calming hand on her arm.

"Where are they then, these fine young men I've heard so much about?" He seated himself on one of the long sofas.

"I'll call them," replied the Princess, as she left the room briefly. "William, Harry, please join us in the drawing room."

A few moments later, two tall and smiling young men entered the room. William as almost as tall as his mother now, with her charm and blonde good looks. Harry hadn't had his early teenage growth spurt yet, so looked much younger than his twelve years. Both boys were dressed in casual clothes – jeans and collared shirts. Diana had told them not to dress up for this meeting – she didn't want to place too much importance on this casual conversation.

William stepped forward first, with a smile and outreached hand. "Hullo, Sir. I'm William. Very pleased to meet you." He shook Natty's hand, and the two were almost at eye level.

"Please call me Hasnat. It's very nice to meet you, too." Natty shook the young man's hand, and turned to the younger boy. "And you must be Harry," he smiled. Harry also offered his hand, and smiled an impish grin.

"Hullo, Hasnat," he said.

"Hullo, Harry," replied Hasnat. It's an honour to meet you, too." Harry beamed.

"Well, lovely then. Let's all sit down. Boys, you know that Hasnat is a surgeon at the Great Brompton Hospital. We've been there many times. He is a heart doctor, and saves lives on a daily basis." Diana jumped in nervously.

"Diana, please. It's not quite like that," Natty protested. "Your Mum likes to make me out like some sort of a hero, but I'm just doing my job. Now, William. How are you doing at your studies? Eton, is it? Do you like Maths and Sciences?" Hasnat inquired seriously.

"Well, Sir, er, Hasnat," William corrected, looking to his Mum for approval. "I do, but I prefer the arts – history, geography, and so on." William was well schooled in the knack of small talk, even at the tender and sometimes awkward age of fourteen.

"That's splendid, William. You'll need a thorough grounding in history for the job ahead of you. And what of sport? Your mother tells me you love water polo and swimming."

Diana was pleased to see Hasnat making such an effort to connect with William. She held her breath – so far, the meeting was going rather well.

"Yes, I do love sports of all kind. I have a swimming meet coming up in just a few weeks, so I'm practicing rather a lot. Now, Harry here – he prefers outside sports like riding and fishing." William always tried to bring his younger brother into the conversation. He knew that his own position made him the centre of attention at almost all gatherings, so he always strived to include his brother.

"Yes, I love riding at Highgrove. I have my own pony and groom. His name is Smokey. The pony, I mean. I'm better than William. He's too cautious." Harry giggled.

"As I recall, your brother was hit with a golf club in the head a few years ago, so it's probably prudent to be a bit more restrained." Ever the doctor, Hasnat couldn't help having a medical view of the situation.

"He's totally fine now, though," Diana jumped in. "Let's have some cakes and tea. Natty, would you like a lager?" Paul had entered the room earlier, and was busy with the tray.

The next fifteen minutes were spent in comfortable, if not warm, small talk. Diana was proud of the impeccable manners of her two sons, and she could see Hasnat's charm turned on – just as Nora had predicted.

"Alright, boys. You can run along now. Hasnat and I have some charity work to discuss. You can go back to your video games."

William and Harry jumped up immediately, shook hands again with the doctor, and said their goodbyes. It was all very civilised on everyone's part.

After Diana had hugged them both, and shooed them out of the room, she and Natty took their drinks to the sitting room where Diana couldn't wait to grill her lover.

"What did you think of them? Aren't they so handsome? And William is so articulate." Like any mum, the Princess was very proud of her two best achievements, and loved confirmation that they were smashing lads, and she'd done a good job raising them so far.

"Yes, they are fine young men – even better-looking than I imagined from their photographs. William especially looks like you, darling," replied Hasnat with a grin, as he took a sip of beer. "They both seem very confident and bright."

"Did you see how protective William was of Harry? He hates that the spotlight is always on him, and not his brother. And Harry's ginger hair – see how the Spencer genes will always come through – even in the House of Windsor!" Diana laughed, but she still seemed tense.

"Don't worry, darling. It went fine. Thank you for letting me meet your sons. I confess even with such a large family of my own, I'm not that comfortable around young people. I'm glad they have such a loving set of families to support them both."

Diana was rather dismayed at Hasnat's casual attitude. She'd hoped for more of an emotional connection between her lover and her two precious sons.

"Yes, of course they have families. But it's vitally important that they connect with anyone that I'm involved with. I could tell William liked you. He doesn't bear people fawning all over him. He can spot a fake a mile away. And Harry loves everybody. Who knows? Perhaps one day soon, we could all go on holiday together to get better acquainted?"

"Wait, slow down, darling. I've just met the princes. That's a long way from a holiday together. I'm not sure I'm the step-fatherly type. Let's just see how our own relationship goes along, Diana, first. Please don't push this."

"I'm not pushing, Natty. It's just that you three are so important to me. I can't imagine my life without all of you in it. We must find a way forward." Diana's bottom lip started to quiver, as her eyes brimmed with tears.

Hasnat took her in his arms, and kissed her. "All in good time, darling. This is a tremendous first step. Let's declare victory for tonight." His arms tightened as he deepened the kiss. Diana had to be satisfied with that.

The two enjoyed a late bite together, and then Natty left within the hour.

"I must check on that patient, Diana. I fear I may have overlooked something, and I want to see if he's stabilised for the night. Besides," he continued with a knowing smile, "You're dying to rush into William and Harry to see if I made the grade, aren't you?"

"Too right, darling," giggled Diana. "You do know me," she waggled a finger. "Alright, go and look in on your patient, and I'll probe how well the great doctor fared with my sons. Ring me later." The two separated with a kiss, and Diana bounded up to the third-floor nursery.

"So, what did you think of the doctor," she asked William and Harry a few minutes later. She had sunk to the floor next to them, and kicked off her shoes.

"He was nice," said Harry casually, his eyes still glued to the television set.

"Yes, he seemed friendly enough," shrugged William. The boys were in the middle of a video game, and were not particularly interested in a third degree from Mum.

"But did you like him?" persisted Diana. "He was very keen on you both. Said you were handsome and very bright. Just like their mother," she quipped.

"If you like him, Mummy, that's all that matters," replied William diplomatically. "I just want you to be happy."

"I am happy, William. He *makes* me very happy. I was so hoping you would all like each other."

"Mummy, can we have some popcorn?" asked Harry.

"Of course, darling," replied Diana vaguely. "But be sure to brush your teeth before bed."

After William and Harry had gone to sleep, Diana spent the next couple of hours discussing Hasnat's visit with several friends on the telephone – ever the Extravert! All had been sympathetic, but cautioned against her rushing things too soon.

"He said he wasn't the step-father type," confided Diana to Nora at around midnight. Paul had brought her numerous cups of tea. "What the bloody hell does that mean?"

"Just what he said, Diana," replied Nora patiently. "Remember, he's never been married, nor had children. You said yourself he was married to his career. You surely didn't expect he'd fall to the floor playing games with the children, did you?"

"Well, no I suppose not," said Diana tearfully. "But somehow this has to work. How can I possibly be with a man who isn't in love with my children the way he is with me?" Diana's terms of love were absolute and idealistic. She expected Hasnat to adore and cherish her two boys as she did – and this just wasn't realistic.

"Give it time, darling. You've said yourself how you get frustrated that Natty seems to forget about everything – even you – when's he working. Some men just can't focus on more than one thing at a time. That's one of the reasons you fell in love with him, remember? He treats you like a woman, not the Princess of Wales?"

"Yes, you're right, darling. But I can't help wanting it all. I suppose I should just be satisfied that they didn't hate each other and move on from there. But I still want more!" The Princess' impatience was clear in her tone.

"There, pet. Don't worry yourself into a state. Like Hasnat said – declare victory for tonight. And didn't you say that William just wants you to be happy? Focus on those wins, and not everything that *didn't* happen." Nora did her best to console her friend.

"I suppose you're right," the Princess sighed. "But I still think going on a holiday together would help everyone bond," she repeated her earlier wish with the familiar Diana streak of stubbornness.

"Well, I don't know how you're even going to get Mr. Wonderful on a holiday just with you, let alone the boys. First things, first, darling."

Diana yawned. "Well, let's not get started on that – you know how I hate that Natty won't be seen with me in public. I suppose that's really the first step, if this romance is ever to go beyond these four walls – without Elsie, that is!"

"Glad to hear you're making a joke, even a bad one. I can tell you're knackered. Shall we ring off for the night?"

"Yes, darling, and thanks for always listening. I'll ring you tomorrow. Goodnight."

"Goodnight, darling and sleep well."

Yet it was another hour, and two more phone calls before Diana turned in. She couldn't get the words out of her mind – "I'm not the step-fatherly type." Eventually she gave in, took a sleeping tablet, and fell into a dreamless sleep.

Her trip to Australia was less than rewarding. The Australian people had always loved her – right from that first visit with Charles and baby William in 1983. But this time, they seemed a bit more critical, more standoffish. The crowds were still there but there was an undercurrent, as the Australian people wrestled with the question of whether or not to keep ties to the monarchy.

The Princess had raised over a million pounds for the Victor Chang Cardiac Research Institute. Chang had been a gifted heart surgeon, and a mentor of Natty's. He had been brutally murdered in 1991, and his Institute carried on his important medical research. In giving a speech at the gala, Diana said, "It has been said that for evil to triumph, good men must do nothing. Tonight, we give heartfelt thanks that a good man, Victor Chang, did a great deal."

Diana returned to London as restless as ever, now convinced that Australia would not provide her with the necessary refuge that she sought.

After her return in early November, what Diana had been dreading had come to pass. The press had discovered her relationship with Hasnat. "Di's New Love; How Top Heart Surgeon Finally Mended A Sad Princess' Broken Heart," "How Princess Di Fell in Love with Hasnat Khan."

Diana had heard rumblings that the story was about to break, when she was still on her Australia trip. She called her *Daily Mail* pal Richard Kay to try to throw some water on the fire.

"The story is absolute bullshit, Richard," she assured the reporter. "I'm deeply upset about this – it can really hurt William and Harry. And the whole thing is absurd.

Me and a Pakistani doctor? I'm laughing myself silly over this."

Richard believed her, and the *Daily Mail* duly published a denial article.

Diana breathed a sigh of relief that she had distracted the press again. But she was premature in her relief. Hasnat was furious with her.

"Diana, how dare you humiliate me like this?" Natty had appeared early one morning at KP, disheveled and quite cross. "You think I'm absurd? You are laughing yourself silly over me? What the hell are you doing, Diana?"

"Natty, please – I was only trying to protect you from the wretched press. Once they've gotten hold of a story like this, your life will be a misery. They'll follow you day and night. You're the one who's always wanted to keep our relationship secret. If I didn't do this, it would all be out in the open and then – well, let's just say you won't believe how your life will change." Diana tried to calm Hasnat down, but he was too livid to listen.

"*I* decide about my life. *I* choose what I want published or printed or whatever. It's not your decision, Diana. You must stop trying to control me. I'm not that man. Bloody hell." He turned on her, and opened the front door.

"Wait, Hasnat. Please. I didn't think. I was tired from the Australia trip. Jet lag and all that. Please believe me, I was just trying to throw the bloodhounds off your trail. I adore you. Please wait."

"Diana, I appreciate that you think you can control the press. And perhaps sometimes you can manipulate them. But you can't twist facts to your own desires. How can I trust you when you just decide on a whim what to tell the reporters and photographers? How???"

"Natty, of course you can trust me. Please. Don't go. Let's talk." Diana was fighting tears now, but even more than that – she knew she was pleading for this man not to leave her. Like all the others had done.

"Not this time, Diana. You're not going to use your allure and kind nature and words on me. I can't take this anymore – even for you. I have to leave. I just don't see a future for us. You must accept that." Without another word, Hasnat walked out the palace door.

Diana broke down in great heaving sobs on the staircase. Paul didn't know whether to try and comfort her, or leave her alone. He was always careful not to overstep the mark with a royal personage. After a while, the Princess returned to her sitting room, where she played a loud Rachmaninoff concerto to try and soothe herself. Before long, her friend Rosa Monckton appeared at the KP gates for tea and consolation.

Diana kept a low profile for the remainder of 1996. As always, she worked out every day – either swimming, rollerblading around KP, jogging, or punishing herself with ninety-minute strength and cardio workouts at the Harbour Club.

Her stream of astrologers, healers, acupuncturists, masseurs, and crystal readers flowed through the gates of Kensington Palace on a daily basis. Although she had finally gained control of her eating disorder, she still relied on outsiders and those who provided soothing cures to try to replenish her spirit. She heard all of them, but truly listened to none. Those that reinforced her own perspective, she kept around. Others that tried to gently show her a different way were cut off.

Her friendships also seemed to dwindle. She missed Lucia in America dreadfully. She lost touch with Carolyn Bartholomew, her onetime flat mate, and fervent supporter throughout the Morton business. Fergie was now lost to her. And somehow, she even missed members of the royal family more than she had expected. Gruff Prince Philip had chiefly been a supporter, as had Princess Margaret. Prince Edward had been a friend to her, and Prince Andrew was always loads of fun. And she quite missed the calm presence of the Queen in her life.

Diana still had her steadfast circle – Nora, Rosa, Elsa, Simone, Annabel Smith, Lana Marks, and a host of others. She had her famous friends like Sir Richard Attenborough and Henry Kissinger, who were helping her find a role on the global stage. And her fashion advisors, gym friends, and a lifetime of fans and chums that she kept up with unwaveringly.

She had always had up and down again relationships with her Spencer family. She and her brother Charles spoke on a sporadic basis. She saw Sarah infrequently, and her mother and other sister Jane even less.

Her only true and steady comforts were William and Harry. She spoke to her eldest son almost daily, and asked his advice about all aspects of her life, be they trivial or complex. He was fast becoming her best friend, and she relied on him heavily.

She and Hasnat did not speak for the remainder of the year. Her usual frenetic tactics would have been to call and chase him endlessly but somehow, she didn't have the stomach for it. She was through being the pursuer in the relationship, and waited for him to come back to her – if he would.

As Christmas approached, Diana knew she was a little depressed. She longed to turn the page on 1996 – the divorce, the rocky road with Natty, and the search for a role for herself all exhausted her.

She watched on telly as the press covered the annual royal proceedings at Sandringham. It broke her heart to see her boys walking alongside their father in their best clothes, as they went to Saint Mary Magdelene's for church service on Christmas morning. How many of these walks had she taken herself through the years? At least the boys look happy, she thought to herself.

The Princess had declined all of her friends' sincere and gracious invitations to spend Christmas with them and their families. She wandered around the palace, lonely but not wanting to be a burden to anyone else. She listlessly looked through her gowns, choosing and discarding a few for the upcoming auction, but her heart wasn't in it. She brooded, cried, and felt very alone.

The day after Christmas, Diana jetted off to Club K in Barbuda with her assistant Victoria Mendham. She and the boys had loved their Caribbean holidays there in the past, and she knew that a few days in the warm sun would warm her spirit. It was a luxury retreat, and very private.

As she soaked up the sun in the final few days of the year, Diana determined that she would not only survive, but thrive. 1997 will be different, she vowed. I will find a new role for myself where my humanitarian efforts can be put to best use. Hasnat and I will reconcile – or we won't. My boys will always be my Number One. I know it will be better. It has to be.

The Princess, ever resilient, was bouncing back yet again. She returned to London refreshed and rejuvenated. And she couldn't wait to see William and Harry before they returned to school!

CHAPTER TEN

The Global Stage

After a brief and cheerful reunion with William and Harry, Diana set off on a four-day aid trip in mid-January to Angola, South Africa. She was elated that finally the British Foreign Office had given her permission to visit the war-torn region. It galled her that she had to beg for clearance to go and help others. And even her pleasure trips abroad needed pre-approval from the monarch.

"Well, look at us now, Paul. They can't say I'm spending millions of pounds on outfits for this trip." Diana smiled at her butler, who had become her dresser/lady-in-waiting/equerry/hairstylist, and press officer for this tour. They had travelled coach for the eleven-hour flight from London, accompanied only by a BBC crew of four who would chronicle her experiences in a documentary called *Heart of the Matter*. She had eschewed a first-class airplane ticket, commenting that it would be absurd to arrive in one of the world's poorest countries wrapped in a cocoon of luxury.

"Ma'am, they certainly can't. This toned-down look suits you." The pair were sitting in Diana's small suite at the British Embassy in Luana. Diana wore simple cotton trousers, and a white collared shirt. Her makeup and hair were understated. She wore her lucky gold hoop earrings.

"Can you believe that just a month ago I travelled by Concorde to New York for the gala ball to benefit the Costume Institute of the Metropolitan Museum of Art? I had a lovely time with Liz – although I think my dress caused a bit of a sensation." She giggled.

"Just a bit, Ma'am," chuckled Paul. It was an understatement in great British tradition.

Diana's dark blue John Galliano dress looked more like a nightgown than an evening frock. It was chic and sheer, and eons away from the fluffy confections she'd worn in the 1980's. The press had gone mad for her in America, and her image in the night-blue dress was splashed across all the U.S. newspapers. She had been accompanied by her dear friend, Liz Tilberis, editor of Harper's Bazaar. The event had raised a load of money for the Museum, and Diana had enjoyed her usual stay at the Carlyle Hotel in New York City. It was now a distant memory, as she sat in the very warm and plain room in the heart of Africa.

"Paul, it feels simply marvelous to do a trip like this on my terms. No heavy itinerary or state dinners. Minimal staff and fuss. I adore it." Her smile faltered slightly. "Albeit I probably shouldn't say that, when I see the poverty and destruction all around us. Did you know that one in three hundred of the local people is an amputee because of an explosion? Did you see all the poor souls limping, and with broken bodies on the roads from the airport? I can't understand why this issue has gone unnoticed for so long!"

"You're too right, Ma'am. It's appalling seeing how many amputees you see everywhere – especially the little ones. And I don't think the issue will go unnoticed from now on, Ma'am. There are sixty international media here to cover your visit. Well done!"

Diana was travelling under the sponsorship of the British Red Cross. Her guide was Mike Whitman, the Director-General. He had briefed her extensively on the risks and dangers of the expedition. He was impressed by her quick understanding of the briefs and their hectic schedule, but also by her willingness to embark upon it, despite her fears.

She visited as many hospitals and rehabilitation centres as could be squeezed into her short visit. Travelling in a dusty Range Rover, clad in a sleeveless blue cotton shirt emblazoned with the Red Cross symbol, chinos, and flats – Diana and the BBC crew documented her visits to as many victims of landmines as possible. She never complained of the heat, dust, or flies. She cheerfully ate simple food prepared on the road. And everywhere she went, she sat on patient's beds, held their hands, hugged them, and listened to their stories. The Princess was moved to tears over and over again, as she heard tales of children, elders, and innocent lives that had been traumatised by daily explosions.

Landmines were explosive devices concealed under or on the ground, and designed to destroy or disable enemy targets. They were typically detonated automatically when driven over or stepped upon. Once discharged, a landmine could cause damage by direct blast effect, by fragments thrown by the blast, or both. Sometimes called anti-personnel land mines, they were left behind when wars ended. No one knew when or where they were located, and so they posed a daily threat of accidental detonation. It was a terrifying way to live.

With most killings and injuries occurring in times of peace, the fact that eighty percent of casualties were civilians, was even more distressing. Children were reported as the most affected age group, which caused the Princess much anguish. The fact that landmines could remain dangerous many years after a conflict had ended, is what made them an ongoing menace, taking the lives of, and maiming tens of thousands of people every year.

The focal point of the tour was Diana's walk across a mine field. Although it had been thoroughly swept for landmines by The Halo Trust, she was terrified to take the walk, but determined to do so on camera to bring far-reaching attention to the global problem. She wore a flak jacket and helmet with a clear visor over her white cotton shirt, yellow pants, and flats. The Princess still trembled as she was given last minute instructions.

Diana walked slowly along the well-studied path, cameras clicking and whirring to capture the moment for all time.

"William, I don't think I've ever been so frightened in my whole life," her voice was almost a whisper, as she sipped cool tea, and talked to her son on the telephone a few hours later. "I tried to call upon all my Spencer strength to look brave, but my stomach was lurching to and fro, and I thought I might even be sick." Diana was calmer now, but still slightly wobbly from her adventure.

"Mummy, you are brave," said her son vehemently from London. "No one else has walked across a minefield like that. You will draw tremendous attention to the plight of this landmine crisis. You're the best, Mum." Diana could hear the pride in her son's voice, and it made her heart soar.

"Well, you'll have to spot if you can see me shaking when you watch it on telly later. I only hope that these bloody cameras that follow me everywhere can finally shine some light on this problem. If so, it will have been well worth it."

The next day was Diana's last in Angola. She visited a village hospital – little more than a small room with six tiny beds – and provided comfort wherever she could.

A nurse ushered Diana to the bedside of a tiny girl with a white sheet pulled up her to neck. She was wide-eyed and pale. The nurse pulled down the sheet to expose most of the girl's bloody insides. She had been fetching water for her family, and stepped on a landmine. All her internal organs were visibly torn apart.

Diana quietly replaced the sheet, and looked directly into the little girl's eyes. She spoke softly to her, smiling and biting her lip to keep from crying. She offered what small consolation she could.

After she left, the young girl asked the nurse who the lady was. The nurse tried to explain that Diana was a Princess from England. The little girl then asked if Diana was an angel. She died a few hours later.

Whilst in Angola, some skeptical British politicians and journalists called Diana a "loose cannon" for her seeming haphazard efforts overseas.

"I'm a humanitarian. Always have been. Always will be," was her simple response.

Back home, the on-again, off-again relationship between Diana and Hasnat was on again. Hasnat had been moved beyond all measure by Diana's compassionate efforts on her Angola trip. There seemed to be an unspoken pact between them not to speak of the future, but to focus on the present, and enjoy every moment they could find together.

"Well, I'm off, Paul. Don't leave the lights on for me." Diana's eyes twinkled as she picked up her bag. She was dressed casually in blue jeans and a black sweater. She was heading to Hasnat's flat for the day, and would be waiting for him there when he got home from a long day at the hospital.

"Your case is in the boot of the car, Ma'am. Did you want me to add in a pair of marigold gloves?" He smiled at his boss.

Diana shoved his arm playfully. "Stop it, Paul. I'm the one who makes the jokes around here. And no, thank you. I've left a pair at Natty's. His place is an awful mess. I don't know what he'd do without me to tidy it up for him." She fussed like any wife clucking about her scruffy husband's habits. "I may be home tomorrow. Or even the day after." She raised one eyebrow, and bestowed a wicked smile upon her butler. "It just depends on when we get hungry enough to go out to eat."

Diana hummed as Paul handed her a jacket, and she skipped out to her car. When possible, she loved to drive herself around London, and took great pride in her ability to put her early Scotland Yard training to good use. She drove fast but not dangerously so, and was able to spot and avoid paparazzi with an uncanny sixth sense. For the hundredth time, she breathed a sigh of relief at her decision to let go her Personal Protection staff after the divorce. The freedom was exhilarating.

She sped the ten minutes to Chelsea without incident, and quietly parked in a side street near Hasnat's flat. She let herself in, having gone gleefully undetected in the modern Chelsea neighbourhood.

Her glee was short-lived as she put down her overnight bag, and surveyed the small flat. It was dismal at best, disgusting at worst. It obviously had not been cleaned since she herself had done it last – weeks ago. There was dirty crockery piled up in the tiny kitchen. The floors were filthy, and the bed was unmade. Empty beer bottles and take-away cartons were littered everywhere. Books and notes were piled up haphazardly in the lounge and bedroom. Dirty clothes dotted the floor, and every available surface. She shuddered to think of the condition of the loo.

Diana sighed heavily, and got to work. For the next few hours, the Princess happily did the washing up, tidied every room, emptied the rubbish, and scrubbed the floors. She changed and washed the linens, and ironed Hasnat's work shirts. It reminded her of the pre-marriage Coleherne Court days, when she used to wash and iron her friend Rory Scott's shirts. She had always loved the job of pressing. There was something soothing and peaceful about taking out the wrinkles, and making a shirt smooth with crisp creases.

Diana had always been tidy – even as a little girl. She lined up her cuddy toys and dolls properly before bedtime. At KP, her wardrobe was kept in pristine condition, with the clothes and shoes impeccably maintained and organised. Woe betide the dresser who missed a spot on a gown, or left a stray thread or button un-mended. Any items that showed the least wear and tear were either thrown into the bin, or donated to a friend or homeless shelter.

Diana took her image seriously, and knew that each time she stepped off the grounds of the Palace, she would be photographed and judged.

She caught sight of herself in the hall mirror – dusty shirt, mussed hair, and a smudge on her cheek. I'm glad there's no photographers lying in wait for me today. I look a fright. But she smiled to herself, as she examined the rail of cleanly pressed shirts. It filled her with a sense of satisfaction that was hard to explain. She spent so much time studying briefs, meeting people, and staying on top of her friends' lives, that it felt good just to use her hands for a change. And to see the efforts of her physical labours.

She eyed the loo, and decided she needed some courage before tackling what was sure to be a ghastly job.

Diana sat on the newly-tidied sofa, and pulled out her mobile phone to call Lucia in Washington. It was still early morning in America.

She answered on the first ring. "Diana! Hello darling. I've been thinking of you. How are you doing after that difficult trip to Angola. I'm so proud of you!"

Diana grinned into the telephone. "It was exhausting and exhilarating all at the same time, Lucia," she replied. "Of course, seeing the damage on the front line was horrific – I'm still having nightmares – but to be able to shine a light on this problem was wonderful. I understand it was covered by news agencies in all kinds of countries – not just Britain or America."

"Absolutely, darling. You were all over the front page. How could you look so beautiful, whilst walking across a mine field? Only you, Diana. Only you. Was it as frightening as it looked?"

"Yes, I'd like to say it was easy-peasy, but I was petrified the whole time. For some silly reason, I kept thinking of my mother. She's always been the queen of putting a good face on things – no matter what. I wanted to show her and everybody else that I could do it. Isn't that ridiculous? A grown woman of thirty-five with children of her own still seeking her mother's approval?" Diana groaned at herself.

"Not so ridiculous at all," soothed her friend. Lucia was twenty years older than the Princess, and knew that Diana relied on her as a beloved mother figure. She cherished this role, and somehow tread the balance of being a good listener with knowing when to give insightful guidance. "I think we always want the good opinion of our parents – no matter how old they are, or even if we don't always agree with their life choices." Lucia made a veiled reference to Frances' almost hermit-like existence in remote Scotland, and the lack of natural warmth between mother and daughter. "I know for myself – whenever my Papa looked at me in disappointment, I was utterly crushed. But in any case," she continued briskly, "I'm certain your mother was extraordinarily proud of what you accomplished in Angola. Heavens, you could have been killed yourself!"

"Pshh," waved off Diana casually. "They had swept the field quite carefully. Although Mike and the rest of the Red Cross staff looked almost as jumpy as I felt. But it had the desired effect, that's the main affair. And perhaps Mummy will ring me once she gets the papers delivered to her God-forsaken island," she trailed off on a wistful note.

"Speaking of affairs, how goes it with the charming Dr. Khan?" Lucia changed the subject with long experience of not letting her girlfriend dwell too long on the negative.

Diana giggled. "You won't believe it, darling, but I'm at his flat right now. I just finished a big clear out and washing up. And I even ironed his shirts. I'm eying the loo, but needed some strength before facing that muck. I love that man dearly, but he is such a dirty beast! I swear Natty lives on fried chicken and beer."

"I'm trying to picture the Princess of Wales on her hands and knees scrubbing the kitchen lino, but I just can't quite visualise it." Lucia chuckled.

"That's exactly where I was thirty minutes ago. I'm surprising Natty with a clean flat, and then we'll go out for dinner. I brought my wig and glasses." Diana sounded like a teenager in love. "He works so hard. It's the least I can do to help him tidy up a bit around here. And I adore doing it. It makes me feel all domestic and wifely and *normal*."

Lucia knew her friend longed for a mundane and typical life – or thought she did. "Well, I don't believe you'd love doing it seven days a week, with three kids under your feet, and queuing up for a bit of sausage and veg," Lucia offered wryly. "But I'm sure Hasnat will appreciate your efforts, and be happy to reward you with a pleasant evening out."

"He'd better reward me with more than just dinner. I haven't seen him in weeks. I'm hungry for a little more than a steak and salad." Diana giggled again.

The two passed another twenty minutes in easy conversation, Diana sharing the latest news of the boys, her work, and the ups and downs of her relationship with

Hasnat. Lucia listened, probed gently, and offered soothing advice.

As a good friend, Diana also asked after Lucia's husband, children, and life in America. They finally rang off with promises to meet up soon.

Diana plucked up her courage, scrounged for the mop and sponges, and resolutely made her way to the neglected lav. Never one to shy away from a tough job, she cleaned with a vengeance, thinking of the night ahead. Diana would never leave a task undone.

Five hours later, Hasnat returned to his spotless flat. Greeting him was a tall, beautiful blonde wearing a full-length white faux fur coat and a smile. And nothing else. Diana greeted her lover with a long and lingering kiss. It was quite some time before the two dressed; and with Diana in her disguise, ate fish and chips at the local chipper.

They returned to the flat much later, and snuggled up together on the sofa, with the Princess chattering all the while, and Hasnat doing his utmost to keep up with her.

"Tell me more about the local hospitals, Diana. How were they equipped? What manner of injuries were they coping with?" Hasnat had an arm casually draped over Diana's shoulder.

"They had almost nothing, Natty." Diana shook her head in dismay. "Tiny little hospitals – rooms really – with beds and people of all sorts. Children, adults – and the babies! All with severe damage from the landmines. Mainly, legs and arms blown off. Sometimes both legs - they were bedridden, hoping some day for prosthetics so they might walk again. The doctors had that rather glazed look in their eyes from lack of sleep, not enough medications, and supplies, and well, lack of everything, I suppose. It was all very somber and depressing. And the heat, too. It was overwhelming, Natty."

"So, what are the doctors doing for their patients?" pressed the doctor, eager to understand the facts of the situation.

"Mainly just trying to keep them alive, darling. In some cases, amputation. In others, just waiting for them to die. Some would go home after their wounds had healed, but to what? A life with no hands? How could a man work or provide for his family? I saw very little in the way of medicines. Everything seemed to be in short supply. The Red Cross brought some well-needed pain medications, but it hardly seemed enough. They are heroes, those doctors. And nurses." Diana's eyes clouded at the memories.

"And you yourself are an angel, my dear," smiled Hasnat, as he gazed into Diana's eyes. "To go all that way to offer your support and caring – with such personal sacrifice and risk. I admire you greatly, Diana."

She preened at the compliment. Natty was rather introverted, even when he wasn't distracted with his work. So, any small words of praise were soaked in like golden rays of sunlight on a dark day. "That means so much to me, Natty. I don't know what it is. I just feel so compelled to help each and every person. To look beyond the wounds, the blood, the smell of death, and see the humanity lying on the bed. It seems hopeless at times, and that just a touch or hug doesn't matter. But I know it does. For even a few minutes, they are taken out of their pain. I try to joke with them, give them a kind word, hug them. It's all I have to give, but I'll keep offering it until someone stops me. There is so much need in the world. Hasnat, I want to go to Bosnia and find a way to get to Cambodia. I really feel I've found my calling. *This* is what I'm meant to be doing in this chapter of my life. I won't stop." Diana's voice was alive with passion and purpose. Her blue eyes sparkled.

"And darling, you *will* get to Cambodia and Bosnia. And anywhere else you set your mind to. I have such faith in you. I think you really can change the world – one person at a time." Hasnat gave her a tender kiss.

"Somehow, we must find a way to work together, Natty," the Princess continued eagerly. "With your talent as a doctor and connections – and my drive and ability to marshal resources almost anywhere – we should start our own hospital. Or mobile caring centre. Or something. Just think of what we could do together!" Diana's eyes were shining at the possibilities. To be able to live and work with the man she loved – it was all she had ever wanted.

"Perhaps I could join you on one of your trips. Not a public one," he amended quickly. "But a private visit to a country that sorely needs medical aid. I could stay for two to three weeks, and talk to local doctors and authorities about setting up some type of clinic. Although as a heart surgeon, I'm not quite certain how that would match up with your landmine crusade, darling?"

"But you could help organise the medical end of the project, Natty. Connections to the right people and non-profits. Help set up distribution of needed supplies. And sort out the sickest of the patients – the ones with the most severe injuries. Surely you could help there?" Diana was beyond thrilled at the idea of a working relationship with Hasnat.

Hee smiled, and the two talked into the night about combining their shared need to reach out and help others, the sickest and most needy, and to make even a small difference. They made love and talked some more. It was an oasis for two busy and driven people – hidden away for a short while from responsibilities, pressures, and obligations. Diana returned to KP two days later.

She resumed her hectic pace of personal appointments, visits with friends, travel, and work commitments. Somehow life seemed to be speeding up.

"Hullo, Paul," greeted the petite Nora, several weeks later. She was breezing by to give her opinion about some of the gowns destined for the Christie's auction for Diana. The Princess was wavering over a few that held special memories for her, and Nora was determined to relegate them to the "go" pile.

"Hello Ma'am," greeted the butler with his customary charm. "The Princess is waiting for you upstairs." He smiled, and took Nora's coat.

She leaned into the butler and whispered. "How is she today? Feeling any better?" Nora and Paul were both very protective of Diana, and sustained each other to help the Princess no matter what.

Paul shook his head. "Unfortunately, Ma'am, she's in a bit of a bad temper today. She's feeling let down." He stopped, not wishing to gossip behind his mistress's back.

"Ah, the *Hello* magazine article. I thought as much. Shhh," she put a hand on his arm. "Don't trouble yourself. I'll just run on up."

"Bless you, Ma'am. She does need a good cheering up today." Paul nodded, as Nora bounded up the main staircase.

"Diana! Are you there? It's your loopy friend, Nora. Where are you, darling?"

"In here, Nor. Come through." Diana was looking out the window of the KP sitting room, with her favourite classical music booming loudly. She turned when Nora entered. She didn't look happy.

"Darling, how are you? Are you still upset about the *Hello* article?" She kissed Diana on both cheeks, and held her hands in her own.

"Oh, I'm alright, I suppose. And of course, I'm still upset with Mummy. I can't believe that she even gave that bloody interview." She paused to turn down the music and steamrolled the conversation further. "I was stunned that she would even speak to the press about me! Remember when she wrote that letter to the *Daily Mail* before I was engaged to Charles? She's always been so against the media and photographers. Why would a woman who has nothing but contempt for all that give them an interview? Especially when she won't even venture to London to see her own daughter or grand-children?" Diana's voice rose and became shrill.

Earlier that month, out of the blue, Frances Shand-Kydd granted an interview to the popular *Hello* magazine. She had spoken frankly about her life, her unhappy marriage to Johnnie, and the impact it had all had on her family, most especially the Princess of Wales. What had infuriated Diana was her mother's assertions that Diana had not been happy with Charles at first; it had only been a mirage of happiness.

"How dare she claim to read my mind? What I was thinking when I married Charles? We *were* happy then. She wasn't there. She was never there," she said bitterly.

"Calm down, darling. I know it's horrible that she did it without speaking to you. Did she ring you before it was published?" The two had sunk to the floor, and were now sprawled on the rug.

"No, although she rang me after. Do you know she actually expected me to be pleased? That somehow, she had set the record straight for me after fifteen years of royal life? Ridiculous! The worst bit was her saying that it didn't matter that my HRH title was taken away from me. That I was happier without it. She's pathetic. I won't speak to her. She can just rot up there in Seil. Have another glass of wine, Mother." Diana's voice was cold and harsh as she rattled out her pronouncements.

"Oh darling, I know it was horrid of her. And you're not in the mood to look at the bright side. Wait!" Nora held up her hand as Diana moved to object. "Alright, could we just agree it could have been worse? She could have said even more loathsome things – who knows what's in her mind? She is a sad woman, darling. And lonely, I'm sure. Maybe just leave it for now. Give it a bit of time. Maybe you'll come around?" Nora finished hopefully.

"Not fucking likely," sputtered Diana. "Everywhere I turn, I'm being betrayed. Fergie is talking to anyone with a microphone, telling them stories about me; I just can't seem to make that girl shut up. Now Mother is pouring out her guts to the press? What next? How about you, Nora? Are you going to spill all my secrets to the British press?"

As usual when worked up, Diana tended to exaggerate. She was feeling very let down by everyone around her.

Nora attempted a joke. "Well, the *Telegraph* only offered me a half million pounds for my story, so I'm holding out for a better offer." She gazed hopefully at her friend. A glimmer of a smile.

"Now that's *really* pathetic Nor," Diana shot back. She paused for a moment. "This has been a rotten spring for treachery. Look what happened with the Versace book?"

Diana was still smarting over the betrayal of her great friends Gianni Versace and Elton John. Diana had donated her fee to the charity, along with a portion of the book's proceeds, in exchange for writing the book's forward. Unfortunately, she had been shocked when she saw the final proof. Images of naked or half-clad models, athletes, and artists alongside stark photographs of certain members of the royal family. In Diana's mind, the book was in exceedingly poor taste. She had withdrawn her foreword and support for the book, and refused to attend the launch dinner. Hundreds of thousands of pounds had been lost to Elton's AIDS trust. Neither Gianni or Elton were speaking to her.

"How could I endorse such a vulgar display? The Queen would have been totally offended. I don't need to do anything more to be in her bad books, do I? I just can't seem to trust anyone. Whenever I let down my guard, I'm disappointed - again. Even that lovely Martin Bashir who conducted my telly interview. I was going to work with him on a book, and then Paul told me he had said some horrid things about me. I don't even want to repeat them. Nora, where can I turn?" Diana's eyes had started to fill.

"Hush, darling, don't lump all those dreadful events together. They are a disparate number of unrelated occurrences over the last few months – not some grand conspiracy theory. And you can turn to me, Diana. You can always turn to me. And so many of your loving friends. And William. Even Paul. Loads of supporters are here for you, darling."

Nora hugged the Princess and dried her tears. Just then the ever-intuitive Paul arrived with some herbal tea for Nora and carrot juice for Diana. Before long, the two chums had enjoyed their refreshments, and strolled down to the wardrobe room to look over some of the earmarked Christie's frocks. Before they hit the bottom step, Diana had launched into her latest racy joke. Hearing the two friends laughing cheered up the butler, who said a silent prayer of thanks for good people standing by the Princess. She'd recently iced out two of her other close confidantes – Simone Simmons, her energy healer; and her acupuncturist, Oonagh Toffolo. She'd been vague with Paul about heated rows, disloyalty, and trust issues. It was all becomingly alarmingly familiar, and he shuddered to think where it would end.

"Richard, what do you think? These hardly even look like me!"

It was May 1997, and Diana was closely examining the proofs from a recent *Vanity Fair* photo shoot. She'd worked with a new photographer – Mario Testino – and was overjoyed with the resulting images. She'd gone to his Battersea studio for a day of shooting, and had thoroughly enjoyed herself. Mario's style was informal and inclusive – he wanted to get to know his subjects before taking their pictures. So, he and Diana talked, ate and drank, and laughed together the whole day. The resulting set of photographs were nothing short of spectacular.

"You look marvelous, Ma'am. So natural and comfortable. My goodness. What a tremendous job Testino has done with you." Richard Kay was all smiles. He had been invited to KP for lunch with the Princess. Although their friendship was low-key, they kept in touch regularly, and enjoyed each other's company. Richard was loyal to her, and protected her image in the press as much as he could. Diana tipped him off occasionally to let him know where she'd be, and conveniently, photographers would appear to snap a picture on her terms. "Are these for the *Vanity Fair* cover?" he asked.

Diana had been working closely with Meredith Etherington-Smith, who was organising the Christie's auction. The two had become close, and had discussed who should model the dresses for the programs and displays. Ultimately, there was really no choice – Diana had to model her own gowns, and it was Meredith who had suggested the Princess break with traditional royal photographers to work with Mario. He had a reputation for bringing out the best in his subjects, and Diana had agreed. Now she was delighted she had.

"Yes, and you know the title of the article – *Diana Reborn*. Isn't that just perfect, Richard? I'm not sure which I like best, the black and whites or colours? Which do you think?" Diana was picking up and discarding photo after photo. Although *Vanity Fair* would make the final decision about which of the shots would make the cover, both Diana and Mario had a heavy influence.

"They are all magnificent, Ma'am. You look luminescent and innocent, all at the same time," replied the tall and lanky reporter. "And look at this one. You remind me of a young Jackie Kennedy here. Something about the turn of the head, and your stately expression. I'm not quite sure what." Richard had picked up a photo with Diana sitting in a one-shouldered gown with her arms crossed.

"Do you really think so?" Diana clapped her hands. "I told you, Richard, didn't I? I thought maybe I had a bit of her look." She was clearly delighted with the resemblance. "I've never had photos like this before. He seems to have really captured my essence. Perhaps I'll have him take our annual Christmas photo. I'm sure he could do wonders with William, Harry, and myself."

"That's a splendid idea, Ma'am. The article will be a hit. As will the auction. The buzz for it is getting stronger every day. It really was a stroke of genius, Ma'am. I'm sure you'll raise a lot of money for your charities."

"Do you really think so, Richard? It's starting to get a little out of hand. But it is for a good cause. Still, I'll be glad when it's over. I'm looking forward to slowing down a bit this summer. It's been a hectic spring, and only going to get worse in June." Diana had sat down on the sofa next to Richard.

"Will you be in New York for the auction, Ma'am?" queried Richard. He definitely liked to keep abreast of the Princess' comings and goings.

"Not for the actual auction, Richard. I think that will just be too much. But I'll be there for a dinner a few days before. And whilst I'm in America, I have so many engagements! I'm trying to meet with President Clinton to discuss the landmine issue. And Mother Teresa has invited me to visit an AIDS hospice with her. I couldn't give that a miss. And I just received an invitation for lunch with Tina Brown and Anna Wintour. At this rate, I may never come back to the UK." She laughed.

"That is rather a packed agenda, Ma'am. If you're speaking at any of these events, I'd be honoured to provide any assistance you need." From time to time, Richard had assisted the Princess of Wales in writing speeches for various fund-raising dinners and awareness campaigns. She didn't always take his advice, as she tended to confer with many friends and associates to perfect her message. But Richard didn't mind. As long as he helped the Princess collect her busy thoughts and shape her messages, he was happy to contribute.

"Oh my. The editors of *Vanity Fair* and *Vogue* together with the Princess of Wales for lunch. That will be quite spectacular. I hope they can behave themselves."

Diana giggled. "I'm sure they will with all eyes upon us. I can't wait. I love seeing the New York collections – or previews of collections. Anna usually puts aside a thing or two for me."

Richard guffawed. "I'm sure that *thing or two* will be a 10,000-pound gown. She must be thrilled to dress the Princess of Wales."

"Well, as much as I'm looking forward to that – what I'm really excited about is the opportunity to meet with the President, and make an impression on him about the urgency of the landmine crisis. If the Americans were to place their support on such a cause, we could make a tremendous difference in the world. Even perhaps a global ban. Wouldn't that be wonderful, Richard?" Diana's blue eyes sparkled, and her face lit up. "And the chance to meet with Mother again. Well, that's rather special, isn't it?" she finished quietly.

Ever since Diana had met with Mother Teresa in 1992, she had stayed in contact with the diminutive nun and crusader to the poor. The rosary that Mother had given her was one of Diana's most prized possessions, and it still held a place of honour on her desk. She always felt calmed and spiritually replenished after even a brief reunion with the humanitarian.

"Rather special, indeed Ma'am. And only you can lump together Mother Teresa, the President of the free world, and the most famous fashion editors in New York into one sentence." Richard was still chuckling.

"Yes, it's to be rather a whirlwind tour. After that, I simply must slow down. The pressure is really building, Richard. At least this summer, I won't have the bloody divorce hanging over my head."

As long as he'd known the Princess, he was always amazed at the lightning speed with which she changed topics and moods. He shook his head.

"Yes, at least that's over. And look at the new life you're making for yourself. Could you ever have imagined last year the impact you'd been making with this landmine effort? It's astounding."

"No, I certainly couldn't. Albeit there's much more to be done. I'm planning to go to Bosnia in August, you know. But what to do with the boys in July? Richard, I just can't compete with Balmoral. The boys just love it there. All the hunting, fishing, hiking. I hate it that my boys love killing things as much as their father and grandfather – but I suppose it's the way of the Windsors." She shrugged her shoulders. "But I can't have them mooching about here in Kensington Palace all month before they head to Scotland. Even with a few scheduled outings and their friends over, they'll be bored to tears."

"Have you any holidays planned for them, Ma'am?" asked Richard "They also love America. What about Disneyland again?"

"Yes, they did love it when they were younger. I think perhaps William might be a little too old for it. He's going to be fifteen next month – imagine! But it's always the same old problem. How do I find a vacation spot that's safe for them – not just from a security standpoint, but away from the wretched photographers? The last few winter ski trips have been nightmares trying to get the least little bit of time to ourselves." Diana nibbled on a fingernail.

"Surely you have friends that can offer you the loan of a resort or safe house? What about Richard Branson?" suggested Richard.

"Yes, maybe," Diana replied absently. "I should ask around. People are always so kind to invite us, you know, Richard. But they don't always understand what they're letting themselves in for. It's virtually impossible to get away unnoticed. I'll have to give it some further thought."

"I will too, Ma'am. I suppose my country home in North Yorkshire wouldn't do, would it?" He smiled ruefully.

Diana laughed again. "No, but thanks all the same, Richard. Now, have you heard this one? What do you call a virgin lying on a water bed?" Diana started laughing before she even got out the punch line. "A Cherry Float!" Richard rolled his eyes. He'd heard loads of jokes like this from the Princess of Wales.

Diana was bent over double laughing at her own joke, as Paul announced that lunch was ready. Diana and Richard were still chuckling as they walked to the dining room.

"Darling, can we discuss this when I return from New York?" pleaded Diana into her mobile phone. I'm just getting dressed for the ballet gala tonight. I'll ring you straightaway when it's over, alright?"

"Of course, Diana," replied Hasnat curtly. "But you can't keep avoiding me. You're flitting all over the world like a woman possessed. You must slow down. We need to talk."

Diana sighed and peeked at her watch. "I know, Natty. And I'm not avoiding you," she lied. "I'll ring you later, and we'll arrange a time for next week. Must run. Bye."

Diana took another deep breath. The relationship with Hasnat seemed to be permanently stalled. After their glorious reunion in the winter, the two had enjoyed a period of bliss. Then Diana seemed to always be busy – with her daily London schedule, the princes, and her overseas engagements. She'd recently made a rush trip to South Africa to visit her brother, and made a short stop to see Nelson Mandela. She seemed to have time for everyone but Hasnat.

For her part, Diana was feeling extremely frustrated. After the divorce, she felt she had shed her old life, and was eagerly embracing new challenges and exciting directions. She'd even had some promising meetings with the new British Prime Minister, Tony Blair. More than his predecessor, he seemed eager to work with her, and carve out some sort of ambassador position. Everything was moving forward. Everything, except her relationship with Natty.

After almost eighteen months together, they were no further ahead in terms of becoming an official couple. Natty constantly put off any suggestions of making their relationship public. They continued with their clandestine meetings at KP, or his small flat. Occasionally they went out to a jazz club, with Diana in disguise. Hasnat changed the subject whenever Diana turned the conversation to marriage or long-term plans. She loved him deeply, and knew he was in love with her, too. But this inertia and lack of action was killing her, bit by bit. She knew in her heart that a marriage between them would never really work, but she just wasn't ready to break it off just yet. The connection between them was so strong. She spoke of her fears endlessly to her friends. Sadly, none of them could really see a future with the intensely private Muslim doctor, but they held Diana's hand, patted her tears, and listened as she tried to work through her feelings.

For now, she was content to put the relationship on hold, and enjoy her trip to New York.

The Christie's auction was a smashing success. Diana's gowns sold for a record-breaking 3.3 million dollars. The John Travolta dress alone went for almost a quarter of a million pounds. The press hailed it as "Diana Cleans Out Her Closet" and "Charities Just Clean Up." In the end, she'd had to split her trip into two, with a breakneck visit back to London in-between. She hadn't been able to arrange to meet the President, but had enjoyed a satisfying breakfast meeting with First Lady, Hilary Rodham Clinton. Her time with Mother Teresa had been as restoring as she'd hoped. She'd also spent a wonderful evening with Lucia and her husband, who had flown in from Washington to see her. It had all been a glittering success.

Back in London, Diana was unwinding with her boys,

on their last break before the end of their school term. The three of them were dressed in casual jeans and shirts, as they enjoyed a picnic lunch in the walled garden at KP.

After Paul had deposited and unpacked the basket, Diana turned to William and Harry with a light shining in her eyes.

Boys, I have a surprise for you. Remember I told you I was seated next to Mr. Al-Fayed at a ballet dinner a few weeks ago. I was there supporting the troupe as well as your Granny Raine." Raine Spencer was on the board of Harrod's department store, the British retail icon that was now owned by the Al-Fayed family. "Well, he kindly offered us to come and stay at his villa in St. Tropez for a couple of weeks in July. And I've just sorted it, and we'll be going." She waited expectantly for a great reaction. And got it.

"Mummy, that's brilliant," exclaimed William. "It's a private villa, right?" Sadly, her firstborn's first reaction was a safety concern.

"Yes darling, it's very remote. And the Al-Fayed's have their own security detail. It's going to be so wonderful. They have boats and jet-skis, and his wife and children will be there. We'll have a marvelous time." She beamed at her eldest son.

"And swimming? And diving, Mummy?" Harry jumped up excitedly. "Will we go on a boat?"

Diana smiled at her youngest son. "Of course, darling. All of that and more. We'll leave shortly after my birthday. We'll have a splendid time, you'll see." She turned to William. "And a big thank you to my super-smart son for conceiving the idea of the auction. It's all because of you that we raised so much money for AIDS and the British Red Cross. So now you're going to be spoiled on our little holiday. You too, Harry." She smiled at her red-headed boy, who was looking slightly downcast. "It's going to be the best holiday ever. And the best summer, too. I promise."

The three Spencer heads bent over their sarnies and Ribena as they eagerly planned what Kensington High Street shopping trips were needed to get them ready for this next adventure.

CHAPTER ELEVEN

Frantic Summer

"Good morning, Your Royal Highness. And may I be the first to wish you a very Happy Birthday." Paul had discreetly knocked on the Princess' bedroom door to bring her a breakfast tray.

"Good morning, Paul. And sorry but you're not the first! I've already had three phone calls, including William before he rushed to Chapel. But thank you all the same."

Diana had no time to be sad or alone, or dwell on the passing of another year. The telephone rang constantly, flower deliveries arrived hourly; and notes, cards and letters piled up in the downstairs hall. Paul counted ninety bouquets of flowers by the end of the day, from famous actors, designers, faraway friends, and other world figures. Diana was delighted with a bouquet of lilies from Charles, as well other floral offerings from selected ex-lovers. Hasnat sent a large bouquet with a note that the Princess read privately.

Determined not to appear as a solitary or pitiable figure, Diana spent her birthday in a very public way. She attended the 100th anniversary celebration of the Tate Gallery in London with her brother Charles as her date. Dressed in a black gown by Jacques Azagury, she was the guest of honor at the celebrity-filled event of 500 guests. The gown had been a birthday surprise from the designer a day before, and she had fallen in love with the black confection. As a royal, she had only been permitted to wear black for funerals, so she relished the new freedom of wearing whatever she fancied, whenever she liked. Her hems were getting shorter whilst her bodices dipped lower. Even her cropped hair matched her sleek new look.

But the best bit of the day was when her son Harry surprised her by ringing her from school. He had collected a group of classmates to sing Happy Birthday. She laughed and wiped away a blissful tear.

As she put the finishing touches on her gala outfit, Diana paused at the landing of the stairs to pirouette in front of her butler. She looked spectacular in the long, sparkly, black Chantilly lace gown that clung to her figure in the most becoming way. She wore the emerald choker and earrings that had remained with her from her royal days. She was tall, slim, and regal in sky-high black pumps.

"Do you think Hasnat would like me in this gown?" she asked Paul wistfully.

"Most definitely, Ma'am. You are definitely drop-dead gorgeous." They both smiled at her own nickname for the handsome doctor. She picked up her clutch bag, and strode purposefully out the door.

On July 11, the Al-Fayed helicopter arrived at Kensington Palace to take Princess Diana and the two princes on a luxury holiday to the south of France. Diana had been showered with offers to visit friends, or use their safe houses for a summer break. She had considered an invitation to the exclusive Hamptons in the United States, but had rejected it as not being safe enough for the three of them. She had almost accepted an offer for a vacation in Thailand, but she was tired of globe-trotting, and decided a sun-and-sand vacation in a sumptuous villa was just the thing.

Mohamed Al-Fayed was a controversial figure in Britain. Born in Egypt, he was a self-made billionaire. After launching a successful shipping company, he and his brothers became involved in many businesses. In the mid-eighties, he had purchased Harrod's, the signature high-end English department store. He owned the extravagant Hotel Ritz in Paris, along with many elegant residences around the world. At times, he had been accused of shady business dealings, and his reputation was mixed. He had undertaken to ingratiate himself with the aristocracy and royalty of British high society, with limited success. Some saw him as *new money* and disdained the entrepreneurial Al-Fayed. He had repeatedly tried and failed to obtain a British passport.

His success in convincing Diana, Princess of Wales to bring her two sons for a private holiday was a giddying triumph for the middle-aged billionaire. It was a way to stick it to the most elite of the upper classes, who looked down on him and his family. He was determined to lavish everything his wealth and access could accomplish to impress and delight this small and elite branch of the royal family.

For her part, Diana felt an affinity to the charming Mohamed. She related to him as an outsider, and took secret glee in pushing the royal family as far as she could. She had been given clearance to take the boys on the holiday, but wondered how the apoplectic Robert Fellowes and other men in grey had reacted to the request. At this point, she was beyond caring. She just wanted a glorious and memorable holiday with her two favourite men!

The helicopter whisked Diana, the boys and their PPOs to Oxted, the Al-Fayed's Elizabethan manor in the Surrey countryside. They had a light lunch with the family, including Mohamed, his wife Heini, and their four children: Jasmine, Karim, Camilla, and Omar. Diana was hoping the children would all get on at the villa, and keep her active young men from getting bored.

The group then boarded Al-Fayed's private jet for the short flight to Nice, where they were transferred to Mohammed's newest toy – a sumptuous yacht named *Jonikal*.

Unbeknownst to the Princess, Al-Fayed had bought the luxury cruiser the day after Diana had accepted his holiday invitation. It was 180-feet in length with several levels, twelve sleeping cabins, three living rooms, a dining room, outdoor lounge, sundeck, and even its own helipad. Diana and the princes were suitably impressed, as they climbed aboard and sped the short distance to the Al-Fayed villa – Castel Ste. Helene.

"Mummy let's have a diving contest," urged Harry a couple of days later. The little family was thoroughly delighting in their stay at the villa. It's private swimming pool and spectacular estate overlooked the stunning views of the St. Tropez bay.

"Right-o, Harry. You're on. You have a go first." Diana smiled at her younger son. She looked tanned and happy in a yellow one-piece swimsuit. Harry obediently showed off his diving prowess off the edge of the outdoor pool.

"Well done, Harry," clapped his mother. "I think your legs wobbled a bit, but good show."

"His legs were definitely not straight. But not rubbish," chimed in William. The other children watched eagerly.

"Your turn, Mummy," encouraged William.

All eyes were on the Princess, as she performed a perfect swan dive into the deep pool. She bobbed to the surface, looking for praise. She'd always loved swimming, and had shown off her diving prowess ever since she was a little girl. At both Park House and Althorp, she'd displayed her diving skills to gain the approval of her parents.

"I think you win, Mummy," exclaimed William. "It was perfect. Sorry Harry." He looked at his brother, who didn't look too disappointed.

"I've had a little more practice than you, darling," Diana said reassuringly, as she climbed out of the pool. "But I think William needs to get in the game." With that, she pushed her elder son into the water with a tender shove. Within seconds, all the children were either jumping or being pushed into the marvelous swimming pool. Harry exacted his revenge by pushing his mum under the water with William. They all splashed and laughed together. It was idyllic.

Castel Ste. Helene was a four-acre estate within the private community of Les Parc De St Tropez. It boasted a main villa with nine bedrooms, large reception rooms, two kitchens, a children's playroom, swimming pool, and terraces. It also housed a waterfront beach house with nine bedrooms, an indoor and outdoor pool, a nightclub with a cinema and a bar, and a gym and sauna. A boathouse, helipad, and jetty completed the self-contained compound, which had an impeccable and comprehensive security system.

Diana and the boys stayed in a luxurious four-bedroom guesthouse with a nearby tennis court.

"It's lovely Nora, really lovely. And just what we needed. The boys are having the times of their lives. Jet-skiing, swimming, and boating. And you should see the video game console and all the games that Mohamed has. William and Harry think they are in video heaven." Diana sighed happily into her mobile phone.

"And how are you getting on with the Al-Fayed family, darling?" asked Nora from a rainy London. "Are they turning on the golden charm?" Nora wasn't as keen for her girlfriend to forge a tight relationship with the notorious Egyptian family, but knew Diana loved the tight-knit middle-eastern family culture.

"Golden is right, Nor. It's rather ostentatious, really. Such a break from cold, royal castles. Everything here is warm and open. You know, even the taps in the loo are made of gold! Not to my taste, but marvelous for a holiday. And yes, everything is first-class – the food, drinks, and entertainment are always flowing. What I love most, darling, is how the family shows affection for each other. They want to spend time together. It's noisy and messy, and I love it."

"Not quite the same as a holiday at Sandringham?" joked Nora.

"Not even close," snorted Diana. "Or even Althorp for that matter. There's something about this Muslim Asian culture that just speaks to me. I feel welcomed just for myself. Like I'm being wrapped in a warm blanket. Very cozy."

"Very cozy, indeed, Diana. It sounds bloody brilliant. Maybe next time you can bring along your poor London chum."

Diana laughed. "I'll do my best, Nor. But wait, let me tell you the best bit. Last night, Mohamed's son Dodi joined us at the villa. I've met him before, but honestly, didn't really notice him. But he was just as pleasant and amiable as the rest of the family. Really attentive, darling. Such a change from you-know-who."

They both knew the Princess was referring to Hasnat. Diana was so conflicted about their relationship. As much as she admired and adored the busy doctor, her needs for attention and love just weren't being met. Based on all the rows they'd been having lately, Dodi's focus on and devotion to her was a welcome balm.

"I can imagine. They actually look a bit similar, Diana. Both tall, dark, and Muslim, haha. You certainly do go for a similar type!" Nora laughed. She was happy to see her friend distracted from the maddening attachment between

Hasnat and Diana, but she recognised that a rebound relationship was not the answer.

"Yes, he's a lot of fun. We're having a splendid hols."

"Diana, how are you feeling about what's happening here in London? The birthday party?" asked Nora cautiously. The papers had been full of news of the impending fiftieth birthday celebration that Prince Charles was planning for his lady love Camilla at Highgrove. It was a sensitive topic for the Princess, but one that Nora knew was on her mind.

"Well, let's just say – watch the newspapers tomorrow, Nora," laughed Diana mysteriously. "You may just see something else to wipe that story off the front pages."

"What are you planning, darling?" asked Nora worriedly.

"Don't be concerned, Nor. Just a little outing on the waters of St. Tropez. A small distraction. You'll see." Her voice changed a little. "Oh, I must dash, Nora. It's time for drinks on the terrace. I'll ring you tomorrow."

Nora knew that Diana had abruptly hung up to avoid a ticking off. Whatever she had planned must be something smashing, she thought to herself, as she hung up her mobile phone.

And it was eye-popping! In her leopard-skinned bathing suit, Diana and the boys took over the St. Tropez waters and world news coverage the next day. They cavorted on jet-skis, dived, and swam in the warm Mediterranean Sea. Diana had even approached the ever-present paparazzi who were swirling around the royals in rented boats. She challenged them as to why they were there, and taunted them by saying "Watch what I do next." It sent the royal reporters and tabloids into a tailspin trying to figure out what she meant. But it had the desired effect. The smiling Princess and two princes appeared on the covers of all the British papers, blanking out the staider coverage of Camilla's fiftieth birthday party. Take that, Charles, Diana thought to herself.

A short while later, Diana's sunbathing was interrupted by a call on her phone.

"He's been *what?*" cried Diana into the mobile. She sat up on the lounger, pulled off her sunglasses, and clutched the phone tighter.

The famous man on the other end of the telephone was crying so hard that he could hardly be understood.

"He's been shot. Gianni has been shot. And killed." Elton John gasped to his dear friend.

"Oh no," screamed the Princess, her eyes filling immediately with tears. "What happened?"

"He was walking, like he always does outside his Miami mansion. He went to get a morning paper. For some reason, he didn't have his assistant with him. He was just shot and killed in cold blood. No one knows why."

"Oh, my god," whispered Diana. "Poor Gianni. And poor Antonio. How is he doing? I don't believe it. Gianni was so young." Diana shook her head in disbelief. She hadn't spoken to her friend, the famous designer since the row about his book. She was heartbroken now that they'd never mended their relationship.

"Antonio is holding up as best as can be expected. They've been together something like fifteen years. He's devastated. Gianni was only fifty years old. It's tragic, just tragic," Elton relayed brokenly.

The two friends consoled each other amidst their shock. Apparently, Gianni had been the victim of a random shooting by a serial killer. He had been the fifth casualty at the hands of this madman. Diana just couldn't believe the vibrant, powerful man's life had been snuffed out – forever. Elton and the Princess agreed to meet at the memorial in Milan in a few days. Diana rang off, and burst into tears as she looked around her opulent surroundings.

Diana tried to enjoy herself for the sake of the boys for the rest of the trip. They had all had a marvelous time, and she had found Dodi to be an attentive and kindhearted companion. He had consoled her in her distress, and they had started to form a friendship. They had spent many private hours together, talking and sharing their histories and dreams. She agreed to meet him in Paris in a few days.

Back in London, Diana helped the boys prepare for their annual Balmoral trip. They had loved their holiday in St. Tropez, and begged to return the following summer. Diana made no promises, but hoped to be invited back to the glorious hideaway.

As always, Diana felt enormous anguish when the boys left her. They were meeting the rest of the royal family aboard Britannia to make its way northward to Scotland. The princes were more excited than sad, and Diana fought back tears as she hugged and kissed them goodbye.

"What are you going to do for the rest of the summer?" asked William anxiously. He was always mindful of his mother's moods, and didn't fancy the idea of her spending the next six weeks lonely at KP.

"Don't worry about me, young man," reassured his mother with a grin. "After the memorial, I may go back to St. Tropez for a few days. We'll see. And I have my upcoming trip to Bosnia to plan. You just be on your best behaviour with Granny. And don't forget to ring me back if I call when you're out fishing."

"Okay, Mum," replied her tall, handsome son. As he grew, he looked more like his mother all the time. A true Spencer, she thought to herself. He'd just had his braces removed, and was flashing his toothy and now-straight smile at anyone nearby.

"And take care of your brother. You know how he's

always getting into trouble," joked Diana to distract herself from looming tears.

"I am not," protested Harry. "I'm just naturally curious, that's all." All three laughed at the statement that had obviously come from a kindly adult – perhaps his PPO.

"That you are, darling. And it's something I adore about you. Now, no complaints - I want a proper hug. I love you both very much. Never forget that. Please give my best to your father – and to everyone really." As much as she loathed Balmoral, it was still difficult to let her sons go off where she had no influence on them. A bitter side effect to the divorce she had never wanted.

After promises to stay in touch daily, the boys left. Diana returned to her sitting room to catch up on phone calls before leaving for Milan.

After returning from the melancholic memorial in Italy, Diana rang Hasnat and arranged to meet him that night in Hyde Park. Gianni's service had been distressing; the only bright spot being that she had made up with Elton. She determined she would live life to the fullest. She wouldn't settle any longer. She even thought she might call Frances – maybe.

Whilst she'd been in Milan, a deluge of gifts and flowers had arrived daily at Kensington Palace. Everywhere Diana looked there were bouquets on almost every surface. A pile of expensive-looking gifts waited for her on the table. Diana raised an eyebrow and looked at her butler. He shrugged and turned up both his palms.

"It's Mr. Fayed, Ma'am," he said simply. "This onslaught of gifts hasn't stopped since you returned from the Villa. I think the Egyptian is smitten." He grinned at the Princess.

She began to read the cards and open the gifts. Dodi was showering her with costly and elegant items – Hermes silk scarves, diamond earrings, a solid gold picture frame, and even a Cartier watch.

Diana looked at the pile in dismay. "It's too much, Paul. I mean, really. I can have whatever I want. I don't need a man trying to buy my love. I'm going to have to turn this off directly."

Dodi had also been ringing non-stop, and the Princess took his calls when possible. It was heady receiving so much attention, after practically begging Natty to spend time with her. The comparison was unavoidable – and not in Hasnat's favour.

That night she met Hasnat in the park and gave him an ultimatum. Either he would agree to go public and take their relationship to the next level, or it was over between them. They shouted, Diana cried, they called each other names. It was dreadful. And Hasnat refused to agree to her terms. They parted acrimoniously.

The next night, as torn lovers sometimes do, they spent the evening together at KP. Their intense bond couldn't be denied, but what was the Princess to do?

Diana spent a magical weekend with Dodi at his extravagant Paris apartment. It was located on the rue Arsene-Houssaye, and was just as opulent and over-the-top as the family villa and yacht. It overlooked the Champs-Elysees from one view, which was spectacular. Diana was introduced to Dodi's butler Rene, and they struck up an immediate affinity. He and Dodi gave her a brief tour of the apartment.

"And who do we have here?" asked the Princess jokingly, picking up a teddy bear seated on one of the elegant dining room chairs.

"That's Teddy, of course," replied Dodi with a smile. "He comes to all my dinner parties."

"I see," said Diana, carefully replacing him in his chair. There were other signs of whimsy throughout the place. Dodi had cuddly toys strewn around, with Harrod's bears in the bedroom alongside a display of model airplanes. There were family photos everywhere, as well as pictures of Dodi with famous actors, producers, and directors with whom he had worked on films.

Dodi Fayed (he had dropped the Al from his own surname) was forty-two years old, rich, handsome, and an unattached divorcee. As the eldest son of Mohamed Al-Fayed, he had been raised in the lap of luxury and was completely spoiled. He had a reputation as an amiable playboy, who loved stunning models on his arm, and was renowned for his generosity to his friends.

He lived rather an aimless life, having only briefly attended Sandhurst Academy in his youth. He also served for a time as a London attaché to the United Arab Emirates Embassy.

He had become an executive producer in Hollywood, having worked on the Oscar-winning film, *Chariots of Fire,* as well as *F/X, Hook* and *The Scarlet Letter.* In fact, he and the Princess had briefly met at the London premiere of *Hook* several years earlier.

He had a very close relationship with his father, who had tight control of the family purse strings. Dodi needed to ask permission of his father for even the smallest decision, which he found stifling at times. He did some marketing work for Al-Fayed, but spent much of his time travelling between London, Paris, L.A., and various Fayed properties in Egypt.

Although ostensibly he also worked in his father's businesses, in reality he had a lot of free time, a trait that made him irresistible to Diana. After almost two years of the infuriating on-again, off-again romance with Hasnat, this never-ending attention from Dodi was incredible, dazzling, and overwhelming.

He had lost his mother at a young age, and the two spent countless hours discussing each of their damaged childhoods. They found they had a lot in common.

Dodi and Diana continued the tour of the ten-bedroom apartment, as Rene fetched them a drinks tray. Diana murmured kind words and compliments, but was not impressed with the ostentatious Louis XVI-gilded furniture, marble floors, and Persian tapestries. There was far too much gold and gilt for her liking – harkening to the gaudy redecorating done by Raine at Althorp years earlier.

As they sipped their champagne and nibbled on caviar, another inhabitant made his presence known. A black dog named Romeo bounded into the sitting room, jumping onto Diana's lap.

"Romeo, stop!" shouted Rene, as he entered the room. I'm so very sorry, Ma'am. I tried to snatch him, but he got round me." Rene looked panic-stricken.

Diana just laughed, as Dodi removed the dog from her lap and deposited him into his own. "It's alright, Rene. No harm done."

The two enjoyed an intimate, candlelit dinner accompanied by the soundtrack to *The English Patient*, music that spoke to both of their hearts.

Although they had kissed aboard the *Jonikal* and at the villa, Diana held back Dodi's more intimate advances. After the sumptuous weekend, Diana didn't want to leave the side of her new man, but there was something in London she needed to take care of. Dodi had invited her for another cruise on the *Jonikal* in a few days' time. This one would be just the two of them, destination Sardinia. Diana couldn't wait.

"Hasnat, we're deceiving ourselves and we both know it," Diana said wearily to her lover, cloaked under the evening sky at Battersea Park, where the two had again agreed to meet. He'd been ringing constantly the last few days, and she'd avoided his calls. They hadn't even embraced when they greeted – each looking at each other with a wary eye.

Hasnat ran his fingers through his mussed hair, stubbed out his cigarette, and sighed heavily. "Darling, I don't know what to say. You know I love you. Desperately." He looked haggard as though he hadn't slept. Which he hadn't.

"Yes, but what is love?" she asked despairingly. "We hide out at your flat or KP. Once in a while, we venture out in disguise. That's not real-world love. That's a dirty, little affair." Fresh from the wide-open arms of Dodi, the Princess was seeing her relationship with new eyes. "I deserve more than this, Natty. And so do you."

"I know, I know, but we've been over this so many times. We want different things. I don't know what to say," he repeated helplessly as he paced the pathway.

"You never know what to say," Diana retorted angrily. "You just want to live in your bubble of work, work, work. With an occasional snog with me at the palace. You don't even really want a real relationship, let alone a marriage."

"Diana, that's not fair," Even when arguing, Hasnat always remained logical. This inflamed Diana's temper. It had been exactly the same with Charles, and she'd been forced into extreme behaviour to get his attention, too.

"No, it's not fair, Natty. And I've been fooling myself all this time. Wishing for something that will never happen. I love you, Hasnat. And your family. I long to be a part of it, truly. But you always shut me out. I want another child. I want to shout to the world that I'm Mrs. Hasnat Khan!" Diana was pacing now too.

Hasnat stopped and took her into his arms. "Do you really, Diana? You want to live in my flat, bring your boys there? You want to give up your lifestyle, your staff, your designer clothes, and wait for me whilst I do my important work twelve to sixteen hours a day? Is that what you really want?"

Diana sputtered. "Natty, you're exaggerating. I wouldn't have to give all that up. You could come and live with me at KP. I have lots of money from the divorce settlement. And you'll get to the know the boys better. And…" Hasnat interrupted her.

"You think I'll be a kept man at the palace?" he asked incredulously. "You really don't know me at all, do you, Diana? You're living in a dream." He dropped his arms as his words fell like dusty ashes.

"And you don't know me!" she snapped. "I've sacrificed and waited patiently for almost two years. Waited in vain. What an idiot I am. Truly as thick as a plank." She looked away. "You're right about one thing, Hasnat. There's no point going over this again and again. I'm through. Don't ring me. Don't come and see me. I'm finished. I need to be with someone who *wants* to be with me. And you'll regret this. I swear it."

Diana ran to the carpark, jumped in her automobile and sat sobbing over the steering wheel. Hasnat didn't follow her. It was over.

"Nora, I had to do it." Diana was miserable. "For my own self-worth. I can't go on begging for crumbs. We've gone around and around like a bloody carousel. I must get off. You see that, don't you?"

"Of course, I see it, darling. You must be brave. I'm sure this is difficult for you. But let's face facts. How happy have you been these last months? You can't be satisfied with half a man." Nora had rushed to her friend's side to ease the pain of the fresh breakup.

"That's it, Nor. And even just spending this little bit of time with Dodi has opened my eyes to what *is* possible. A man that really wants to spend time with me and makes *me* a priority. You know I've never had that, darling. Not with Charles, certainly. With James – perhaps a bit. But that too was a secret affair. And I was still married. But now, I'm divorced, Hasnat is single. There's no good reason why we can't be together. But still he's always resisted."

"You've done the right thing, Diana. You want more, need more. It's not as if you're just looking for a good shag. You want a marriage, more children, to show off Hasnat to your friends, and integrate him into your life. And he's deathly terrified of becoming Mr. Princess of Wales."

"Well, there's nothing like a good shag, but everything else you say is true," Diana replied with a watery smile. "And he's never had the guts to talk to his family about me. I know they like me. But he's afraid of his mother. I don't think they see an English girl, any English girl that would be suitable. Let alone a Princess with a press pack hounding her day and night." She paused. "But I still love him, Nor. What am I to do about that?"

"Nothing much, darling. Don't bite my head off when I say time heals all wounds. But it is *partially* true. Try not to think of him, don't do what you usually do and analyse every word and deed a thousand times in your head."

Diana laughed half-heartedly. "You know me too well, Nor. Well, I've broken it off at last. That's a massive step for me. I just need to be strong and follow through.

That's what William says, too." She sounded a little more resolute.

"And you have Dashing Dodi to distract you for the rest of the summer. Just have fun with him, Diana. I'm not saying to use him, but just go to dinner, watch the sunset, laugh with him. Go on a cruise, enjoy the Mediterranean, and the adoration of a man who can't get enough of you. That will help you get over Hasnat. Just don't get too serious. Rebounds never work."

"That's great advice as always, darling. What would I do without you?"

"Well, let's not find out. And I know that no matter how great my advice is, you don't always take it. Or, at least not all of it. But congratulations on taking such a big step. I know how hard it can be to let go, when you feel such a connection to someone. Be easy on yourself." Nora *was* proud of how strong Diana was becoming and hoped it would last.

"Yes, Ma'am," answered Diana smartly. "Now let's have some coffee, and you can help me pick out some bathing suits for the *Jonikal*. I want to look my most alluring. For Dodi, of course," she giggled.

Diana actually took Nora's advice, and basked in the hot summer sun with Dodi, seemingly without a care in the world. The large crew took care of their every need, and even anticipated ones they didn't know they had. The weather was hot and sunny every day, which suited the Princess just fine. She'd always been a sun worshipper and looked forward to her annual Caribbean trips – especially with the boys. Charles had preferred ski vacations, and Balmoral, of course. He had gotten bored of lying in the sun and lounging about, as he called it. But Diana never did.

The difference on this trip was the budding romance between Diana and Dodi. Literally together twenty-four hours a day, they never seemed to tire of each other's company. Rising late, they enjoyed a light breakfast together. Then Dodi might do a little work or make a few phone calls. This was Diana's opportunity to catch up with William, Harry, and her own circle of friends. The afternoons were spent swimming, sunning, reading, and talking. They never ran out of subjects to discuss. Dodi was a terrific listener, and extremely supportive of Diana's passions for banning landmines and her other charity work.

After a late afternoon shower, the two would dress, and have drinks on one of the decks before a late supper. They would listen to music, perhaps even dance. But always they talked. Diana had never found a man who was so eager to get to know the real *her*. She confided a lot of her history, and the scars resulting from some of the traumas of her past. She detailed her successful battle with bulimia, including the setbacks. She even talked about her episodes of cutting herself when she had been so desperate to be seen and heard. She confessed her hopes and fears for William and his weighty future as King of England. And the two of them made their own plans for the future, talking about the possibilities of spending time together in Paris and America.

In turn, Diana held Dodi's hand as he spoke of the loneliness after the loss of his mother, his own failed marriage, and his challenging relationship with his father. He spoke of trying to find more purpose in his life, and Diana eagerly shared ideas where he might use his influence to make a difference in the world.

As with any new lovers, they simply couldn't get enough of each other, and would whisper and snuggle in bed late into the night. It was an oasis of time that really helped ease Diana's bruised ego. Dodi made her feel like a woman again. He was an attentive and passionate lover. Her senses were alive, and she glowed with happiness.

Incredibly, the press didn't find them for a few days, so they even had the freedom to frolic and swim off the end of the yacht without notice. Somehow the ship's captain had been able to chart a course that had eluded the paparazzi, so the mood amongst the passengers and crew was light and carefree.

Inevitably, they awoke one day to an intrusive flotilla of boats loaded with photographers. Their private holiday was over. Photographers snapped them whenever they appeared on deck.

"Why don't we give them something good to print?" joked Diana one day. Dodi's playfulness and youthful exuberance was rubbing off on her.

"Like what, darling?" asked Dodi, as he toweled off after a swim.

"How about a kiss?" she dared.

Without missing a beat, Dodi stood up and pulled the Princess towards him. She put her arms around his neck and they kissed.

"That will give them something to talk about," said Dodi with a touch of smugness.

That will give *you* something to think about, Natty, thought the Princess.

Sure enough, the blurry photograph was plastered across the front pages of all the tabloids the next day with headlines like "The Kiss" and "Princess in Love."

"That may have been a mistake, Dodi," said Diana with a rueful grin. "They'll be all over us now like a rash." The Princess was regretting her reckless attitude.

Dodi shrugged with naïve certainty. "I can handle whatever they throw at us. I'll take care of you, Diana."

Diana simply smiled. She was a little bothered though. Sometimes these little tricks of hers with the press backfired. And Dodi truly didn't know the magnitude of the media scrutiny he was about to face.

They parted a few days later. Although Diana was a bit down about leaving the idyllic life aboard the *Jonikal* with Dodi, she was very eager to make her humanitarian trip to Bosnia two days later. She was beginning to get restless with the idle life, and yearned to jump back into her busy diary, and helping to make a difference in the lives of others.

"When will I see you again, darling?" Dodi clutched her tightly as they kissed. They had returned to London, where Diana would be getting packed for her trip to Sarejevo, Bosnia. He had a desperate look about him and a panicky edge to his voice that made the Princess uneasy.

"I'm only going to be gone three days, Dodi," she said lightly. "I'll ring you when I'm there, and we can make plans when I return."

"I'll meet you," Dodi replied quickly. "And we can spend a few days in Oxten. No one will be there; we can have complete privacy. Please say yes, Diana."

"Yes, that sounds lovely, Dodi. We can get away from the photographers there. And it will be wonderful to spend a weekend with you, before my Greek trip with Rosa. You know that's been arranged for months."

"That's fantastic, darling. I'll make all the arrangements. You don't need to worry about a thing. I'll see you in three days." He gave her another tight squeeze and kiss.

A little warning bell was ringing inside Diana's head. She didn't like men who were needy and desperate (or N&D as she and Nora called them). As much as she loved attention, it needed to be on her terms. But she shrugged it off. A little break would be nice, but the cruise *had* been brilliant.

Diana was thrilled to have the press redirect their energies towards the issue of landmines, and away from *The Kiss* for the next couple of days. She donned casual clothes again, as she visited as many landmine victims as she could, in field hospitals and aid centres. She was starting to believe this interest in her new cause would be sustainable, and eventually culminate in a world-wide ban of anti-personnel landmines. This was a controversial issue in Britain, however, as these landmines were essential to their arsenal in certain types of warfare. But to Diana, it was simply an issue of protecting and preserving humanity.

One of the lasting images of the trip was Diana's impromptu visit to a cemetery. She had asked the driver to stop at the side of the road, to see for herself how many people had paid the ultimate price with their lives. As she walked amongst the headstones, she met another slightly older woman, there visiting the grave of her son. Although the two women did not speak the same language, they gravitated towards each other. The image of the pair holding each other's faces, with Diana providing silent comfort, hit the newspapers and raced around the world. This, more than all the other visits she'd made, brought widespread global attention to the landmine issue.

"Dodi, it was almost indescribable. It was like we reached each other on a whole different level. We looked into each other's eyes, and I could feel her pain as if it were my own son. I tried to will strength and courage into her. I can only hope I helped her. It was such a moving experience."

"Diana, I really do think you have the hands of a healer. I'm sure you changed that mother's life today. You made her feel that her son's life was not lost in vain. I can't tell you how proud I am." She could hear it in Dodi's voice, and it made her smile.

"Come home, darling. I miss you dreadfully. I can't wait to see you tomorrow."

"Me too, Dodi. This trip was marvelous, but I miss you too." She rang off.

The couple spent a quiet few days together, before Diana's trip to the Greek Islands with Rosa. As before, they spent hours talking and planning, as well as walking the beautiful gardens, and making tender love. Dodi at his best was gentle and devoted. She had never felt so cherished.

And then disaster struck. Dodi got word from his publicist in America that a woman named Kelly Fisher was claiming to be his jilted fiancé, and suing him for breach of promise.

"What the hell is this all about, Dodi?" asked Diana as they watched the television coverage together. A beautiful and tearful Kelly gave a television interview with a famous woman defense lawyer. She was claiming she and Dodi were to be married in just a few weeks, and Dodi had broken it off once he'd met Princess Diana.

"Darling, what she's saying just isn't true. Yes, we were lovers, but we were never engaged. She's making it all up, just to get some attention. You know she's an actress – she's looking for her time in the limelight, that's all."

"Look me in the eye and promise me that's the truth, Dodi," glared Diana. "I don't need any more bad press about being a homewrecker." She thought of the Oliver Hoare nuisance call debacle, and shuddered.

"I promise, darling. How could I be spending time with you if I was meant to be married in a few weeks? It just doesn't make any sense. Listen, whilst you're with Rosa, I'll fly to L.A. to get this sorted. Once you return, it will all be over. Everything will be all right. You know better than anyone how hangers-on try to manufacture their own stories just to get some reflected star power. It must have happened to you countless times." Dodi could be quite persuasive when he chose to be.

"Yes, you're right, which is why I'm suspicious of people who are overly-eager or try to get too close too soon. Just don't fuck with me, Dodi. If you're really with this girl, just tell me." Diana was slightly mollified, but still apprehensive.

"I'll do better than that. I'll show you." And he engulfed her in a kiss that showed her without a doubt how he felt about her. Diana had to be satisfied with that.

"I need another husband like I need live-in paparazzi," confided Diana to her friend, Rosa. At Dodi's insistence, the two had taken the Fayed private jet to Milan, where they had boarded a small boat for their cruise. Although not as lavish as the *Jonikal*, it was still an enchanting vessel, and Diana was longing for some much-needed girl time.

Rosa had stood by Diana through the death of her father, bulimia, and the separation and divorce from Charles. And the Princess had supported her friend through her own family troubles.

"So how *do* you feel about Dodi, Diana?" asked Rosa as they sunbathed aboard the *Della Grazia*. She smiled at her friend, who was rubbing suntan oil into her already-bronzed skin.

"I fancy him, I suppose. He's very attentive and loving. But I don't love him. I hardly know him."

"That's a relief, darling. I was afraid you might be jumping from one man who disappointed you to another." Rosa was pensive.

"Do you think Dodi will disappoint me?" Diana asked curiously.

Rosa paused. "I don't know him, but no, I don't think he'll disappoint you. I think he might bore you, though. His life seems rather – aimless. Especially in contrast to yours. And Hasnat's."

"Yes, you might have a point," said Diana slowly. "And I don't like the way he's always giving me things. He left me a message on my mobile last night listing all the things he's bought me. That's so annoying. I don't want to be bought, Rosa. I have everything I want. I just want someone to be there for me, to make me feel secure. I'm not sure if Dodi is that man. It's just too soon to tell. But he is scrumptious in bed." Diana's trademark giggle was back in full force.

"Sounds like you are being sensible, Diana. Just have fun with him. Summer romances can be such a wonderful experience. When are you seeing him again?"

"As it turns out, very soon. I was meant to go on holiday with Lana Marks – you know my designer friend. She just called me yesterday, and had to cancel. Her father died suddenly of a heart attack. Poor lamb, she's rather distraught. I can't wait to see her when she's up to it. But the trip is off. Dodi had invited me for one last nine-day cruise, and now I can accept. My last bit of holiday before I see the boys again. Time to make a few more hot holiday memories."

"You've had quite a summer, Diana. For someone who wanted to keep things quiet, you've hardly spent a day at KP," commented Rosa.

"Yes, and here I thought the summer of '97 was going to be dead boring. Was I wrong. Too bad the press feels the same way. They're as vile and unsquashable as cockroaches."

Rosa clucked, as the two talked with the ease of old friends. Diana told her all about her trip to Bosnia, and plans to visit more such places in the coming months. She spoke of how well the boys were managing at boarding school. And of her new friendship with Charles, with an ease that was a happy surprise to both of them. Diana left the ship feeling all talked out.

Her reunion with Dodi was warm and sensual. There was no more talk of Kelly Fisher. They resumed their glamorous life aboard the *Jonikal,* getting to know each other on an even deeper level. Two days before they were due to return to London, Dodi confessed he thought he was falling in love with her. Diana was immensely flattered, but merely thanked him with a hug and a kiss. It was too soon for any of that. She started to itch to get back to her London life. The lazy and idle existence was not really for her. She was an active and busy soul, and couldn't wait to see William and Harry again.

They were due to return to London on August 30th. As they left the ship for the last time, the two embraced and promised each other more luxury trips like this in the future. Dodi mentioned an Alaskan cruise or heading to the Caribbean in the winter. Diana was noncommittal.

As they boarded the Fayed jet, Dodi convinced Diana to detour to Paris for one last night together. He wanted to show her the villa once owned by the Duke and Duchess of Windsor – the banished ex-King of England and his wife Wallis Simpson. It was now owned by Mohamed. And Dodi wanted to take her out to dinner in Paris, and spend the evening at his apartment before taking her home to London the next day.

Diana reluctantly agreed. She had enjoyed her holiday with Dodi, but her boys were always her top priority, and she was impatient to see them and get caught up. But with all the renewed paparazzi frenzy around them, she had no choice but to stick with Dodi, and the private jet to get her home safely. He was starting to wear a little on her nerves. She was feeling uncomfortable with his cockiness in being able to handle the press in Paris. But he was her ride home, so she agreed with the change in plans.

"Darling, it's Mummy. Are you having the best time at Balmoral? Have you been keeping count of all the things you've killed?"

Diana and Dodi had reached his apartment. The Princess had arranged to have a hairdresser sent up, and was catching up on a few phone calls before she and Dodi went out to dinner.

"Oh, Mum. It's not that bad. And you know we do more than that. Hiking, riding, picnics. I love Scotland. But I can't wait to see you. It's been ages." He lowered his voice. "Did you get the video game for Harry's birthday that he wants?"

"Yes, I did, William. And perhaps a treat or two for you as well. Listen, I must run, but let me speak to your brother for a moment. I love you and we'll have a special day together tomorrow – just the three of us."

She spoke to Harry who was just as happy to be seeing her back in London tomorrow too – until he was called by his cousins to play a game. Mother and son happily rang off.

"Nora, it was ghastly! I don't know what Dodi was thinking, dragging me to that mausoleum." Nora had rung through after the Princess had finished with the boys.

"So, is this the castle where King Edward VIII lived with that American divorcee after he abdicated? Does Dodi want you to live there or something?"

"I bloody well hope not," Diana replied with a short laugh. "It's dreadfully old-fashioned, and somehow quite sad. But luckily, we only stopped there for thirty minutes on the way from the airport. But the media! They were insane, Nor – the most aggressive I've ever seen. Dodi couldn't believe the way they were swarming all over us. I don't know how we're going to make it out to dinner to Chez Benoit tonight. But I adore this French restaurant, so let's hope for the best."

"Do be careful, darling. You know much more about how to avoid the paparazzi than Dodi. Just enjoy your last night, and we'll see you in London in the next couple of days. Maybe lunch at San Lorenzo soon?"

"That sounds smashing, darling. And don't worry. Dodi has loads of security people here. We'll fight our way through. I'm on a mission to see my boys now. I'll ring you tomorrow. I'll bring you some French chocolate. Ta ra."

CHAPTER TWELVE

The Most Dreadful Week

The telephone rang in the butler's pantry at Kensington Palace at five a.m. on Sunday, August 31st.

"Kensington Palace," an unrecognisable voice answered.

"Paul, is that you? It's Nora. Tell me it isn't true. Have you spoken to Diana? She's alright, isn't she?" Her voice shook with fear.

"Yes, it's me. And Nora, no. She's not alright. She was in a crash last night."

"I saw it on the television. A car crash. In Paris. They said Dodi and the driver were killed instantly. And the Princess was seriously injured. She's in hospital. But she's alright? Isn't she Paul?" she repeated almost hysterically as she gripped the phone.

"No, she's not. They, they, they... couldn't save her. They couldn't save her," Paul's voice broke and he started sobbing.

"NO," cried Nora. "Paul, what happened?" She felt as if she'd been punched in the stomach.

"I don't know all the details yet, Nora," he gulped between sobs. "The news is hazy from Paris. But it's true. Buckingham Palace confirmed it. Robert rang me. Dodi and the Princess were out for dinner. They were going back to Mr. Fayed's apartment, I think. The paparazzi were chasing them in a tunnel. And they crashed. You're right that Mr. Fayed and the driver were killed straightaway. I think the bodyguard is seriously injured. The Princess survived the accident, and was taken to a local hospital. She had a lot of internal injuries. They tried to save her. But they couldn't. They…they…they couldn't save her." Paul was almost incoherent with grief.

"Paul, they couldn't save her?" Nora asked stupidly. "They couldn't save the Princess of Wales? Why? Why?"

"I don't know, Ma'am. We're still trying to piece everything together. It seems her heart stopped, at least once." He was sobbing uncontrollably now. "In the end, she died of a broken heart. Oh my god, Ma'am, what are we going to do without her?"

Nora was having trouble absorbing this shocking information. Her best friend was dead. Dead. Diana dead.

"Where is she, Paul? Where is she?" Nora was almost shouting.

"She's at the La Pitie-Saltpetriere hospital in Paris, Ma'am."

"Alone?" fired Nora. Her shock was now turning to practical matters. "We've got to bring her back to London. How is she getting home?"

"I don't know, Ma'am," continued Paul, trying to regain his composure. "We're waiting for instructions from Buckingham Palace and St. James Palace. I don't know the precedent for this sort of incident. Technically, she's not a royal anymore. And I'm sure the Spencers will want to have a say." His voice trailed off helplessly. "I don't know what Her Majesty will want to do. Or His Royal Highness, the Prince of Wales."

"Paul, what are we to do without her?" Nora whimpered. "And the boys? Oh my god, what about William and Harry? Those poor boys without their mother."

"They are safe at Balmoral with Her Majesty and the Prince of Wales. I don't know if they've been told yet, but they couldn't be in better hands at the moment. They'll be well taken care of in Scotland. Oh, it's just too atrocious, Ma'am."

"Steady on, Paul. You must be strong. I'm sure you'll be needed in the days ahead." Nora did her best to revive the distraught butler. "I'm sure there will be... arrangements?" Nora had no idea what was involved in a royal funeral. A funeral! It just couldn't bear thinking about. She struggled to maintain her composure.

"Yes, Ma'am. Quite right. In fact, I'm sorry but I must ring off. As you can imagine, the telephone just won't stop ringing, and I need to know what to do next."

"Yes, I understand, Paul. Please let's keep in constant touch. I need to know everything that's happening to her. I *must* know. And Paul." Nora hesitated. "I can't even begin to tell you how sorry I am. You two were more than just boss and butler. You were friends. I'm sure you are devastated. Should I come over?" Nora was desperate to be with someone who had been close to the Princess.

"Thank you, Ma'am," Paul managed to choke out. "I'm numb right now. I still can't believe she's gone. And no, please don't come over just yet. I may be needed in Paris. I'll ring you later."

"Alright, Paul." Nora paused again. "You do realise this is going to be massive. Diana was loved all over the world. This is going to be a tragedy on the scale of which we've never seen. Diana, why? How are we ever going to cope?" Nora was crying in earnest.

Diana's best friend and dear butler wept together, as the world woke up to the most shattering news they could possibly imagine.

On the far side of the globe, the Spencer family showed its strength. Earl Spencer spoke to the press on camera.

"I always believed the press would kill her in the end," Spencer almost spat from outside his Cape Town home. "But not even I could believe they would take such a direct hand in her death as seems to be the case.

It would appear that every proprietor and every editor of every publication that has paid for intrusive and exploitative photographs of her, encouraging greedy and ruthless individuals to risk everything in pursuit of Diana's image, has blood on his hands today." The Earl hissed out his family's first statement.

Sarah Spencer asked Paul Burrell to fly to Paris to take some burial clothing for the Princess. Paul quickly packed a new, unworn black cocktail frock, makeup, and black pumps. He also brought Mother Teresa's rosary – a cherished possession of the Princess' – to be placed in Diana's hands in the coffin. Colin Tebbutt, Diana's chauffeur, accompanied Paul, by air, to the hospital where Diana lay in a quiet, secluded room. A nurse lovingly dressed her, and ensured she looked as perfect in death as she always had in life.

At Balmoral, Her Majesty the Queen had been woken shortly after the crash at 12:33 a.m. She had sat with her husband, mother, and son waiting for further news. When the worst had been confirmed, Prince Charles decided to wait until morning to wake his sons to plunge them into unspeakable grief.

Tony Blair, the new British Prime Minister, spoke from the lawn of his home constituency:

"I feel like everyone else in this country today. I am utterly devastated. Our thoughts and prayers are with Princess Diana's family, particularly her two sons. Our hearts go out to them.

We are today a nation in a state of shock, in mourning, in grief that is so deeply painful for us.

She was a wonderful and a warm human being, although her own life was often sadly touched by tragedy. She touched the lives of so many others in Britain, and throughout the world with joy and with comfort. How many times shall we remember her in how many different ways – with the sick, the dying, with children, with the needy? With just a look or a gesture that spoke so much more than words, she would reveal to all of us the depth of her compassion and her humanity.

We know how difficult things were for her from time to time. I am sure we can only guess that. But people everywhere not just here in Britain, kept faith with Princess Diana. They liked her, they loved her, they regarded her as one of the people. She was the People's Princess and that's how she will stay, how she will remain in our hearts and in our memories forever.

I will remember her personally with great affection. I think the whole country will remember her with the deepest affection and love, and that is why our grief is so deep today."

Tony's words were heartfelt and destined to be prophetic. All of England, in fact much of the world, woke up that morning and took a collective gasp when they heard, read, or watched that their beloved Princess Diana was dead.

At Balmoral, two young princes were delivered the worst possible news, broken to them by their dear Papa. It was decided that it would be best for William and Harry to stay under the protective guard of their grandparents, away from the voracious press and prying eyes of London well-wishers.

After the boys had been told, Prince Charles and his mother had a row about how to handle the funeral arrangements. The Queen insisted it was a private matter to be handled by the Spencer family. Charles countered that a royal or state funeral was the only possible option given how much Diana meant to the people of England, not to mention she was the mother of the future King of

England. Charles asked for the use of the Queen's Flight to go to Paris, claim Diana's body and bring it back to England. The Queen was adamant that it was none of their affair, and refused her assent for the royal aircraft to be dispatched.

"What would you have them do, Mother? Load her into the back of a Harrods's van?" Charles was furious.

The Queen relented.

The royal family attended regular Sunday church services at the local church, as always. They believed keeping up a sense of normalcy for the boys was paramount. The faces of Her Majesty, the Duke of Edinburgh, Queen Elizabeth the Queen Mother, the Prince of Wales, and two young princes looked pale and strained as they were driven to the church. No mention was made of the Princess during the service, nor was she listed in the prayers for the royal family. Her name had been struck once she had lost her title of Her Royal Highness. In a surreal moment, Harry turned to his father and asked, "Are you sure Mummy is really dead?" Prince Charles dumbly nodded.

After the service, the Prince flew to Paris with Diana's sisters Jane and Sarah, to reclaim his ex-wife and bring her home. He took the Queen's flight, along with the Welsh Guard, to afford the proper dignity to the newly-deceased Princess of Wales.

Diana had been given the last rites by a local priest. Charles and Diana's sisters spent separate quiet intervals alone in the Princess' room with her, before the return trip to London. They all emerged looking ravaged and distraught.

Diana arrived at RAF Northolt airport in London at seven p.m. Sunday night. Dignitaries and officials greeted the Prince and the coffin, which was draped with the Royal Standard. As the hearse drove to St. James Palace where Diana would rest in state, hundreds of cars were stopped all along the motorway as Londoners silently watched the hearse drive by.

"We're going to have to hold a state funeral," whispered Jane to her sister. "This response is unbelievable."

In fact, the reaction to Diana's death all over the country was nothing short of extraordinary. An eerie silence crept over the land as people were glued to their televisions, watching the coverage of Diana over and over again – highlights of her short life and the emerging details of her death.

Within a short time of her reported death, bouquets of flowers started to appear at the gates of both Buckingham Palace and Kensington Palace. And then the people started arriving. Their grief spilling onto the streets of London, thousands of people needed to share their anguish with perfect strangers. The flowers piled up and a private nation went public with their weeping and sobbing.

In Paris, an anguished father collected the body of his son Dodi Fayed, and as per Muslim tradition, buried him within twenty-four hours. Mohamed Al-Fayed was in a state of shock and disbelief that his oldest son had been killed in a senseless accident.

The bodyguard, Trevor Rees-Jones was in intensive care with life-threatening injuries. It was unknown whether he could possibly survive.

The driver of the car, Henri Paul, who had also been killed instantly, was buried privately.

By Monday morning, the wall of flowers outside Kensington Palace had grown to a sea of colour. The public outpouring of grief was now intermingled with anger. Eight paparazzi had been arrested in Paris following the crash. They were blamed for speeding and crowding the Fayed limo. Their blinding flashbulbs and noisy pursuit on motorbikes, was cited as the cause for the Fayed driver, Henri Paul, to lose control of the car and smash into the thirteenth column in the Alma tunnel. What was even more reprehensible was that after the car had stopped, the photographers had continued to take pictures of the passengers – both dead and alive – rather than calling for help.

Press everywhere were vilified for their relentless pursuit of the Princess and her image. It was a black day for the media.

"I just had to come." Nora stood at the front door of KP as the butler opened it. The two clung together, wordlessly.

"Come in, Ma'am," Paul invited miserably.

By unspoken consent, they avoided the Princess' sitting room and made their way to the drawing room, where they sat on opposite sofas.

"How are you holding up, Ma'am?" attempted Paul. He looked as if he hadn't eaten or slept. Which he hadn't.

Nora didn't look much better. She was hollow-eyed, and couldn't stop wringing her hands. She shrugged. "As well as you'd expect. Strangely, I don't feel anything much yet. Still in shock, I suppose. Glued to the telly. And you? How was Paris? How was she?"

"As beautiful as ever. Hardly a mark on her. Most of the damage was internal." He raised a red-rimmed pair of eyes to hers. The irony was not lost on either of them. "The Prince was remarkable. Took charge of everything. Appeared calm but obviously in turmoil. He didn't have to do it, you know? He could have left it up to the Spencers. I'm impressed he did the right thing for Diana, even if she was his ex-wife."

Nora didn't have the energy to argue with him about all that the Prince could have done when his ex-wife was alive. "That's something, I suppose," was all she said. "Have you spoken to the boys? How are they doing? I can't imagine what they're going through. They won't put my calls through to them at Balmoral."

"No, I haven't been able to reach them either. I understand the Duke of Edinburgh is exhausting them every day with long hikes in the moors, fishing, and other outdoor activities to keep them busy. And they've locked away all the televisions and radios, and forbidden newspapers everywhere but Her Majesty's apartments." It was clear the royal hotline was reaching Paul from Scotland.

"When is the family coming down to London? Today? Any word on funeral arrangements?"

"There is a committee working on the plans right now. The Spencers, representatives from all three palaces, members of the royal family, etc." Paul replied with a sigh. We've finally agreed on a royal funeral at Westminster Abbey for this Saturday. And rather than a military procession, there will be members of various charities walking behind the gun carriage. It's brilliant how the palace is going to be able to get it all organised in such a short time. It's what the royals do well, though," he finished dutifully. "And I'm not sure when the family is coming down to London. I haven't been advised."

"The Abbey. My goodness. That is fitting. I pray I'll get an invitation." Nora looked at the butler intently.

Paul nodded. "You will, along with 2000 other mourners to include friends, charity workers, celebrities, people from all walks of life. People who loved the Princess," Paul's voice cracked.

Nora rose to sit next to him, and patted his hand. "I'm sure Diana will be looking down from heaven overwhelmed at how well loved she is - was. She'll be most agonised about the boys. The person they need most right now is her. It's just so tragic, so utterly pointless. I saw on BBC that she wasn't wearing a seat belt. Could that possibly be true? She was always so conscientious about that. I remember her telling Clemmy to buckle up numerous times." Nora wiped away a tear.

"Somehow it's true. None of them were wearing seat belts. I don't understand it either. The Princess *always* wore one. I can only guess at her state of mind if she skipped it that night. And those foul photographers! She must have been so frightened with them chasing after the car on motorbikes. At the same time, she was probably worried about one of them getting hurt."

"Yes, that would be her, alright," agreed Nora. "I can just hear her saying 'slow down, for god's sake, slow down.'"

"I know," said Paul. "I heard that it wasn't the Fayed's regular driver that night. And he'd been drinking! How on earth did Dodi get Diana into that vehicle? She knew better than that. She was probably the best stunt driver in that car!" exploded the butler.

"I saw that there was a press frenzy that day in Paris. After *The Kiss* photo, they went mad for Diana and Dodi. He was probably just trying to get her safely home. I saw that they changed plans more than once that day." Nora couldn't get enough of the coverage of the crash.

"And have you heard Mr. Al-Fayed is now talking about a conspiracy theory, and claiming that the death of his son and the Princess was rigged? Utter rot," declared Paul.

"I fear that details about this accident will be coming out for years to come, Paul. It's getting more complicated every day, every hour, really. Paul, I know it's a matter of time until the royal family reclaims Diana's home. Would you mind if I took one last look through KP? I have so many memories here – happy and sad. I promise I won't touch or take anything."

Paul nodded sadly, and the two toured Diana's home of the last fifteen years. They both cried as they looked at her sitting room – just waiting as she left it. Her desk with her personalised notepaper, and pen with Quink, waited for her to dash off a quick thank you card. Cherished photos stared out from the walls and tables. Nora even believed she could smell the last candles and flowers that had scented the room. Even the stuffed hippo in the corner seemed to look sad. The butler and the friend parted a short time later with promises to stay in touch about the funeral arrangements.

Aside from the crowds' anger about the press and their responsibility in Diana's death, another issue was becoming considerably larger by the hour. "Where is Our Queen?" "Speak to Us Ma'am" and "Show Us You Care" screamed from the daily headlines. The grieving people of England couldn't understand why the Queen and her family remained at Balmoral, whilst they themselves were all suffering in London. The queues to sign Books of Condolences for the Princess had grown to a twelve-hour wait. People were prepared to stand for hours to pay their respects at St. James Palace. The flower walls – particularly at Kensington Palace – had swelled enormously with notes, cards, candles, balloons, and teddy bears being added to the growing pile.

And as the public looked northward for their Queen, they also looked up at the flagpole over Buckingham Palace; the empty flagpole. Outrage was rampant that the Union Jack was not being flown at half-mast, out of respect from the royal family. It didn't matter that the Union Jack never flew over Buck House. Only the Royal Standard flew there; and only when the Queen was in residence. It was immaterial. The people needed a sign from their monarch that she cared, and shared in their heartache.

The people were angry at the lack of emotion and sadness being shown by the royal family. Within palace and parliamentary walls there was growing concern that this could be the greatest royal crisis since the abdication. Prime Minister Blair read the mood of the people correctly, and urged the Queen to show herself in London and say something about her former daughter-in-law. The sovereign insisted on adhering to protocol and precedent. She stayed at Balmoral to protect her grandsons.

Nora rode an unearthly quiet tube to bring her daughter Clementine to Kensington Palace to place a bouquet of flowers in honour of her godmother. Like so many thousands of others, Nora just couldn't stay away.

The grief and sadness of the people was palpable. You could see it, hear it, smell it, touch it, even taste it. People clung together crying, or clutching one another as if in need of life preservers. They keened as they rocked on their hands and knees. They stood blankly staring at the cards and notes, reading but not seeing anything. The smell of the flowers was overpowering – a dizzying and sickeningly cloying perfume.

Diana wouldn't have wanted this. She would not have wanted people sad and broken about her death. You didn't even know her! How can you claim grief for someone you only saw on the front page of newspapers? Nora's grief was also turning to anger.

"Mummy did Auntie Diana know all these people?"

asked Clemmy with her hand tightly clasped to her mother's.

"No, darling, but they felt they did know her. It's hard to explain really, but because she cared about ordinary people like you and me – somehow that touched them. She helped everyone – those who were sick, or weak, or poor. Even though she was a Princess, she was real."

"Yes, Mummy. She always hugged me and teased me. I miss her," Clemmy's lip started to quiver. It was unavoidable with the unending distress all around them.

"I miss her too, Clemmy. But I'm sure she would love the note you wrote to her. Let's place the flowers with the rest, darling."

"Thank you for being my friend, Aunt Diana. You are an angel in the sky now. Love, Clemmy xo."

Clementine placed her bouquet on top of the others. Mother and daughter read a few of the cards, and then quietly slipped away.

It was announced the next day that Her Majesty, The Queen and the rest of the royal family would return to London the day before the funeral – a full twenty-four hours ahead of schedule. This was received quite positively by the public, who were eager to see their monarch and spiritual leader. When the Union Jack was raised and then lowered to half-mast over Buckingham Palace, a great cheer resounded on The Mall. Princes Andrew and Edward were dispatched to walk about casually at the palace and inspect the flower offerings, to test the reaction of the people to the royal family. The men in grey were concerned how the Windsors would be received on the streets of London. Security was tight. Thankfully, the princes went unmolested. The palace breathed a sigh of relief. Things were starting to turn around for the royal family.

The Queen, the Duke, the Prince of Wales, and the two young princes came outside the walls of Balmoral to inspect the flower shrine that was growing outside the palace gates. The world watched with great compassion, as William and Harry in their dark suits spoke to people in the crowd, and witnessed for themselves the overpowering love displayed for their mother. They looked so young and defenseless.

Friday, the royal family returned to London. It was rumoured that the Queen was going to speak live to her people from Buckingham Palace at six p.m. This would be the first live broadcast from Her Majesty in over fifty years. She and the Duke had gotten out of the car just outside the gates of Buck House, and slowly walked around, looking over the flowers and other tributes. The response was muted, but the Queen was touched when a young woman handed her flowers. "Would you like me to place them for you?" asked the monarch. "No, they are for you, Ma'am. You deserve them too." Her Majesty nodded, as she accepted the floral offering.

At Kensington Palace, Prince Charles and the two young princes also inspected the flowers. By now, officials were estimating that ten to fifteen tons of flowers were scattered throughout London. It was an overwhelming tribute to a beloved princess.

"The Queen's statement was sincere and moving:

"Since last Sunday's dreadful news, we have seen, throughout Britain and around the world, an overwhelming expression of sadness at Diana's death.

We have all been trying in our different ways to cope. It is not easy to express a sense of loss, since the initial shock is often succeeded by a mixture of other feelings: disbelief, incomprehension, anger - and concern for those who remain.

We have all felt those emotions in these last few days. So, what I say to you now, as your Queen and as a grandmother, I say from my heart.

First, I want to pay tribute to Diana myself. She was an exceptional and gifted human being. In good times and bad, she never lost her capacity to smile and laugh, nor to inspire others with her warmth and kindness.

I admired and respected her - for her energy and commitment to others, and especially for her devotion to her two boys.

This week at Balmoral, we have all been trying to help William and Harry come to terms with the devastating loss that they and the rest of us have suffered.

No one who knew Diana will ever forget her. Millions of others who never met her, but felt they knew her, will remember her.

I, for one, believe that there are lessons to be drawn from her life, and from the extraordinary and moving reaction to her death. I share in your determination to cherish her memory.

This is also an opportunity for me, on behalf of my family, and especially Prince Charles and William and Harry, to thank all of you who have brought flowers, sent messages, and paid your respects in so many ways to a remarkable person. These acts of kindness have been a huge source of help and comfort.

Our thoughts are also with Diana's family and the families of those who died with her. I know that they too, have drawn strength from what has happened since last weekend, as they seek to heal their sorrow, and then to face the future without a loved one.

I hope that tomorrow we can all, wherever we are, join in expressing our grief at Diana's loss, and gratitude for her all-too-short life. It is a chance to show to the whole world, the British nation united in grief and respect.

May those who died rest in peace and may we, each and every one of us, thank God for someone who made many, many people happy."

Every television in the United Kingdom was tuned into this speech. It was an amazing homage by a sitting Queen for an ex-daughter-in-law. The nation felt vindicated.

That night, the hearse carried Princess Diana back to her home at KP. William and Harry followed in a limo, and said their private goodbyes to their mother at their home. Paul Burrell kept an all-night vigil with the Princess before the funeral on Saturday morning.

Over 50,000 people slept on the streets of London waiting for the funeral cortege. 35,000 police were on hand to manage the crowds. A world-wide television audience of 2.5 billion people was expected to watch the funeral live.

At 9:08 a.m., the clock at Westminster Abbey tolled. It would sound every minute until Diana reached the Abbey. The seven-hundred-pound lead-lined coffin was raised onto the gun carriage by six Welsh Guardsmen. The Royal Standard draped over it, with a white lily flower arrangement from Prince Charles, behind a wreath of white roses from William and Harry. An envelope marked *Mummy* on top of the wreath sent an agonising gasp throughout the crowd at every turn in the road.

The carriage made its way slowly out of the gates of Kensington Palace to a deathly silent welcome. London had been declared a no-fly zone for the day, and all traffic had stopped. Over two million people lined the streets, and as the Princess passed by, all you could hear was a resounding silence with intermittent wailing along the route, marked by the somber bell toll.

The gun carriage passed by the west gate of Buckingham Palace where an extraordinary thing had happened. The entire royal family, including the Queen, were waiting. Dressed in black, they made a solemn spectacle. As the carriage passed, Her Majesty, Queen Elizabeth II nodded in deference to the late Princess. This was an unprecedented mark of respect.

As the clock continued to toll, the gun carriage passed St. James Palace. It was here that the most heartbreaking sight of all occurred. Five males of distinction fell into step to walk behind the mounted casket – the Duke of Edinburgh, Earl Spencer, the Prince of Wales, Prince William, and Prince Harry. They looked down as they walked, but remained composed. The five hundred-plus charity workers all fell in behind the royals, and they all walked the remaining short distance to Westminster Abbey.

Inside the Abbey, Nora watched the procession enter the cathedral. The sight of the two young princes following their mother was almost more than she could bear. She'd been seated next to Mary Robertson, one of Diana's earliest employers, when she had nannied for them. Mary had flown in from America for the service. The two clutched each other's hands to give strength.

The Abbey was packed. Nora had caught a glimpse of Hilary Clinton earlier, as well as Tom Cruise and Nicole Kidman. She'd also spotted Henry Kissinger amongst all the other dignitaries and world leaders.

She'd seen the Spencers arrive, and sit opposite the royal family. Frances looked shattered.

The funeral began at precisely eleven o'clock. Diana's favourite hymn was played – *I Vow to Thee my Country.* Nora recalled it had also been played at her wedding, fifteen years ago. Heartbreaking.

Diana's sisters each faltered through readings, and the Prime Minister read from the bible. Sir Elton John performed *Candle in the Wind,* but had changed the lyrics for the Princess of Wales, and how her candle would never burn out. How fitting, thought Nora. Diana had always felt a kinship to Marilyn Monroe, for whom the song had originally been written. What an appalling coincidence that they had both been taken too soon at age thirty-six. *Goodbye England's Rose* seemed so right. She didn't know how Elton got through it. She herself was weeping.

But the biggest shock was when Diana's brother, Earl Spencer, strode to the pulpit to read the eulogy. It was nothing less than a fiery attack on the royal family. Gasps of breath followed one after the other, as the Earl beat mercilessly on.

"She would want us today to pledge ourselves to protecting her beloved boys, William and Harry, from a similar fate, and I do this here Diana, on your behalf. We will not allow them to suffer the anguish that used regularly to drive you to tearful despair.

And beyond that, on behalf of your mother and sisters, I pledge that we, your blood family, will do all we can to continue the imaginative way in which you were steering these two exceptional young men, so that their souls are not simply immersed by duty and tradition, but can sing openly as you planned."

The Queen stared ahead in stony silence, as Harry cried. But the Earl was not finished.

"I would like to end by thanking God for the small mercies he has shown us at this dreadful time. For taking Diana at her most beautiful and radiant, and when she had joy in her private life. Above all, we give thanks for the life of a woman I am so proud to be able to call my sister, the unique, the complex, the extraordinary, and irreplaceable Diana, whose beauty, both internal and external, will never be extinguished from our minds."

His voice splintered, as he knelt before his sister's

coffin. The Abbey went silent.

Suddenly, a rumbling started, almost like the sound of rain pounding on the roof. Nora looked at Mary questioningly. What could be happening? Then, it hit her. It was clapping. Large video screens had been placed in Hyde and Regent Parks, so that the public could watch the funeral. They'd hung on the Earl's every word. Applause rolled up the aisle of the Abbey in a thunderous wave. Soon, everyone began clapping, a spontaneous outburst of emotion for the Princess. Nora doubted anyone had ever applauded a royal funeral at Westminster Abbey before. You were never one to do it by the rule book, Diana, Nora smiled to herself.

As the applause died down, the casket was raised again, and carried down the aisle, where a moment of silence was observed.

Then, the coffin was raised into the hearse, to make its journey to Diana's final resting place at Althorp. The Spencers had truly reclaimed her in death. She was to be buried on the estate on an island in an ornamental lake known as The Round Oval.

Nora found out later that as the hearse and its guard slowly drove northward, people lining the route, tossed bouquets of flowers continuously at the car and windshield. At many points, the car had to stop to remove flowers for visibility and safety's sake. The unearthly silence of London followed the procession to its final destination. Whilst the hearse drove to Northamptonshire, the Spencers and the Windsors rode the royal train for the interment. Given the Earl's eulogy, that couldn't have been a comfortable journey.

The final committal was private with only the families, and Paul Burrell, in attendance.

As the Abbey gradually emptied, Nora turned to the woman next to her, and invited her for a cup of tea. The two women shared memories of the Princess in happier times. Nora and Mary said their goodbyes an hour later, each drained by the trying day. They vowed to keep in touch, but both knew that wouldn't happen.

Nora returned home, and saw a note that her husband had taken Clemmy to the park. Grateful for a moment alone, she put on the kettle and went to see if there were any messages. The answerphone was lit up. It was a message from Hasnat.

"Nora, it's Hasnat Khan here. I saw you at the funeral, but I just couldn't speak to anyone. Can you ring me back please?" His voice sounded tortured. She picked up her mobile to ring him.

He answered on the first ring. "Hello, is that you, Nora? Thank you so much for ringing me. How are you holding up?" He strove for politeness.

"Hasnat, I'm terrible, if you want the truth. I just want to crawl into a hole and die. And you?" Nora laughed sharply.

"Can we meet for a drink? I need to talk to you. Please."

Nora hesitated, and then agreed to meet him at an out-of-the-way pub in thirty minutes. She changed out of her mourning clothes, and drove to meet him. He looked terrible. Pale, unshaven, hands shaking, he held an untouched beer in his hands.

He rose to greet her. They shook hands. They'd only met a couple of times.

They sat down, and Nora ordered a glass of white wine. Hasnat stared at his beer, and then looked up at her, his eyes filled with pain.

"When did you speak to her last? Did you talk to her on that final day?" He quizzed her, wanting to know every last detail of Diana's life.

"Yes, I did speak to her last Saturday." With a start, Nora realized it was just a week ago today. Why did it feel like a lifetime? "She was happy and enjoying her holiday, but very eager to get back home. She wanted to see the boys."

"Anything else? Did she say anything about me?" Hasnat pressed her again.

"I'm sorry, Hasnat, but no she didn't. She did say she was happy the summer was over. She'd had a great break, but wanted to get back to her normal routine."

"Did she mention *him?*" Nora knew he meant Dodi.

"Hasnat, Diana wasn't in love with Dodi. It was just a summer romance. Nothing more."

Hasnat sat back in his chair. "I tried to ring her. I knew something was wrong. She wouldn't answer me. I think she changed her phone number. She didn't want to talk to me."

"Yes, you know she changed her number all the time. Hasnat, don't torment yourself. I know that she loved you very deeply. And there's nothing you could have done for her. Just leave it."

Hasnat became very animated. "But I *could* have saved her life, don't you see? I'm a heart surgeon. I've been combing whatever medical records I can get my hands on, and I'm sure, I'm absolutely certain, that I could have repaired her heart. I know the procedure that would have worked. If only I had been there." He looked tormented and lost.

Nora took his hands into her own. "We can't make sense of this senseless act. Who knows? Maybe there will be an inquest and over time, we'll be able to make peace with it. But for now, Hasnat, I'm begging you to let this go. You couldn't have been there. They did all they could for her. Let her legacy speak for her. Please."

Hasnat took a sip of his beer, and nodded. He left her minutes later.

"Was is truly awful?" asked Nora several hours later.

Paul's voice soundly oddly calm. "No, actually it was rather amazing," he replied. "Her resting place is private, lots of trees, you can hear nature all around. No flashing lightbulbs or clicking cameras. It was peaceful and very respectful. I can't say much more than that, Nora, but I felt her spirit there, I really did."

"Oh Paul, I'm so glad," she replied fervently.

"Do you remember she used to love the song *A Nightingale Sang in Berkley Square*?" Paul asked quietly. "She told me she played it for the Prince a long time ago."

"Yes, I do. It's a haunting melody."

"Don't laugh, Nora but I swear I heard her singing it, ever so softly. She had a lovely singing voice, you know?"

Our homeward step was just as light
As the tap-dancing feet of Astaire.
And like an echo far away,
A Nightingale sang in Berkley Square.
I know 'cause I was there, that night in Berkley Square.

"Paul, that's exquisite," choked Nora. "And I'm sure it was her. Diana always liked to get in the last word." They both attempted a strained smile, as they abandoned themselves to private memories of their dear friend, the beautiful, kind, flawed, and beloved Diana, Princess of Wales.

Epilogue

Diana, Princess of Wales died tragically on August 31, 1997, but her legacy lives on to this day.

Her sons William, (Duke of Cambridge) and Harry (Duke of Sussex) are princes who would make their mother incredibly proud. Not only are they warm, compassionate and caring philanthropists in the style of Charles and Diana, they both seem to have found marital and family happiness that eluded Diana throughout her short life.

Prince William went on from Eton to graduate from the University of St. Andrews with a Master of Arts degree, where he met his future wife, Catherine Middleton. He followed in the Windsor family footsteps, by embarking on a military career at Sandhurst, and became a helicopter pilot for the RAF Search and Rescue Force.

He gave up his career to assume more official duties as the second-in-line to the throne. He and his wife Catherine have three children: Prince George, Princess Charlotte, and Prince Louis. By all accounts it's a very happy marriage.

Prince Harry also attended Sandhurst, and completed two tours of duty with the Army in Afghanistan as a Second Lieutenant. Harry founded the *Invictus Games* – a Paralympic-style sporting event for injured servicemen and women.

Harry settled down in his thirties and married the American actress Meghan Markle in 2018. They have a son Archie, and a daughter, Lilibet Diana.

Both William and Harry have talked publicly and lovingly about their mother, her impact on their lives, and how much they still miss her every day.

Although the media blamed the behaviour of the paparazzi who followed the car, a French judicial investigation in 1999 found that the crash was caused by the driver Henri Paul, who lost control of the Mercedes at high speed, while he was intoxicated and under the effects of prescription drugs. Paul was the deputy head of security at the Hotel Ritz at the time of the crash, and had goaded the paparazzi waiting outside the hotel earlier. His inebriation may have been made worse by anti-depressants and traces of an anti-psychotic in his body. The investigation concluded that the photographers were not near the Mercedes when it crashed. After hearing evidence at the British inquest in 2008, a jury returned to a verdict of "unlawful killing" by Paul, and the paparazzi pursuing the car. Diana's death turned out to be a tragic accident.

In 2005, HRH Charles, The Prince of Wales married his long-time love Camilla Parker Bowles. Although entitled to carry the title of HRH Princess of Wales, instead she is known as HRH Duchess of Cornwall, most likely out of respect for Diana's memory. It is widely believed Charles will make her his Queen Consort when he becomes the King of England.

Dr. Hasnat Khan entered into a Pakistani-arranged marriage in 2006. The marriage dissolved two years later. He remains in the UK working as a consultant cardiothoracic surgeon at Basildon University Hospital.

He is single, with no children.

The Ottawa Mine Ban Treaty, which opened for signatures months after Diana's death, has been signed by 122 countries, prohibiting the use, stockpiling, production, and transfer of landmines. The International Campaign to Ban Landmines won the *Nobel Peace Prize* a few months after the Princess' death. Well done you, Diana!

Glossary of British Terms

ace excellent, very good

afters dessert (after the meal)

albeit although

anteroom empty or spare room

anyroad anyway

arse behind, bum

awayday a day of local royal engagements outside of London

bag official folder of royal business

barmy crazy, unhinged

barracks army quarters

Battenberg cake a light sponge cake with jelly that when cut into, reveals a checkerboard pattern

beast meanie, nasty person

beyond the pale unacceptable, slightly indecent

bin garbage

bill check

biscuit cookie

bits details, parts or pieces

blimey an informal exclamation of surprise (derivative: *God blind me)*

bloody (profanity) damned or an adjective: very

bloomin' slang for bloody

bollocks nonsense or B.S.

bolt-hole escape or getaway

boot trunk of a car

bother care

bow a man's nod of the head to royalty

brilliant wonderful, excellent, terrific, great

bugger bastard or creep or I'll be damned (I'll be buggered)

butler head of all domestic staff in a household

cad someone dishonourable

cap young boy's hat (part of a uniform)

carpark parking lot

chap man or young man

chapel church service at boarding school

cheek nerve

chief bridesmaid maid of honor

chin wag familiar chat, friendly catch-up

chips french fries

chuck up the sponge throw in the towel, admit defeat

chuffed pleased, excited

chum friend

cinema movies or movie theater

clearing up cleaning up

clock slang for believe (in shock)

clotted cream rich thickened cream served with tea and scones

collect pick up

come round come over

cooked his or her own goose sabotaged themselves, master of their own troubles

cortege funeral procession

country tweeds set of sturdy woolen clothes for outdoor pursuits, including suits, or jackets and skirts

cow derogatory term for idiot or fool

crisps potato chips

cross angry

cuddly toys stuffed animals

cuppa short form for a cup of tea, never coffee

currant bun a sweet bun containing currants or raisins

daft silly, mad, crazy

deference showing respect, as staff show to royal employees

de rigeur French term for the standard or expected way of doing things

dialling tone dial tone

diary schedule or personal agenda

directly soon, right away

done and dusted complete, finished

Dowager Queen ex-Queen consort, wife of deceased king, now retired

drawing room formal living room for entertaining

dresser a female staff member who attends to the wardrobe and accessories of a female royal employer

drinks tray portable bar served at home

dungarees jeans or blue jeans

enroute on the way

equerry an officer of the British royal household who attends or assists members of the royal family

Eton mess dessert consisting of a mixture of strawberries, broken meringue and heavy whipped cream

exeat school holiday, typically from boarding school

fancy like or believe

fairy cake cupcake

fetching attractive, pretty

film movie

fizzy water carbonated water drink

flat apartment

fly-bys ceremony where British military air regiments fly over Buckingham Palace

footman a liveried staff member whose duties include admitting visitors and waiting at table

forthright honest, direct

fortnight two weeks

frock dress or evening gown

fuddy duddy worrier, fusspot

full english breakfast a hearty breakfast that includes some or all of the following: back bacon, fried, poached or scrambled eggs, fried or grilled tomatoes, fried mushrooms, fried bread or toast with butter, and sausages. black pudding, baked beans, bubble and squeak, and hash browns

get on get along or manage

ghastly horrible, awful

give leave give permission

give over be honest, come clean

glum sad, feeling down

go turn, chance

gobsmacked shocked, amazed

grace-and-favour usually applied to a home provided free-of-charge or for nominal rent by the Queen either due to familial connections or services to the crown

grand good, great

handbag women's purse, bag

happy families a scene where everyone is (or pretends to be) happy together

hob kitchen stovetop

hols shortform for holidays

hospice hospital for terminally ill people

howl cry loudly

in the event in any event, as it turns out

jam roly-poly a flat-rolled suet pudding which is then spread with jam and rolled up, (similar to a swiss roll), then steamed or baked

jelly babies jelly beans

jolly happy or very

junket trip, outing

kilometre measure of geographic distance, approximately .6 of a mile

knackered exhausted, tired

lad boy

lady-in-waiting a woman staff member who attends a queen or princess (accompanies on engagements, holds flowers, performs small duties), sometimes a relative or favoured friend

lav short for lavatory, bathroom

least said, soonest mended to sweep under the carpet, avoid conflict or difficult conversations, say nothing

leave off take off or stop it

lemon refresher natural lemonade

let her hair down relax, be informal and casual

lie-down nap or sleep

loads lots or many

loo bathroom, washroom

look in check on

lot group, crowd

Ma'am shortform for Madam, a form of address for senior royalty

mad crazy for, or enthusiastic about

maid a staff member who performs household cleaning duties

masses lots

Maths Math or Mathematics

meant to supposed to

men in grey courtiers, Buckingham Palace officials

mobile mobile phone, cellphone

mooch lie around, be lazy

nail varnish nail polish

nappy diaper

nick to steal

nursery child's bedroom/suite, also the collection of nannies & children

on leave on holiday or break from work

on offer offered

operating theatre hospital surgery

overstep the mark overstep your bounds, go over a limit or boundary

pablum baby cereal

paracetamol pain reliever such as aspirin

Personal Protection Officer (PPO) private royal protection, bodyguard
poach to steal
polo a team sport played on horseback, favoured by royals and wealthy aristocrats
poppycock nonsense, garbage, made-up facts
post position, job OR mail
pound measure of British currency, approximately equal to 1.5 US dollars
prat idiot, fool
private secretary an administrative assistant to a member of the royal family
proper genuine, accepted, authentic, real
provost senior administrator or chancellor
pudding dessert
put a foot wrong make a mistake
put paid to put an end to, stop
put-up job a set-up
queue lineup
Quink ink for a fountain pen
rail rack, as in clothes rack
RAF Royal Air Force
rather quite
recce short for recognizance, an advance inspection of a location to ensure its readiness for a royal visit
Ribena blackcurrant-based uncarbonated and carbonated soft drink and fruit drink concentrate
ring to call on the telephone (ring up)
rocket arugula
rot garbage, rubbish
row argument
royal set-pieces fixed, traditional annual engagements like Royal Ascot, Trooping the Colour, Opening of parliament
rubbish garbage, nonsense
sack to fire

safe room a hidden, self-contained and well-stocked room for emergencies

sarnie sandwich

school run drop off and pick up a child from school

scrummy short for scrumptious, lovely or fine

second-in-line second in the succession to become the next British monarch (Prince Charles is first-in-line)

shag have sex

sire to father (as in a horse)

sitting room informal living or family room

Sloane or Sloane Ranger stereotypical young upper-middle or upper class girl (woman) who pursues a distinctive fashionable lifestyle

smashing wonderful, terrific

smidgen a bit, a little

sod off derogatory as in get lost or go away

sort to deal with, sort out, organize

spot on just right, exactly so, correct

stand in good stead serve you well

stiff upper lip don't show emotion, be strong

stodgy boring, old-fashioned, dull

stone a measure of weight, approximately 14 pounds

straightaway immediately, right away

succession order in which the next monarch will ascend the throne

ta thank you, could also be goodbye

tea trolley tea service on a wheeled cart

telly television

tether rope

thick dumb, stupid

tomfoolery silliness, hijinks, fooling around

turn up show up, appear

Trooping the Colour a ceremony performed by regiments of the British and Commonwealth armies to celebrate the monarch's birthday

turkish delights small candies with gel and fruits

upper crust slang for aristocrat

valet a personal male attendant to a prince or king, responsible for his clothes and appearance

vex angry or to make someone else angry, put out

walkabout a royal event when the principals greet the public face-to-face by walking up and down cordoned off sides of a street

washing up doing the dishes

wee pee

well done, you good job

wet blanket killjoy, someone who doesn't want to have fun

whilst while

willie slang name for a man's penis

woolgather to be distracted, having one's mind on something **else**

working clothes the children's' formal clothes for official engagements, suits and ties

wrangle argue or row

Author's Note

Concluding Diana's journey with *Diana, A Spencer Forever*, was a fitting end to this years-long adventure of weaving historical facts with fiction. I hope I brought the Princess to life for you as I imagined her daily life, how she thought and felt, and the impact she had on millions of people around the world. I trust I have been respectful to her, her family and the royals. Farewell to our beloved Princess.

The complete series:
Diana, A Spencer in Love
Diana, A Spencer in Turmoil
Diana, A Spencer Forever

At Home with Diana - the companion book to the series opens the doors and windows of Diana's homes and royal residences, and tells her story from that unique perspective. A great travel guide!

The Royal Key - where *The Time Traveler's Wife* meets *Downton Abbey*, in a healing love story that transcends time.

To learn more about the British royals, upcoming author events, and to sign up for my newsletter, please explore my website at **debstratas.com.** Shop at my new **Foreverrroyal.ca** online store. Visit my **Debstratasauthor** Facebook page. You can also follow me on Twitter at **@deb_stratas** and **debstratasauthor** on Instagram. I'd love to hear from you!

Feedback is a gift. Please return to the amazon page where you bought this book to leave a review and brief comment. I thank you so much!

Manufactured by Amazon.ca
Bolton, ON